72,900 words.

Away With You

by Grant Atherton

with grateful thanks to

JAKOB PAULUSSEN

for all his valuable help and advice

Cover art by
SelfPubBookCovers.com/BeeJavier

Grant Atherton's Website
GrantAtherton.co.uk

WARNING

This book contains sexually explicit scenes and adult language and may be considered offencive to some readers.

Away With You, Copyright (c) May, 2019 by Grant Atherton

All rights reserved. No part of this book may be reproduced, scanned or distributed in any printed or electronic form without prior written permission from the author. Please do not participate in or encourage piracy of copyrighted materials in violation of the author's rights. Purchase only authorised editions.

This book is a work of fiction. While reference might be made to actual historical events or existing locations, the names, characters, places and incidents are either the product of the author's imagination or are used fictitiously, and any resemblance to actual persons, living or dead, business establishments, events or locales is entirely coincidental.

CHAPTER ONE

The rhythmic beat of techno-trance and bursts of laughter from the dance floor. The popping of corks and clink of glasses from around crowded tables laden with food and wine. The sharp insistent reports of party poppers launching coloured streamers over the bobbing heads of chattering guests.

The sounds of celebration.

I raised my voice above the din as Karen made her way towards me. "At last I get to talk to the blushing bride."

She stopped in front of me and poked me in the chest. "If I'm blushing, it's your fault. You were supposed to give a speech of congratulation, not a stand-up comedy routine about my dissolute past."

Grinning, I lifted my glass to her and said, "A few well-chosen anecdotes are all part of the tradition. We wouldn't want to disappoint the guests, would we?"

It was Karen and Richard's wedding day. We were in Karen's guest house, The Fairview. The whole of the ground floor, including the bar and restaurant, had been transformed for the occasion.

Guests had come from far and wide, acquaintances old and new, some I hadn't seen for years. And now the ceremony and speeches were over, we were all whooping it up and making merry.

I took a step back, the better to check Karen over. "You look amazing," I said. She did, too. Her flame-hued untamed hair, dressed with silver thread, tumbled down over the top of a cream-coloured wrap held in at the waist by a silver chain. Simple and elegant.

I glanced over to where Richard and Nathan were chatting in a group with fellow police officers from the local station. "Even Richard has scrubbed up well. It's good to see him out of uniform for a change."

She followed my gaze and smiled. "We didn't do so badly for ourselves, did we?"

Returning the smile, I said, "We did okay."

I let my gaze linger on the group for a few moments before turning my attention back to Karen. I said, "I have to say, though, I was surprised not to hear the bit about 'love, honour and obey' in the vows."

Karen gasped. "Mikey! Like that was ever going to happen. I thought you knew me better than that."

"Too right I do. I was talking about Richard's vows, not yours."

"Oh, very funny."

"Well, you have to let him know who's in charge. Start as you mean to go on."

"It's a partnership of equals," she said, sniffily.

"So it's just me you boss around then?"

"You deserve it. You're hopeless." She added, "But my work is done. You have Nathan to keep you in check now."

I glanced over at him again. His group were laughing at some shared joke, and his square-cut face was creased in a wide grin. A warm glow spread through me.

"Ten months and counting," I said. "The three of us have settled into family life very well, thank you."

"Three?"

"Don't forget Rocky." Rocky was our German Shepherd, an ex-police dog living out his retirement with us at Woodside Cottage.

"I'm not sure I'd count a dog as family."

"Don't you dare let Nathan hear you say that. He dotes on that animal." As I spoke, I took the nearly empty wineglass from her. "Don't go away," I said. "I'll go top these up."

I narrowly avoided a couple of over-excited children chasing each other around the tables and headed over to the reception desk where a second makeshift bar had been set up.

With glasses replenished, I turned back just as a dark-haired woman in a black sequined evening dress appeared in the archway leading to the restaurant. She was holding a glass of wine and swaying slightly.

My spirits sank.

Willow Brookes. Down for the day from London. An unwelcome reminder of the past. Not one of my favourite people and not one whose acquaintance I was eager to renew.

She caught sight of me.

A sardonic smile spread across her face, and she slinked towards me, putting me in mind of a cat stalking its prey.

I feigned a welcoming smile as she approached and gritted my teeth.

She stood before me, hand on hip, the other hand gripping the edge of the desk to steady herself. "Michael MacGregor of all people." She slurred her words. "I'm surprised to see you here."

"Why wouldn't I be?"

"After that embarrassing public outing in the media? I thought you'd be hiding away somewhere and licking your wounds."

The smile died, and my good mood dissolved. I should have known she was out for blood the moment she headed my way.

I said, "Ancient history, Willow. And all forgotten. I'm sure by now the chattering classes have found new sources of salacious gossip to brighten up their lives."

"I don't think Donna's forgotten."

"Perhaps not. But at least she has a sizable divorce settlement to help ease the burden. And I'm happily settled in a new relationship. So I have no reason to hide."

"A new relationship?" She feigned surprise. "I thought you were into anonymous sex these days. Or did I read that wrong?"

The muscles in my jaw tightened. I drew in a long slow breath and said, "Like I said, ancient history. And whatever sort of relationship I choose is no concern of yours, is it?" Before she could reply, I cut her short with a curt nod and left her, making my way back to Karen.

Willow wasn't to be spurned so easily. She followed me back to where Karen was now chatting with Nathan.

I tried to fob her off with some crack about her needing to find new victims - I could well do without Willow dragging up my past in front of my nearest and dearest - but she wasn't listening.

Her focus was elsewhere.

She greeted Nathan with a squeal of delight and linked her arm through his.

"Where have you been all evening?" she said, and with a pout, added, "I hope you've not been avoiding me. I'm in need of a real man right now." She cast a quick glance my way as she added that last statement. No doubt to let me know the implied comparison was for my benefit.

She beamed up into Nathan's face. "And how is my favourite policeman?"

In earlier times, during those long-past days of our youth before we'd all gone our separate ways, Willow had chased after Nathan with a passion. Unable to see how pointless it was, she had pursued him relentlessly, taking no heed of his lack of response. And all these years later, her interest seemed undiminished.

She was in for a shock.

Nathan stiffened. "Much the same as ever," he said.

If that was his way of telling her she was still wasting her time, the message failed to get through. She tightened her grip on his arm and said, "Are you going to keep me company this evening?" She put on a little-girl-lost tone of voice and batted her eyelids. "I'm all on my ownsome tonight."

Not the most subtle of pickup lines I'd ever heard.

Karen glanced over at me, a despairing look on her face, but said nothing.

Nathan eased himself free of Willow's grip and said, "Much as I'd love to, Mikey and I are heading off home soon." Turning his attention to me, he said, "Before we leave, I'll introduce you to some of the local team." He nodded over to the guys he'd been chatting with. "When you have a moment." He turned away and headed back to his group.

This time, Willow's surprise was genuine. She kept her gaze on Nathan, following his passage across the room, and then turned and stared at me, wide-eyed, as the implication of his words sank in.

I held her gaze, savouring the moment, and said, "That's right, Willow. He's my favourite policeman too."

I stepped away from them both and said, "If you'll excuse me, I'll leave you two to catch up." To Karen, I said, "See you later before you leave."

I went to join Nathan and, after expelling a long slow breath and willing myself to relax, I squeezed his arm and said, "Thanks for rescuing me."

One of his group, a bald-headed man with a round face and cheery grin, said, "You're not the first. We've been on rescue missions all afternoon. Ever since Willow first hit the bottle." He held out a hand. "Andrew Lynch. Charwell HQ. I'll be standing in for Richard at the local station while he's filling his boots on honeymoon."

We all joined in the general laughter, and Richard flushed.

I took Lynch's hand and shook it. "Pleasure to meet you."

"The pleasure's mine," he said. "I'm a big fan of your radio show. The Chief tells me you're working on another series." He nodded towards Nathan as he spoke.

"You won't have long to wait," I said.

My series on the psychological aspects of real life murders was as popular as ever. And it was a sad fact that there would always be plenty of material for more shows.

"And I hear you're a keen runner too." He patted his well-rounded stomach and said, "I could do with losing a few pounds. So if you need some company, let me know."

"Be my guest. I'd welcome some company."

Even after all these months, I was still getting used to the inherent friendliness of life in Elders Edge; twelve years of London anonymity had inured me to the pleasures of small-town communal living. There had been a time when I had sought that anonymity, eager to leave behind what I had believed to be the oppressive confines of my hometown. But now I was back, I was glad to be part of that life again.

Nathan introduced me to those in the group I hadn't yet met, and we all passed a pleasurable hour in light-hearted conversation before Richard made his excuses, pleading the need to leave. He and Karen were honeymooning in the Scottish Isles, and the journey would be a long one.

At that point, the group broke up.

Lynch had arranged to have his car brought round from the local garage after its service, and he headed off to reception to pick up the keys while Nathan and I helped Richard track down Karen.

Once we'd found her, the four of us went through reception on our way to the entrance. Lynch was at the desk speaking to an oil-stained mechanic in dark-blue overalls, and we signalled our farewells as we passed by.

Willow was on the far side of the room talking with someone I recognised from the old days: Ralph Ferguson, an old school friend. I'd tried to engage Ralph in conversation earlier at the bar, an attempt to catch up on the intervening years. But he had seemed reluctant to talk and excused himself, returning to his group. He and Willow appeared to be arguing.

Karen caught my look as we headed out to the car park. "Don't worry," she said. "She'll soon be out of your hair. She's catching the train back to London tomorrow." Karen was all too well aware of the long-standing animosity between Willow and me.

Groaning, I said, "She's staying over?"

"Just the one night. And she's leaving first thing."

I sighed inwardly, but let my bad humour pass. I wasn't going to let negative thoughts about Willow spoil my mood.

Once outside, we crossed over to Richard's Astra and, before they climbed in, I gave Karen a hug. "Thank you," I said.

She pulled away and regarded me with raised brows. "For what?"

"For being the best friend I ever had."

She punched me lightly on the arm. "Get away with you."

I shook Richard's hand and said, "Make sure you look after her. Or it'll be pistols at dawn."

He laughed. "No worries, Mikey. You can pack your pistols away."

"We'll look after each other," said Karen. "You just make sure you look after this place while I'm away."

After hugging Karen too, Nathan said his farewells, and we stood side by side and watched them drive away.

As we climbed the steps back to the entrance, Nathan draped an arm around my shoulder and gave me a squeeze. "We've seen a few changes over the years," he said.

Over by the desk, one of the guests was helping Willow to a chair. Willow was shaking, and her face was pale. The concerned guest took the glass of wine from Willow's trembling hand and put it on the counter.

"Not all of them for the better," I said.

CHAPTER TWO

"You're very quiet." Nathan sounded concerned, the dark brows creased in a frown.

We were on our way home from the wedding reception.

The weather had taken a turn for the better and we were strolling back through Tinkers Wood, making the most of the mild evening air. From either side of the well-trodden path, overgrown rye grass brushed against our legs, leaving pollen traces on the fabric of our trousers.

I should have been enjoying this.

A short distance ahead, peering over the top of a garden already in bloom with spring colour and half-hidden by moss-covered elms, Woodside cottage awaited our return.

As we approached, I flashed Nathan a reassuring smile. "Nothing to worry about. I was just thinking back to our early days before I hightailed it to London."

It wasn't the only thing on my mind. I was still rattled by my spat with Willow. But I didn't want to burden Nathan with details of my verbal scuffle. This was supposed to be a day of celebration, one to be enjoyed and savoured.

"Those old familiar faces?"

Nodding, I said. "Seeing some of those people after all these years conjured up a few memories. Not all of them good."

I delved into my pocket for the house keys as we reached the perimeter wall and pushed open the gate on creaking hinges.

Nathan shot me a quizzical look and followed me through to the garden. "Willow?"

There were times I swear he could read my mind.

"The way she acted around you this afternoon reminded me of how she was back then."

He answered with a grunt.

Crunching gravel underfoot, we trod the brick-bordered path to the rear of the cottage, to where night-scented wisteria climbed the white stucco walls.

Scratching sounds and the occasional yelp emanated from the other side of the door as I slid my key into the lock.

"Brace yourself," I said as I turned the key. I pushed open the door and stepped back.

The words were barely out of my mouth before Rocky was on us, a bouncing blur of spirited yelping fur. He bounded around, slapping his tail against our legs, jumping up at us, happy to see us home.

"Jeez," I said as I tried to steady him, "you'd think we'd been away for months." I dropped to a crouch, held his head between my hands and tried to calm him with soothing words.

He ran a large wet tongue over my face, broke free, and launched himself at Nathan, paws against his chest.

Nathan pushed him down and issued a stern, "Sit."

Rocky immediately squatted, tail slapping the ground, and stared up at Nathan.

I wiped the back of a hand across my face as I rose to my feet and said, "How come he always listens to you and not me?"

"You're too soft with him."

I pulled a face and followed Nathan over to the far side of the garden where a rickety old wooden bench crouched by the wall. As we sank onto it, the weatherworn boards groaned under our weight.

We sat side by side while Rocky ran around the garden, snuffling the ground, padding through the grass, and pressing his nose to everything he passed over, before relieving himself against the large beech that guarded the gate.

Nathan followed Rocky's movements, his face a picture of pleasure, the hard square lines softened by the fading light.

And as I watched him, the gnawing unease that had built up inside me melted away.

Given my high public profile, the media storm stirred up by my divorce had been inevitable. And the resulting publicity had been demeaning. Eventually, the storm had passed and, in the calm that followed, I had found what once I'd lost.

I reached out and put a hand on Nathan's thigh.

Moments like this reminded me how much had changed since those turbulent times and how much I had to be grateful for.

Willow's mocking reminder of my less-than-admirable past had momentarily unsettled me. But I wasn't doing myself any favours by dwelling on it.

I leaned back and closed my eyes. Around us, early evening scents filled the air, and a gentle breeze rustled the leaves.

All was now well with the world. Nathan still worked too hard, and I sometimes had to stay over in London when business took me away but, on the whole, not much interfered with our comfortable domestic routine, and life was good, the painful events of the past behind us.

I said, "I was thinking back to our teenage years. I was so jealous of Willow back then."

"Jealous? What did you have to be jealous about?"

"I was still coming to terms with how I felt. It wasn't easy. She was more open about her feelings than I could be. The way she chased after you."

"Did she?"

"Oh, please. All the girls chased after you. With Willow at the head of the pack. You must have been blind not to see that."

He grinned and slow-punched my arm. "I only had eyes for you."

"Might have helped if you'd let me know that."

"You got to know soon enough," he said, still grinning. He leaned over and planted a kiss on my forehead.

Rocky bounded back to us, dropped his head on Nathan's knee, and stared up at him. Big brown eyes full of unconditional love.

Were humans capable of that? Could they love so absolutely? No matter what?

Nathan turned towards me, a warm smile spread across his face.

I guess that was answer enough.

Returning the smile, I patted his thigh and squeezed it.

Rocky saw his chance to get some attention and licked my hand. I reached out and ruffled the fur between his ears. "So constant," I murmured.

"I think he's just hungry," said Nathan.

Rising to his feet, he said, "Come on, boy. Let's get you fed." He headed indoors with Rocky at his heels. Over his shoulder, he said, "And besides, I wasn't totally oblivious to Willow's amorous attentions. Which is why I stayed out of her reach as much as possible."

I followed them inside and through to the kitchen.

"After seeing all those faces from the past this afternoon, I kept thinking how different it would have been if I hadn't screwed up and done a runner. I was such an idiot."

"You had your reasons."

"I hurt a few people."

"Ancient history."

"That's exactly what I told Willow."

In the act of opening the wall cupboard over the sink, he stopped, twisted around and said, "Willow? What does she have to do with it?"

I hadn't meant to blurt that out. But it was too late to take it back.

"She had a pop at me earlier," I said. "She never forgave me for the way I treated Donna. Not that I could blame her."

"I didn't know they were acquainted." Nathan reached into the cupboard and took out a can of dog food. Rocky wagged his tail faster, anticipating the treat to come.

I said, "Karen introduced them. We were all living in London back then, before Karen's divorce."

I grabbed a couple of clean bowls from the drainer, passed one to Nathan, and filled the other with water. "Donna and I socialised with Karen and her husband in those days. Willow was more Karen's friend. Karen introduced her and her husband to our little group some years after Willow moved down to London."

"She's married?" He spooned the contents of the can into the bowl and put it on the mat by the door.

"Yes, Owen. Nice guy. We got to know each other well and spent a lot of time together. It was Owen who got me into running back then.

But Willow took Donna's side when we broke up. And, from then on, I was definitely persona non grata."

I placed the water bowl on the floor by Rocky's food. "Karen had already moved back to Elders Edge by then. And after what happened, I lost touch with the others."

Rocky gulped down his food, turned his attention to the water, and lapped the bowl almost dry. Seemingly satisfied, he licked his chops, trotted through to the living room, and curled up in his basket by the coffee table.

Nathan said, "Sounds to me like you were well out of it."

"I was sorry to lose touch with Owen. He was a good friend. One of the best." I turned and leaned up against the counter. "Willow was a different matter."

"So what happened between you two?"

I folded my arms and shrugged. "Who knows? We never did hit it off. Even before the divorce. She wasn't the most stable of people." I crossed over to the sink and washed my hands under the tap. "Her first partner died in a car accident. Not the most promising of starts. So I tried to make allowances. But you can only go so far."

"I heard something about that, but not the details. She'd already left Elders Edge by then."

"She was pregnant at the time. So I know it can't have been easy. If I had to make a professional judgement, I'd say she never recovered from the trauma of her partner's death and took out her pain on others."

"Ouch." He handed me the empty can. "So she has children?"

"Just the one. Simon. But Owen's the only father he's ever known. I've not seen the boy for some years, but he must be in his early teens by now." I rinsed the can under the tap and dropped it into the recycling bin. "Not that I'm likely to see any of them again after tomorrow."

"Tomorrow?"

"Willow's staying over at the Fairview so I may bump into her before she leaves. Karen asked me to drop by in the morning."

"Is that necessary?"

I shrugged. "Probably not. But you know Karen. She wants to keep the agency manager on his toes. I promised I'd watch over him."

Nathan grunted and headed into the living room. I followed him through and, while he settled himself on the couch, I slipped a CD into the player. A moment later we were listening to the rousing strains of Finlandia.

As I slumped down next to him, he twisted around, swung his legs over the arm of the couch and lay full length with his head in my lap.

Rocky left his basket, trotted over to us, and stretched out across my feet.

Nathan stared up at me with troubled eyes and said, "I didn't know Willow had been giving you a hard time. I hope you didn't take it to heart."

That mind-reading act again. I smiled and ran a finger down his stubbled cheek. "You said it yourself; it's ancient history. Nothing is going to spoil today. I won't let it."

The look of concern faded. He returned the smile and closed his eyes. "The end of a perfect day," he murmured, and the gentle rise and fall of his chest beneath my hand slowed as he drifted into a peaceful slumber.

I watched him for a while, staring down into that calm untroubled face, and a sharp pang of guilt ran through me.

It's not as if I could change the past. And there would always be times, like today, when it would come back to haunt me. But the remorse I felt for the hurt I had caused was mine to bear, not Nathan's, and I resented his being troubled by reminders of my mistakes.

But words were just words. And nothing Willow could say would change my life one iota.

And so I pushed away all thoughts of the past, leaned back, closed my eyes, and let the music carry me away.

CHAPTER THREE

The following day dawned cold but dry and brightened over the morning to a clear blue sky. The perfect weather for my daily run. I donned a pair of sweatpants and shirt, and Nathan dropped me off at the Fairview on his way to police headquarters in Charwell so I could make the most of the weather and jog home after my visit.

He was due back in town later so, after arranging to meet him for lunch at the local station, I waved him off and headed into the reception.

The place was a mess. Dried puddles stained the parquet tiles, and litter was strewn around; paper hats, sandwich wrappers, napkins.

A serious-looking middle-aged man in a grey suit that had seen better days peered at me through a pair of heavy-framed spectacles from behind the desk.

I headed towards him.

At the other side of the room, a young man and woman were cleaning up the detritus from the day before, he bundling up the food-stained tablecloths, and she sweeping the floor. I recognised the young woman as Mia, one of Karen's regular staff and, when she glanced up and offered a timid wave, I greeted her with a cheery 'hi'.

At the desk, I learned the agency manager was called Robert Dunn. I introduced myself as a friend of Karen's and explained how she had asked me to drop by to make sure he was coping okay.

The expression on his face told me all I needed to know about just how tactless that introduction was.

He bristled and said, "I assure you, I'm quite capable of fronting a business of this size without having my capability questioned."

Time for some diplomacy. "I didn't phrase that very well," I said with a smile. "I wouldn't dream of questioning your management skills."

I nodded over towards Mia and her colleague. "Staff are in short supply at this time of year," I said. "Karen thought you may need a hand getting this place back into shape after yesterday's party."

That seemed to have the desired effect. He apologised for his presumption, sounding somewhat abashed, and said, "I just have the two of them here today. I'm sure they'd appreciate some help."

Great. I'd talked myself into a morning of forced labour. In future, I'd try thinking before opening my mouth.

Accepting my self-imposed lot with some reluctance, I said, "I'll start in the bar. That's where most damage is usually done."

As I turned away, I remembered that Willow may be around and I preferred to avoid her if possible. Another verbal shootout was the last thing I wanted.

I turned back to the desk. "Is Willow Brookes still here?" I asked. "She was staying over after the wedding."

My enquiry was met with a shake of the head. "Mrs Brookes signed out early this morning. Sorry, you missed her, but I understand she had a train to catch at ten."

Good. She was safely on her way out of my life. "No problem," I said. "It was nothing important." I made my excuses and headed for the bar.

The mess in there was much the same as everywhere else; soiled tablecloths, spilt food trodden onto the wooden floors, party streamers hanging from the light fittings, plus a broken glass hastily kicked against a wall.

I picked up all the loose debris and piled it into one corner before arming myself with a mop and a bucket of hot soapy water from the kitchen and setting to work cleaning the floors. Once they were back to a presentable condition, I tackled all the other surfaces and, by noon, my work was done. I gathered up the bundle of tablecloths from where I'd dumped them and carried them through to the reception area, asked Mia where the dirty laundry was stowed and followed her directions to a storeroom under the stairs.

After nearly tripping over an inconveniently placed bag just inside the door and cursing, I dropped the tablecloths into the laundry basket, grabbed the bag from the floor and shoved it onto a shelf. An address tag hung from one of the handles. I checked the name, looking for someone to blame for leaving it lying around so carelessly.

It read 'Willow Brookes'.

What the hell?

Something didn't add up here.

I pulled the bag back off the shelf and carried it over to where Dunn was leaning over the desk, opening the post. He looked up as I approached and peered at me over the top of his glasses.

Holding up the bag, I said, "I just found this in the storeroom. It belongs to Willow Brookes. You are sure she left?"

Dunn straightened up, face scrunched in a frown, reached under the counter and produced the guest register. He opened it on the counter top and ran his finger down the last page. He said, "According to this, she signed out at 8:30."

"Did she have her bag with her?"

"I didn't see her. But let's find out, shall we?" He raised a hand and called out to Mia to come over to the desk.

Mia was the type who always presumed the worst. She was biting her lip as she scuttled towards us, her pudgy face a show of apprehension.

"Nothing to worry about, Mia," I said, trying to put her at ease. "We're trying to find out why Mrs Brookes left her bag behind."

"I put it in the storeroom."

"Yes, I know. But why?"

"She asked me to."

"Why?"

"She wanted me to look after it."

There were times getting information from Mia was an uphill struggle. "Why don't you tell us exactly what happened."

While I was trying to wring a sensible explanation from Mia, Dunn called over the young man and sent him upstairs to make sure Willow hadn't returned to her room.

Mia went on to explain that Willow Brookes had signed out as planned, had asked to leave her bag while she ran an errand, and would be back to pick it up in time to catch her train. "I thought she must have been back already to collect it."

"Did she say where she was going?" I said.

Mia shuffled uneasily. "She asked for directions to the local police station."

"The police?" Dunn sounded concerned.

"I doubt it's anything to worry about," I said. "There were several of her old acquaintances from the local station at the reception yesterday. She probably just wanted to catch up."

"Enough to miss her train?"

"If you knew her as well as I do, you'd know she's not one of the most reliable of people. She probably changed her mind."

Dunn didn't seem convinced. "You'd think she'd let us know."

I turned back to Mia. "Did she say anything else?"

Mia shook her head, lips pressed tight.

We were interrupted by the return of the young man. He confirmed that the room had been vacated and all Willow's belongings removed.

To Mia, I said, "What kind of mood was she in? Do you remember?"

Mia didn't seem to be on sure ground here. She shuffled again and said, "I can't really say." She thought about it for a moment and added, "She wasn't very friendly though. I remember that. She was a bit snappy."

So no change there then.

Dunn said, "Time's getting on. You have to wonder if maybe something has happened to her."

I glanced up at the clock on the wall behind the desk. It was after twelve. "I'm heading over to the station anyway," I said. "I'm meeting my partner there for lunch. I'll track her down and send her on her way back."

My suggestion was met with an enthusiastic response, and I cursed inwardly. Another confrontation with Willow Brookes was the last thing I wanted. But the consensus seemed to be that tracking her down was now my responsibility.

Even in her absence, she was giving me grief. I had better things to do with my day than chase after some capricious woman who had probably changed her plans, oblivious to the inconvenience she was causing to others. But, once again, I'd talked myself into yet another chore I could have done without.

I was still cursing under my breath as I headed out the door.

CHAPTER FOUR

My old friend Miles Barber was on desk duty at the local station that afternoon. He was leaning over the counter scribbling into a notepad when I pushed my way in through the glass entrance door. I crossed towards him and he looked up with a cheery grin in response to my greeting.

Sgt Barber was an old hand at the station, and we'd worked on cases together in the past.

It was a slow day, and he was the chatty type, so it was no problem getting him to tell me about Willow's visit.

"After yesterday's shindig, she was a bit the worse for wear," he said. "She always was a heavy drinker. You'd think she would have learned to hold it better by now."

Once I'd told him of that morning's events, he offered the opinion that Willow was probably intoxicated, was sleeping it off somewhere, and had missed her train as a result.

I agreed that, as possibilities go, it was right up there at the top of the list, but suggested it might be best to track her actual movements just to be on the safe side. "Was she meeting someone here?" I asked.

"Strictly business. She was here to make a complaint. Serious stuff."

That brought me up short. It hadn't occurred to me it might be anything other than a friendly visit.

"I'd presumed it was a social call. Someone from last night."

He snorted. "I promise you, if you'd seen the look on her face, you'd know it was no social call. One thing you got right though, it was about someone she met last night. That's what I hear, anyway."

"That's what you hear?"

"I was stuck on the desk this morning, so I passed her over to Andrew Lynch - you met him yesterday. If you want the low down, he's the one to talk to."

He stiffened as though struck by a sudden thought. "Come to think of it, I'm sure he said he was taking her back to the Fairview afterwards."

"Strange she never made it then. Is the Sarge around?"

He waved me over to the waiting area. "Grab yourself a seat," he said as he picked up the phone. "He's about to go on his break, but I'll see if I can track him down."

There were three others seated in the waiting area; a heavily tattooed woman with pink hair sobbing into her hands, a shabbily dressed young man smelling of body odour and marijuana, and an older man with long greasy hair who muttered to himself and glared at each of us in turn.

Fortunately, I didn't have long to wait. Lynch appeared a few minutes later, chubby face creased by a wide grin.

I rose to meet him and he greeted me with a hearty handshake.

He looked me up and down. "Been for your morning run?"

"I wish."

We moved towards the centre of the reception and, once we were out of earshot of the waiting area, I talked him through that morning's developments. Nodding towards Barber, I lowered my voice and said, "I hear Willow came by to make a complaint. I'm trying to find out what happened to her."

The grin disappeared, and he shot Barber a reproachful look. "You'd best come through to my office. I'm about to take my break, but I can spare a few minutes."

He led me down the featureless main corridor to an office at the far end. We were barely through the door before he was sounding off about Willow. "That Goddamn woman causes trouble wherever she goes. We're busy enough as it is without having to deal with time wasters like Willow Brookes."

My thoughts exactly. "What happened?"

He pulled aside one of two mesh-back chairs standing behind his desk and offered me the other one. As we seated ourselves, he explained her visit. "She made a complaint against one of the guests at the wedding reception. Totally without foundation and not something that need concern us here. I persuaded her to drop her charge and sent her on her way."

"I hear you drove her back to the Fairview."

"Near enough. I was heading in that direction. I had a bill to pay at Tanners Garage. So I dropped her there. It's no more than a few minutes away."

"So she was definitely on her way back to the Fairview?"

"No question."

"She never made it. You're sure you saw her go that way?"

He hesitated and shook his head. "I'm not certain I saw which way she went. I got a call from the station while I was on the forecourt. Some disturbance up at Yates's farm on the clifftop. So my mind was on other things."

He paused for a moment as he thought it over some more and said, "I took the shortcut back through the High Street so I wouldn't have passed her on the Esplanade, anyway."

He spread his hands in a show of remorse and pulled a face. "Sorry, I don't know. I guess I presumed she went in that direction. It's where she said she was going after all."

I needed to think this through. It wasn't beyond reason to suppose that Willow would get sidetracked and change her plans. She wasn't known for her consistency. But this was so last minute. Even for Willow, it seemed out of place.

"She said nothing on the way over in the car?" I said. "Anything that might show she'd had a change of plans?"

"Not a word. She wasn't in a communicative mood. I think she was pissed at me for not taking her complaint seriously."

And maybe that was the point. If she wasn't getting the action she'd demanded from Lynch, she may well have taken matters into her own hands.

"Just thinking out loud here," I said, "but you don't suppose her vanishing act is somehow related to the complaint?"

Lynch frowned. "Why would it be?" He didn't sound convinced.

This is where, once again, diplomacy was called for. I needed him to consider the possibility he was wrong, that Willow's complaint was genuine. But I had to be careful about how I approached this without seeming to question his professional judgement.

"There are only two possibilities," I said. "Either her complaint was genuine... "

He opened his mouth to protest, and I help up a warning hand to stop him. "This is purely hypothetical," I said. "Just humour me for a moment." I continued, "Alternatively, her complaint was false, and she was looking to make trouble for this person."

"That's more like it."

"What I'm trying to get at here is that her complaint didn't come out of nowhere. Whether or not it was genuine, her intention was clear enough; she wanted to press charges against someone - for right or wrong - and that intention was thwarted."

He accepted my argument with a nod.

"She clearly had it in for this person, for whatever reason," I said, "and if she thought she was being pressured into changing her mind, she may have taken matters into her own hands, decided to confront whoever it was she made the complaint against. I wouldn't put it past her. You know how impulsive she can be."

His frown deepened. "I wouldn't call her rational, that's for sure."

"I know it's not really any of my business," I said, "but could you tell me what she was complaining about?"

Lynch stared at me for a moment and then turned away and drummed his fingers on the desktop as if thinking it over.

He turned back to me and said, "I'm reluctant to go into specifics but, as it's you, I don't suppose it will do any harm to fill you in on the basics." He drew a breath and said, "She claimed one of the guests assaulted her; manhandled her and then slapped her around."

"That's serious stuff."

"It would have been had it been true."

"Have you any reason to believe it wasn't?"

"Well, first of all, there was no physical evidence."

"And what else?"

He leaned forward. "Mikey, you saw how she was yesterday. She was out for trouble, getting into fights, being generally obnoxious. She even picked on some poor child for bumping into her. Gave the kid a real ear-battering. And then had a go at the mother. If what she claimed was true, do you really suppose she wouldn't have screamed the place down at the time?"

"Even so, she wasn't exactly sober. She may not have been clearheaded enough to deal with it right then. Did she say who it was?"

Lynch grimaced and shook his head. "I'm not sure it's appropriate to name names. And besides, I wouldn't be surprised if Willow had found her way back to the Fairview by now. Which would make any further discussion pointless."

I glanced at my watch. It was getting on for one o'clock. "One way to find out," I said. I dug out my mobile and speed-dialled the Fairview. Robert Dunn answered.

Willow had not returned, and Dunn sounded worried. "Her husband was supposed to meet her at the station. He called after you left. She's not been in touch, and he couldn't reach her on her mobile." Sounding more hopeful, he said, "Any news at your end?"

I told him I was still checking it out and would get back to him.

After finishing the call, I relayed the conversation to Lynch and said, "This is getting more serious by the minute. Unreliable she may be, but I can't believe she wouldn't contact her husband. And not answering his calls is the clincher. Something's wrong here."

Lynch still wasn't convinced. "Willow's a grown woman. We can't spend valuable resources trying to track down someone who's been off the radar for a few hours."

"Agreed," I said, "But we could at least follow up on her complaint. If she really has been dumb enough to take matters into her own hands, she could have put herself in harm's way."

Lynch still wasn't playing ball. Why did I feel like I was banging my head against a brick wall? Was this someone he knew? Someone he was covering for? I tried putting out a few feelers.

"I saw her arguing with Ralph Ferguson at the reception," I said. "It wasn't him, was it? Or maybe one of the guys from the station?"

"Willow argued with a lot of people." He shuffled uneasily in his chair. "Look, Mikey, this guy Willow made the complaint against, he's a decent guy. No way would he have done what she accused him of. He's just not the sort."

So it was someone he knew. "A friend of yours?"

"Not someone I know personally. But I know enough about him to vouch for his good character."

Why so evasive? Okay, so it's not like I was part of the Elders Edge station's regular team, but he must know by now that I'd worked closely with the station in a professional capacity in the past and could be trusted.

Time for a change of tack.

In the circumstances, it would be easy to use my relationship with Nathan, his boss, as a means of putting pressure on him to give me what I wanted. Not very honourable and something I was reluctant to do. Especially to someone I had only just met and who seemed an okay guy. But I couldn't understand why he was so cagey, and so needs must. But maybe I could take a more indirect approach.

I nodded and said, "Fair enough. In the end, it has to be your decision." I leaned back in my chair as if acquiescing. "The Chief's on his way back. I guess I could ask his advice if Willow hasn't turned up by then."

That seemed to have the desired effect. I could almost see the cogs turning in his mind at the mention of the Chief. And he must have known Nathan would want all the details.

"Okay, have it your way," he said and slapped his thighs in a show of resignation. "I just want you to know that all I'm trying to do here is save you some embarrassment. And I assure you, it's not going to help any."

"Embarrassment?"

Lynch chewed on his lower lip before answering. "The guy she made the complaint against was you."

CHAPTER FIVE

"How fucking dare she? Who the fuck does she think she is?"

I was in Nathan's office. Pacing the room, punching the air, mad as hell. And giving Nathan a hard time.

He had returned from Charwell a few minutes earlier. And I hadn't calmed down any. My heart was pounding and my face flushed and damp.

"Have you any idea the damage this could do to me?"

"It won't come to that." Nathan stood behind his desk, well clear of my jabbing fists.

"You remember what happened last time?" I said. "All that crap in the media." I turned once more and stormed across the room, still gesticulating. "I am not going through that again."

He moved towards me, rounded the corner of the desk and stepped in front of me, forcing me to a sudden halt. "Enough." He grabbed my arms and pinned them to my side. "Wave your arms around much more," he said, "and you'll take off."

I stiffened, jaw clenched, and fought to get my breathing under control.

"Try to stay calm and let's work our way through this." He held onto me for a moment longer until I'd composed myself and then released his grasp. "Did you learn any details?"

"Details?" My heart rate shot up again. "Why would I need details of something that never happened, anyway?"

"Because it's in the details you find the lie. You know that as well as

I do. Just get a grip of yourself, Mikey, and think this through objectively. Getting worked up isn't going to help."

Through clenched teeth, I drew in a lungful of air, and slowly brought my breathing back to normal again. Finally, trying to keep my voice even, I said, "It's difficult to be objective when it's personal."

"You're like two different people, calm and collected when dealing with others, but the moment you're personally involved, you're off on an emotional rampage. This isn't very constructive." The jaw was set firm, but his eyes were troubled, and the dark brow creased with worry.

A surge of regret swept through me, tempering my mood, and the anger slowly subsided.

I pressed a hand to his chest to steady myself, took another breath, and said, "Sorry, I had no right to dump that on you."

He pulled me to him, wrapped his arms around me, and stroked my back.

I let him comfort me, sheltered in his warm embrace. "I didn't mean to put you in the firing line."

He held me for a few moments longer and then, loosening his grip, he lowered himself onto the nearby couch and drew me down beside him. "We'll get this sorted, okay?"

I nodded, and he rose again, crossed over to the phone on the desk, and called reception. "Send Lynch in to see me the moment he gets back from his break," he said. "And no other interruptions."

He returned to sit beside me and squeezed my arm.

"Lynch must have been sure there was no case to answer. You have nothing to worry about."

I wasn't so sure. "I hope not."

"Of course, he will have to write it up in the incident log. We have to do this by the book. But he'll make it clear that Willow withdrew her allegation. Okay?"

"Okay." I grimaced, disappointed, but accepted his decision. I had harboured a private hope that Lynch might keep Willow's claim off the record. But Nathan's involvement would have put paid to that. There would never be any question of his not following procedure to the letter.

He wrapped an arm around my shoulder and pulled me to him.

"You're in the clear. This is not going any further."

But of course it would. And no matter how much he tried to reassure me, he must have known it too. Public profiles invite public scrutiny. And if the merest whisper of this got out, the media would be all over it like a rash. All my past indiscretions would be dredged up again.

I could just about bear any crap thrown my way. But, by association, Nathan would be splattered by the same shit storm. And that pained me more than anything.

Would we never be free of the past? I pressed a hand against his thigh. He had forgiven me before. But how far does forgiveness stretch? "You don't believe it, do you?"

He drew away and glared at me. "What the hell?"

I lowered my head.

"God knows, you've done some stupid things in your time. But you're not that stupid. How could you even ask such a question?"

As a statement of moral support, it could have been better phrased. But the intention behind the words was clear enough, so I accepted them with good grace. "Sorry. I was just thrown for a loop. This whole thing came out of nowhere and it shook me."

He pulled me close again and gave me an extra hug. "No one will believe it."

"I don't understand why she would do such a thing."

"You said yourself she took Donna's side during your divorce. Could that have been why? A way of getting back at you?"

"Even for her, that seems extreme. But whatever the reason, she has some explaining to do."

Nathan pointed a warning finger at me. "When she turns up, I don't want you going anywhere near her. You leave her to me to deal with. You hear?"

"What? I'm just supposed to sit back and ignore being accused of assault?"

"That's exactly what you're supposed to do."

I kept quiet. There seemed little point in arguing my case until it became an issue.

"I mean it, Mikey. It would only make matters worse."

I avoided responding directly. "You have to find her first," I said.

"In fact, she may have turned up for all we know."

"That's easily settled." He rose and crossed over to the phone once more. A few moments later, he was speaking with Robert Dunn at the Fairview. As he finished the call, he said, "If you bothered to check your phone now and again, you'd know how things stand."

"What's that supposed to mean?" I dug my phone out of my pocket and checked the screen. Four missed calls. All from the Fairview.

Nathan said, "Robert Dunn has been trying to get hold of you. Willow's husband called again. She's still not been in touch, and he's getting frantic."

"Sorry," I said, "I was so wound up, I was in no mood to take any calls."

Nathan returned and dropped to my side again. He said, "It seems to be the consensus here at the station that she changed her plans and didn't bother to let anyone know. Is that likely?"

"She's not the most reliable of people, that's for sure. And she can be impulsive. But her husband knows her better than anyone. And if he's worried, I guess it must be out of character, even for her."

"Then we have to presume there's cause for concern."

"So what happens now?" I said.

"For the moment, it's a local matter. I'll have enquiries made around the town, including the hospital, of course. And we'll try to track down anyone she knew from the old days. But if she hasn't turned up within forty-eight hours, we'll ramp it up and put her details out on the PNC Database."

"I'm not sure she stayed in touch with anyone from back then," I said. "Apart from Karen. Her sister lived nearby, but she moved away some time ago. There was someone she was close to at school, though. Amelia?"

"Amelia Cole. I remember her. They were inseparable."

A knock at the door interrupted us. As it opened, Nathan rose to greet the visitor.

It was Lynch.

Nathan waved him towards a chair and took up his position on the other side of the desk. "I need details about Willow's complaint." Straight to the point, as usual.

Lynch flushed and cleared his throat, "I didn't want to make a big deal of it."

"You were just doing your job. So let's go through it. Exactly as she reported it."

Lynch swivelled his chair around so he had us both in view. "She said she and Mikey had a row - she didn't go into detail - and that he grabbed her by the arms. She pulled herself away and as she stepped back, he struck her several times across the face with the back of his hand."

Anger welled up inside me again. I exploded. "That fucking woman."

A stern reproach from Nathan. "That's not helpful. Mikey."

"It wasn't meant to be helpful. I'm just so fucking furious. Have you any idea what it's like sitting here and listening to this bullshit?"

"Would you like to wait outside while the Sarge gives his report?"

I stiffened momentarily and then bowed my head. "Sorry. I'll be quiet. I need to hear this."

Lynch shuffled in his chair. "She told me the incident took place on the outer deck. And when I asked her to be more specific about the time, she became evasive."

I said, "Surprise, surprise."

Nathan shot me a dour look and asked Lynch to continue.

Lynch said, "I reminded her that the outer deck was a public area and had been in use throughout the day. But she was unable to tell me if there were any witnesses to the incident. And she kept changing the details. At that point, I put on some pressure and warned her about the consequences of making false claims."

"Is that when she withdrew her complaint?" asked Nathan.

"With some reluctance," said Lynch. "But her story was all over the place. She'd obviously not thought it through. And she knew she'd been caught out in a lie. That's when I drove her back to the Fairview - well, as near as possible - and I made it clear that making a false claim was, itself, an offence and she should consider herself fortunate I didn't pursue the matter."

Nathan picked up a pen from the desk and twisted it over and over in his fingers as he thought over Lynch's words. Finally, he dropped the pen and said, "Put the case to rest. But just to be on the safe side, I'd like a breakdown of her movements during that entire period. I want to know who she spoke to and where she was at every moment. And the timing of the alleged assault. Okay?"

Lynch nodded his agreement and said, "And I'll make a few discrete enquiries around the station and at HQ. There were several of our guys at the reception who should be able to vouch for Mikey's movements."

"Good. Then we'll let it rest there." Nathan rose from his chair to signal the end of the meeting.

As Lynch took his leave, he came back to the couch and sat beside me again.

I said, "It strikes me as odd she should make such an outrageous claim and then disappear when challenged about it. You have to wonder about her mental state."

"That's something for us to worry about," said Nathan, "not you. And if she tries anything like that again, I'll make damn sure she learns the consequences of making false accusations." He squeezed my leg. "Okay?"

I nodded. There was something about his confident manner that was always so reassuring. And now the shock at hearing of Willow's claim was wearing off, I was more at ease. I said, "Everyone should have their own personal policeman. It makes life so much simpler."

I got a grunt in response.

It was easy to forget sometimes how much I depended on him. He was the one who kept me grounded, the one I could always rely on. Knowing I had his support mattered more than anything.

He glanced at his watch. "Well, your personal policeman is starving. So let's go get a late lunch, shall we?"

As he rose again, we were interrupted by another knock at the door and Sgt Barber stepped in. "Sorry for the interruption, Chief, but I thought you'd want to know. They found Willow Brookes."

"At last," I said. "That Goddamn woman has a lot to answer for. I'm going to make her regret what she did."

Sgt Barber looked troubled. He swallowed hard and said, "Maybe I should rephrase that." A pause. "They found Willow Brookes's body."

CHAPTER SIX

A chill breeze blew in from the sea, and I turned my collar up against its biting sting. The taste of the briny sea air was in my mouth.

Nathan and I were tramping over the wet sand towards the rocky outcrop where a luckless beachcomber had found Willow's body early that afternoon.

Gulls wheeled high above us, their cries cutting across the rhythmic pounding of the sea along the receding shoreline to our right.

"Should I be here?" I said.

"Why wouldn't you be?"

"With this assault claim hanging over me, I thought-"

Nathan grabbed me by the arm and brought us both to a sudden halt. "A false claim. One that's been put to rest. Case closed, okay?"

"It might not seem that straightforward from the outside."

He snorted. "I make my decisions according to internal police procedures, not the misguided presumptions of outsiders."

"Just saying."

"Well, forget it. I need your input here." He let go of my arm, and we walked on again.

Nathan said, "I think we should let Richard and Karen know."

"Dear God, no," I said. "Not while they're on honeymoon. Let's give them that, at least."

"Karen was her friend. She'd want to know."

"She'll find out soon enough. And it's not like she can do much about it."

Miles Barber had been quick to set up a first responders team. Nathan and I had followed on behind. Already, bright yellow barrier tape cordoned off a wide area around the rocks and a blue and white plastic tent had been erected over the body at the base of the crumbling cliff wall. Protecting the body from outside exposure - and from unwanted attention - would have been a priority.

A green and yellow paramedic response vehicle was parked on the nearby slipway running down to the beach. A paramedic in green and yellow response vest stood by it, talking into a radio.

At the access point, a uniformed officer greeted Nathan with a salute and handed us both protective coveralls, gloves, and overshoes.

We donned them and made our way over to where Sgt Lynch was barking out orders to several other uniforms.

Lynch greeted us with a grim expression. "Not exactly the outcome we were looking for."

Nathan acknowledged this with a grunt and said, "I asked Mikey here to give us the benefit of his expertise in crime scene assessment."

Lynch said, "I'm not sure we'll need your help on this one, Mikey. Looks like we have a jumper here."

"What makes you so sure?"

That came out sharper than intended. But I get snippy when people make assumptions. We all do it. Human nature. And I'm as guilty as everyone else. But not in a situation like this. Reading crime and accident scenes is what I do for a living, and it requires better judgement than that. We need to keep open minds no matter how obvious something may appear on the surface. And in his position, Lynch should have known better.

He looked up towards the clifftop. "The trajectory seems about right, judging by where the body landed. And the extent of blunt force trauma suggests high impact damage."

"It could have been an accident. She may even have been pushed for all we know."

"Maybe, but Willow has a history that suggests otherwise. It wouldn't be the first time she'd tried to take her own life."

Nathan said, "When was that?"

"Way back. Just before she moved to London."

"I knew her then," said Nathan, "but I didn't know about the suicide attempt."

Lynch said, "I got it from that friend of hers, Amelia, not long after it happened. We were all part of the same crowd back then. It was an overdose. Relationship problems, I think. But they tried to keep it quiet."

"I remember the family left in a hurry," said Nathan. "You've seen more of her recently, Mikey. Do you have any thoughts on her state of mind?"

"I didn't get too involved with her. I tried to stay out of her way as much as possible. But she was certainly emotionally volatile."

Nathan said, "What do we know so far?"

Lynch nodded back to where the body lay. "It's a real mess back there." He shot a glance my way, and said, "For the moment, it's reasonable to presume she fell from the clifftop. As for the how and why..."

He pointed up to an overhang beneath which the cliff face had crumbled. "You can see how dangerous it is up there. These cliffs are subject to erosion. And this whole stretch is fenced off with warning signs every few yards. No one in their right mind is going to risk getting too close to the edge just to get a better view."

Nathan said, "Any recent land-slips?"

Lynch confirmed otherwise. "Already checked it out." He continued, "As for foul play, sure it's a possibility. But not very likely."

"Even so," I said, "it's as well not to presume too much at this early stage. There's a danger of looking for supporting evidence at the expense of any other kind. Best not to make assumptions."

Nathan butted in. "Nothing is ever ruled out, Mikey. You should know that. Unexplained deaths are always treated as potential crimes." There was a frosty edge to his tone, and I hoped I hadn't overstepped the mark.

To Lynch, I said, "No offence intended." I nodded towards where two constables crouched on the rocky surface carrying out fingertip searches. "I can see you're covering all the bases."

Lynch grinned. "No offence taken. We're all on the same side here. And you're right, of course. We shouldn't make assumptions."

"Let's go take a closer look," said Nathan.

I braced myself mentally and followed them towards where the tent flapped and shuddered in the quickening breeze. The seaweed-strewn sand gave way to pebbles and then to rocky ground, and we had to pick our way carefully over the uneven terrain.

The rocky outcrop where the body had been found stood proud of the surrounding area, and this stretch of beach widened where it ran back into a deep indentation in the cliff face.

We reached the tent, and I said, "This part of the beach gets cut off when the tide comes in, doesn't it?"

Lynch confirmed that it did. "This stretch has been accessible for the last hour, and we have about three left before the tide reaches the bay."

I said, "So the body could have lain underwater for a while?"

Lynch shook his head. "It's still shallow here at high tide. About waist height. And this shelf of rock never gets covered. Lucky for us, 'cos we're not likely to lose any possible forensic evidence."

Nathan nodded toward the paramedic response vehicle. "I presume the medics have examined the body?"

"Just to confirm she's dead. We're waiting for the Pathologist to make his examination."

"He's on his way? We'll need to work quickly before the tide comes in."

"He should be here in plenty of time, Chief."

Nathan grunted. "Okay, let's do this." He pulled back the tent flap and stood to one side so we could all get a good look at the body.

I swallowed hard and forced myself to look at the crushed remains of what had once been Willow Brookes.

The body was a ragged mess of shattered limbs and bloodied clothing. A blood-soaked overcoat covered most of the injuries, but the contorted shape beneath the garment told how extensive they were. The skull had shattered, making the face unrecognisable, and deep tears and lacerations covered the exposed limbs. A bone protruded from one leg where it had broken and was folded back along the side of the body. These were injuries consistent with a fall from a height.

In this game, it's not as if I hadn't seen my share of corpses. And although I would never be fully accustomed to the spectacle of violent death, it was no longer quite the sickening distressing experience it had once been.

But this was different.

This was someone I had known in life. And it was hard to reconcile the difference between the living breathing person I had once known, active and vibrant, with all her tics and traits and behaviours, and that cold dead thing she had become, drained of the life force that, for good or ill, had made her the unique being she once was. Despite my animosity towards her when she was alive, I was sorry Willow had to end her life like this.

I turned away and stared out across the beach to where bright pools of water, stirred by the breeze, caught the sun's rays and flashed and sparkled in a parody of animated life.

Nathan said, "We are sure it's Willow?"

"There was some ID in her shoulder bag," Lynch said. "And I recognise the clothes she wore when she came to the station."

"And has her husband been informed? Nathan asked.

Lynch confirmed that details had been passed to the local force, and an officer was being dispatched to break the news.

I'd forgotten about Owen. The shock of Willow's sudden and unexpected death had put all thoughts of him from my mind. But now my thoughts were with him and his son. He would surely be aware by now that something was badly wrong. And he was about to have his worst fears confirmed.

And something else. Something that, in light of more pressing concerns, we had forgotten.

I interrupted Nathan and Lynch's conversation.

"You were right, Sarge," I said to Lynch. "You don't need me here." I squeezed Nathan's arm. "I'm sure you both have a lot to do so I'll get out of your way. I'll catch up with you later."

After bidding them both goodbye, I set off back the way we came. It was my more immediate intention to look around the clifftop so I could get a better picture of what may have happened. But my leaving was as much about finding time to think through the broader implications of Willow's death.

Once the investigation was underway, Owen would learn of the events leading up to his wife's demise. And that included her visit to the police station, one of the last places she had been seen alive. Owen would want to know why she was there.

Earlier, Nathan had assured me that details of Willow's complaint would go no further. Circumstances had rendered that assurance baseless.

Willow's death would soon be public knowledge. And the reason for her visit to the police would be public knowledge too.

Tragic enough that Owen would have to cope with the loss of his wife, he would also have to deal with her assault claim against me.

And whilst that would increase his suffering to a level that was unimaginable, it wouldn't make my position any less difficult to cope with either.

I was about to be caught up in his nightmare and life for both of us would soon get a whole lot rougher.

CHAPTER SEVEN

By the time I made the clifftop, I was panting. I grabbed hold of the guardrail at the top of the steps and paused to catch my breath as I took in the view.

From the town centre, this point could be reached with little effort by following the main road along a gradual incline. But the only means of access from the shore was via steep concrete steps set into the face of the cliff, and it had taken me several exhausting minutes to climb them.

The wind blew in from the sea. It was stronger here, and sudden gusts carried with them the occasional muted sounds of activity from the beach below.

The cove itself, where the police were at work, was hidden from view around a curve in the cliff's face.

Following the well-worn grassy verge, I made my way in that direction, keeping a safe distance from the chain-link fence that prevented access to the crumbling edge.

I passed a number of brightly painted signs, posted at regular intervals and warning of the dangers of straying too far from the path.

In places, the land had slipped away, taking parts of the broken rusty fence with it, and leaving several gaps.

One gap marked a spot above the bay. And it was from here, presumably, that Willow had fallen to her death on the rocks below.

Standing well back from the edge, I crouched down and examined the ground in that direction as best I could.

There were no signs of human activity. Not that I should have been surprised. At a location like this, open to the worst of the elements, any signs of disturbance would have soon vanished.

I rose again, turned my back to the sea and scanned the surrounding terrain.

To my right, the large expanse of flat grass gave way to scrub-land and a few stunted windblown trees. Beyond that, a denser wooded area stretched to the headland and then another sharp drop to the sea below.

To the left, the road from town led into a small car park at the side of which stood a shuttered burger shack. Way over in the distance before me was Yates's farm.

There was a clear line of sight to this spot from both the burger stall and the farm. The burger stall had been closed for the winter, so it was unlikely someone would have been around to witness any dubious activity.

The farm, however, was a different matter.

I headed towards it.

This is where Sgt Lynch had investigated a disturbance earlier that day. Coincidence? Lynch had made little of it, so it was probably nothing of note. But it was, at least, worth checking.

Plaster-coated brick buildings stood around a cobbled square. Access was through a wide wooden gate anchored between two of the smaller outbuildings. The gate faced the clifftop and the main house stood opposite on the far side of the yard. Four plump hens wandered about the square, pecking at the dirt.

The metal-hinged gate squeaked as I entered, and two geese, reacting to the noise, waddled towards me from the across the yard, honking a warning.

A figure wearing coveralls appeared in the open doorway of an outbuilding to my right, obviously alerted by the noise, and shooed away the geese as I approached him.

"Mr Yates?"

"That I am."

He was about my age, maybe slightly older, shorter than me and of a stocky build with unkempt thinning blond hair. He was wiping his hands on a piece of ragged cloth, and there was a cautious edge to his voice when he spoke.

"You with the police?" he said.

"Why do you ask?"

"I heard sirens. Don't often hear them out here. Something going on?"

I explained who I was and why I was here. "You'll find out soon enough," I said. "The uniforms will probably be around asking questions later. We have a body down on the beach."

He scratched his chin. "Real sorry to hear that. Not sure what I can do to help, though."

"It looks like she fell from the cliff," I said. "You can't see the exact spot from here, but if you were out and about, you may have seen something, or maybe you saw her passing by."

"A jumper?"

"We're keeping an open mind on that for the moment."

"Don't know what I can tell you. Lots of people passing by. Dog walkers, mostly. But I'm too busy to take much notice."

"Is there anyone else here who might have seen something?"

"Just me and the missus. And she's been down in the town all day. She runs our veg stall down in the market there."

"No suspicious-looking people hanging around? No unusual activity?"

He shrugged. "Can't help you there."

"What about earlier today? You called the police. What was that about?"

He pulled back his head, forehead creased, and stared into my face, perplexed. "You tying 'em together? That what you're thinking?"

"I'm not thinking anything. But at the moment, it's best not to rule anything out. So what happened?"

"Not sure anything did."

Now it was my turn to be perplexed. "What's that supposed to mean?"

He swallowed and said, "I was jumpy is all. Thought I heard someone moving around in one of the sheds and it spooked me."

"And was there?"

"No idea. I got the police out. They found nowt either."

That puzzled me. Yates looked like the sort who could handle himself. Not someone to be easily intimidated by a mere noise. I wondered why he hadn't checked it out himself. The surprise must have shown on my face because he immediately launched into an explanation.

"See, you won't know this. Something happened a few years back. Me and the missus had a break-in. Early morning. Two of them. They had a reckoning we kept a lot of money up here. Weren't right pleased to learn they'd got it wrong." He rubbed his head. "Still have a scar where they whacked me."

He waved a hand towards the gate. "Look around out there," he said. "We're right out of town here. No one else about. We're an easy target for them as fancies their chances. I don't take risks anymore. That's for the police."

"Understandable," I said and offered him my sympathies. "Would you mind if I looked around the shed?"

He hesitated and shrugged again. "No reason not to. But you'll not find anything. The police didn't."

He led me across the yard to a smaller brick-built shed at the side of the house.

Inside, the air was stale. Several old metal oil drums, festooned with dust-laden cobwebs, were pushed together in one corner. Above them, a length of rusty chain hung from a crossbeam. In the opposite corner stood a stack of plastic containers of various colours and sizes, most of them bearing warning symbols of one kind or another. A few rusty hand tools lay scattered around the concrete floor.

"So what did you hear?" I asked.

"It was like the chain here banging against one of the drums. I heard it from inside the house. The door was closed, so I knew it was no animal."

I took a closer look around the building and examined the door and the single small window. "Seems to be a solid enough structure, no gaps for the wind to get through. So I think we can rule that out."

"To be honest with you," he said, "I felt daft afterwards. It wouldn't have bothered me at one time. I suppose, as it turns out, it was just someone sheltering from the wind. Or could have been kids nosing around."

"Given your experience, I'm sure it was best to err on the side of caution." I took a last look around and said, "I think we're done here.

Nothing much to see."

He pushed open the door and stood aside to let me through. We headed back to the gate where I took my leave of him after reminding him that the local police would be around later asking questions about the body on the beach.

Instead of taking the steps back down to the beach, I took the easy route back into town across the car park.

Sometimes in my line of work, you get an instinct for when something isn't quite right. A feeling that something is amiss. It's not something you can explain, just a feeling you get based on years of experience. I had that feeling right then.

I would have given anything to know what really happened there that morning.

CHAPTER EIGHT

I stared at the screen. My mouth was dry, and there was an empty feeling in the pit of my stomach. I tried to steady my nerves with a few slow breaths but was finding it hard to stay calm.

Nathan and I were seated in one of the smaller meeting rooms at Elders Edge police station. On the desk before us, a monitor displayed an image of the main interview room. By its side sat a microphone.

"I'm really not looking forward to this," I said.

Nathan didn't need to ask why.

"You have nothing to worry about," he said.

"He's sure to find out Willow was here. And he'll want to know why."

"All incidents reported to the police have to be handled with regard to the privacy of victims, witnesses and suspects. And as the matter has now been put to rest, specific details of Willow's complaint remain confidential."

The formal cop-speak did nothing to reassure me.

It was the day after the discovery of Willow's body. After learning of her death, Owen Brookes had travelled up the evening before, and Andrew Lynch had seen him settled in at the Fairview. This morning, Lynch had picked him up and brought him to the station where he was now about to be interviewed by Sgt Miles Barber.

We didn't have long to wait. The door of the interview room opened. Miles Barber entered, followed by Owen.

Barber carried a manila file, a tan shoulder bag, and a clear plastic wallet containing what appeared to be several personal items. He offered Owen a seat and handed him the bag and wallet as they settled themselves on either side of the desk.

After opening the file on the desk before him, Barber retrieved a printed sheet of paper, slid it across the desk to Owen, and offered him a pen. "Just a formality, Sir. But if you could check the contents of the bag and the wallet and confirm receipt by signing the form."

Owen stared at the items before him, and after a cursory look at their contents, he signed the form, pushed it back to Barber and dropped the pen on top of it.

"I'm sure it's fine," he said. Strain coloured his features. The grey pallor aged him beyond his thirty-five years, the usual infectious boyish grin replaced by a grim tight-lipped expression that betrayed his pain.

"Dear God." I turned away, ashamed at worrying more about my own anxieties than his suffering.

Nathan shot me a sympathetic look.

Miles Barber tried to put Owen at his ease, asking if he needed a drink before they started the interview.

A rapid shake of the head and Owen said, "I don't really understand why you need to interview me at all. It's not as if I was here."

"We're trying to establish your wife's state of mind and movements before the… before the incident in question."

"You say they found her at the foot of some cliffs. Are you saying she jumped?" The challenge in Owen's voice anticipated Barber's answer and dared him to voice it.

Barber's answer was cautious. "We're still waiting for the autopsy report, but at this stage, nothing is being ruled out. We have to consider all possibilities."

"There is no way Willow would have taken her own life. She had no cause." Owen's face reddened, and he folded his arms.

Barber held up a calming hand. "Which is precisely why we need your input. Anything you can tell us about your wife's general disposition, if she had any particular concerns, any recent changes."

"I thought maybe you could tell me."

Barber looked puzzled.

"I'm told she disappeared soon after filing a complaint here," said Owen. "So if anyone knows her current disposition, you do."

Barber shuffled in his chair, clearly ill at ease. "I'm aware of her visit. But it's not connected to the current investigation."

Owen wasn't about to let it go. "So why was she here?"

"We're not at liberty to reveal those details."

"So you're closing ranks?"

"I beg your pardon, Sir." Barber's sympathetic tone faded.

"Michael MacGregor is one of your own, isn't he?"

I gasped and pushed back in my chair. A knot tightened in my stomach.

Nathan said, "What the hell?"

In the interview room, Miles Barber tried to regain control. "If we could get back to the point of our discussion, Mr Brookes."

"She was here to make a complaint against MacGregor. An assault, wasn't it?"

"Where did you hear that, Sir?"

"Sorry." Owen's tone took on a sarcastic edge. "I'm not at liberty to reveal those details."

For once, Barber was thrown off-kilter.

Owen said, "Fortunately, the police weren't the only ones Willow spoke to. So this time, there's going to be no cover-up."

"This time? Cover-up?"

Owen grimaced. "Let's just say that recent events have shaken my confidence in the integrity of the police." He leaned towards Barber, and said, "So are you going to tell me what happened?"

I said, "Can we stop this?"

"Let's see where it goes first," said Nathan.

Barber continued. "Your wife was advised to drop her complaint after being told of the consequences of making a false claim."

"And of course, she wasn't put under any pressure, was she? It couldn't possibly be that you were covering for one of your own?"

"There were serious flaws in Mrs Brookes account of the alleged incident. The complaint was judged to be without foundation."

"How very convenient. And of course, that judgement had nothing to do with MacGregor's close connection to the local police. Not to mention he just happens to be in a relationship with your Chief."

Nathan reached across the desk and pressed a button on the microphone. "End this now."

Barber reacted by rising to his feet. "This interview is over for the moment, Mr Brookes. We'll continue at a later time when you've had time to compose yourself."

He made his way over to the door, opened it, and stood aside to usher Owen out.

"Believe me, this isn't over by a long way," said Owen. He scooped up the bag and wallet from the desk. "Let's see what the media think about it, shall we?"

Barber followed him out of the room and closed the door.

Nathan leaned over and turned off the monitor. His face, reflected in the blank screen, was creased in a scowl.

All I could do was stare at it, frozen in place. Owen's threat had hit me like a physical blow. "I have to talk with him," I said. "Try to persuade him not to involve the media."

"No." Nathan's tone was firm. "That's the last thing you should do."

"I can't go through all that again. You can't have forgotten what it was like."

"I'll deal with it. You must not get involved."

My expression must have told him I wasn't convinced.

"Listen to me, Mikey." He swivelled his chair around to face me full on. "Willow's assault claim was put to rest. Case closed. There was no charge to answer. And that will be the official response to any media enquiry."

"You can't believe that will be the end of it? The media aren't interested in the truth? Scandal and gossip sell newspapers, not facts."

"I know only too well how the media works. So why give them more ammunition? Owen Brookes is in no mood to listen. He'll go to the press, anyway. And any pressure you put on him would be misconstrued as intimidation. You'd be playing into their hands."

I tried to protest, but he held up a restraining hand. "Confronting Owen isn't going to help. You need to keep your distance."

I opened my mouth to answer but closed it again. I knew better than to pursue the argument. Once Nathan made up his mind about something, no amount of pleading would persuade him otherwise.

I pushed myself to my feet. "No point my hanging around here then. I wouldn't want anyone to think I was interfering."

"Mikey." There was a reprimand in his tone.

I gripped the chair's toprail with both hands and squeezed it hard. "Sorry, but I'm not in the best of moods right now. And there's nothing to keep me here anyway, so I may as well go home."

Nathan rose too. He took me by the arms and stared into my face as if looking for something. A moment later, he pulled me close, wrapped his arms around me and cupped the back of my head with a hand.

His voice softened, and he hugged me tight, "I know this is hard for you," he said, "but we're in it together. You know I'm always here for you." He pulled away, held me by the arms once more, and tried a smile. "Okay?"

Thawing a little, I returned the smile and said, "I'm lucky to have you."

"Works both ways."

I wasn't so sure about that. Where I was concerned, he always seemed to be on the losing end of a bad deal.

He kept me back for a few minutes while he made sure the coast was clear. Once he'd confirmed it was and reminded me to keep a low profile, he walked me to the main door, and I headed home.

I'd intended to drop by the Fairview on my way back to check in with Robert Dunn and make sure everything was running smoothly.

Now it didn't seem such a good idea.

Not if I was to be sure of avoiding Owen.

But wouldn't that send the wrong message? Suggest I was afraid to face him? The act of someone with a guilty conscience?

Maybe I should brave it out, show him I had no reason to hide away.

And perhaps if I spoke to him, explained what happened, I could dissuade him from going to the press.

At the junction with the High Street, I stopped and stared into the window of an electrical goods shop, feigning an interest in a display of Smart TVs while I struggled to reach a decision.

Should I carry on down the High Street towards home or turn off and head over to the Fairview?

Owen was in a bad place right now. And the last thing we needed was a rift between us. He needed my support at a time like this.

And he couldn't really believe I would assault Willow. He was distraught and his judgement was clouded. Shouldn't I try to reason with him, make him see how wrong this was? And maybe I could persuade him to go easy on me and let the police concentrate on the investigation into Willow's death rather than wasting time fending off the media.

I turned away from the window and headed towards the Fairview.

CHAPTER NINE

The air was rich with the smell of the sea.

Shops and other commercial buildings lined the road on either side. And with the High Street behind me, I was within sight of the seawall running alongside the Esplanade adjacent to Salem Row at its far end.

This is where Willow was last seen alive.

Salem Row was on my way to the Fairview, and I'd stopped to look around. I walked towards the Esplanade, scanning the surrounding buildings. It was as if, by doing so, I could conjure up Willow's presence and follow her to her final destination.

What had changed her mind? What had led her away from the Fairview and thoughts of home, and persuaded her, instead, to take the treacherous path that had led to her demise?

"Michael MacGregor?"

The sound of my name snapped me out of my reverie and I turned towards it.

A broad-shouldered man in dark-blue overalls crossed towards me from the forecourt of a small open-fronted building. He was tall with brown hair and an angular stubbled face with chiselled features. He carried a pack of cigarettes. "It is Michael MacGregor, isn't it?"

The face was familiar. I couldn't quite place it until I glanced up at the signboard on the metal-framed construction behind him. It read 'Tanner's Autos'.

This was the man I had seen speaking with Andrew Lynch at the wedding reception. It was only two days ago, but seemed an age away.

As we had never met, I supposed he knew me from my TV appearances. It always surprised me to be recognised, given that most of my work was through radio with just the occasional foray into TV. Or maybe it was from a photo in one of the media rags at the time of my divorce scandal. I hoped not.

I held out a hand in greeting. "Mr Tanner?"

The creased brow gave way to a smile when I pointed to the signboard. "Your local publicity is better than mine," I said.

He took my hand and shook it. "I'm a big fan. I never missed an episode of your crime series." Before I could thank him, he said, "I hear you're mixed up in this Willow thing."

My muscles tensed, and there was a tightness in my throat. "Mixed up?"

"Helping with the investigation." He opened the pack in his hand, shook out a cigarette, and offered me one.

The tension eased away. I really shouldn't be so alarmist. I declined the offer, and said, "You've heard about it?"

"The police have been round most of the morning asking questions. I still can't believe it." He pulled a lighter from his pocket, lit the cigarette, took a deep drag, and expelled a cloud of smoke. "I was laughing and joking with her yesterday. There was nary a hint of her doing something like this."

It seemed to be a foregone conclusion she'd killed herself. I didn't bother disputing it. "You knew her?"

Another cloud of smoke. "From way back. We were catching up on old times yesterday."

Following his line of thinking, I said, "I hear she'd done something like this before. Back in those old days. You know anything about that?"

He stared at me, face creased in a frown, the cigarette halfway to his lips. "First I've heard of it. She was a real party girl back then. Always up for a good time." He drew on his cigarette again. "You never know what's going on in someone's head, do you?"

True enough. My job would be so much simpler if we did.

He took a last draw of the cigarette, dropped it to the tarmac, and ground it underfoot. "That's my break over. Back to work for both of us."

I'd never stopped working. But I didn't contradict him. "I don't suppose you saw where she went after you'd finished chatting."

"She crossed over and took the left turn at the end of the road. That's the last I saw of her."

That was odd. The Fairview was to the right. To the left, the Esplanade ran past a row of shops and ended at the coastguard building. Beyond that was a dead end.

He must have noticed my puzzlement. "That old schoolfriend of hers, Amelia Cole, runs a newsagents just around the corner. She probably went to see her."

"Did you tell that to the police?"

He shrugged. "Didn't think to. They were calling on all the shops, anyway. And she may not have gone there. It was just a thought."

I thanked him for his time and raised a hand in farewell as I crossed the road towards the Esplanade.

All too often, our experiences inform our present actions. Regardless of how long ago they were. And Amelia Cole seems to have been close to Willow at a point of emotional turmoil in her life. Maybe she could throw some light on Willow's more recent behaviour.

The newsagents was just around the corner next to the beauticians. It was an old-fashioned glass-fronted shop with a faded sign above the window announcing it as Cole's Newsagent and Confectioners.

Going by the old 'birds of a feather' adage, the straggly haired, frumpy woman behind the counter didn't strike me as the type to have associated with the more sophisticated-looking Willow. I'd conjured up a completely different image in my mind.

She was leaning on the counter, checking her mobile screen, and looked up at the sound of the bell as I entered the shop.

The practised smile faded and her eyes narrowed. "Are you from the police?" It sounded more like an accusation than a question.

I treated her to one of my more winsome smiles. "Near enough. I work with them. Is it that obvious?"

She wasn't to be won over. "How many more of you do I have to speak to? I do have a shop to run, you know."

She didn't look exactly rushed off her feet. But I let the claim pass without comment.

I told her who and what I was, that I was part of the team investigating the death of Willow Brookes, and how my role and approach differed from theirs. "It's my job to build up a profile of Willow in the hopes of understanding her recent state of mind. It could help explain her actions."

Amelia didn't seem impressed. "The police wanted to know if I'd seen her around here the other day. I hadn't."

"It's not the present that concerns me. I'm trying to learn about her past. I hear you used to be close friends."

There was a wariness in her tone when she replied. "Once. A long time ago. But I'm not sure how that helps."

"You heard what happened? That she may have taken her own life?"

She raised a hand to her throat in a calming gesture and screwed her eyes shut. The sound of her breathing was the only thing that broke the silence for several seconds. She nodded. "Yes, I heard." Her voice had softened. "She was always so full of life. It's hard to believe it could have ended like this."

"Something must have changed her," I said. "It wouldn't be the first time, would it?

Amelia opened her eyes and stared at me in silence.

"She tried to take her life once before. An overdose, wasn't it?"

She clutched the gold chain that hung around her neck and twisted it. "I don't know anything about that." She averted her gaze, and the stiffness in her voice matched the stiffness in her posture.

"Sgt Lynch told me about it. I understand he learned it from you."

"I know no more about it than anyone else." Her face flushed. "We'd gone our separate ways by then."

"You had a falling out, didn't you?"

"I don't know where you heard that, but it's not true. We drifted apart, that's all. People do you know." There was a defensive edge to her tone. "And anyway, she moved to London soon after."

"You never kept in touch?"

"There wasn't much point. We had our own lives to get on with."

"Was there anyone else she may have stayed in touch with? Any of your old crowd?"

"Not that I know of. You could try her sister, though. She may have been in contact with her. She runs a dog training centre and kennels over in Colton Drey."

"They still live locally? I thought they'd moved."

"They?"

"I met Laurel and her husband when they visited Willow in London."

Amelia laughed. It had a hollow ring to it. "You're behind the times. They divorced some time ago and Laurel moved back here."

"I hadn't realised. I didn't know her that well."

"It's not something she likes to talk about."

"I'm sure the local police will have spoken to her already, but I'll check it out."

I questioned her some more, trying to build up a picture of Willow during those early days, her interests, significant relationships, family life. Amelia gave me nothing, as if distancing herself from any association she may have had with Willow. For someone who had once been close to Willow, that seemed odd.

The jangle of the bell interrupted us. A freckle-faced boy dragged a harassed-looking woman into the shop by the hand and headed for the counter, his eyes fixed on the row of bottled sweets.

I stepped away to give them room.

The interruption thwarted further attempts to extract useful information from Amelia Cole. Not that I would get any more from her, anyway; her uncooperative attitude made that obvious enough. And so I signalled that I was leaving and mouthed a goodbye.

I left the shop and resumed my journey to the Fairview.

This was the second time in as many days my instincts had told me something was being held back.

And I was still no nearer to figuring out what it was.

CHAPTER TEN

I retraced my steps and continued my course along the Esplanade. As the Fairview came into sight, my confidence, like the sea to my left, ebbed away.

Was I doing the right thing? The choice I faced was simple enough; endure another public trashing of my reputation, or try to stop Owen leaking details of Willow's complaint. That would risk being accused of pressuring the victim's husband. But which was worse? Either way, I was on to a hiding for nothing.

I was still debating my options when a police patrol car sped past, overtaking me from behind. It pulled up ahead by the steps leading up to the Fairview terrace, and the rear offside passenger door opened.

Owen stepped out.

A tightness gripped my throat. I faltered and slowed to a halt.

As he made his way to the steps, he caught sight of me, stopped, and turned to face me.

There was a time he would have welcomed me with a cheery smile and a slap on the back and earned himself an affectionate hug in return. Those familiar greetings that pass between old friends.

But not this time. The remembered boyish grin was now a tight-lipped grimace, and the once amiable twinkle in his eyes was the cold blank stare of someone who took no pleasure in seeing me again.

I picked up the pace once more and headed towards him, clenching and unclenching my fists in a feeble attempt to ease the tension in my muscles, willing myself to relax.

He stood his ground as I approached, legs apart. A confrontational stance if ever I saw one. He was clutching the plastic wallet and handbag. The cold, flinty gaze and tight expression didn't bode well for what I'd hoped might be a civilised discussion. As if that was going to happen, anyway. Wishful thinking, I guess. But at least my dilemma had been resolved. I had no choice but to face him now.

I drew up in front of him, and we faced each other in silence, each waiting for the other to make the first exchange. His face was worn, and the grey pallor accentuated red-rimmed eyes.

The whine of a passing motorcycle cut through the rhythmic lapping of the sea and faded into the distance.

Owen was the first to speak. He held up the plastic bag and waved it in my face. "Just picked up what's left of my dead wife. But, hey, not to worry. At least you're off the hook now."

He clamped his mouth shut in a grim, tight line, and I flinched.

"I know what you've heard, Owen. But it's not true." I held out my hands, imploring. "Please believe me. I would never do such a thing."

He wasn't buying it so I pushed the official line to support my plea. "You've just heard the police response. If they thought there was a case to answer, they would have pressed charges."

I hadn't meant to tell him I'd witnessed his interview. Given his comment about the police closing ranks, he wasn't likely to believe me, anyway. But what the hell. He was going to think the worst, no matter what I told him.

A flicker of confusion crossed his face and then enlightenment dawned in his eyes. "You heard my interview. Is that where you've just come from?" The contemptuous tone was back. He shook his head. "Why am I not surprised? It must have been a shock to learn you'd been caught out. Were you hoping to keep it under wraps?"

"What do I have to say to convince you, Owen? I'm telling you, I did not assault Willow."

"They think she killed herself." He thrust his face towards mine. "And if she did, then something drove her to it. It didn't come out of nowhere."

We all strive to make sense of the world. And when tragedy strikes, we look for reasons, for something or someone to blame. And right now, I was it. Owen was angry, railing against the injustice of his loss. And I was the focus of that anger.

But I had to tread carefully here. This was a man struggling with grief. The last thing I wanted was for this to turn into a futile, escalating war of words. Or something worse.

Trying to keep my voice low and even, I said, "Whatever it is you've heard, you must also know I strenuously deny it."

"Why would she make it up?"

"I don't know that any more than you do."

"Maybe her instincts were better than mine."

"What?"

"I need to spell it out? I know you argued. Is that why you hit her? Because she saw you for the kind of person you really are and told it like it was?"

He raised a clenched fist. "I swear, if I thought I could get away with it..."

I braced myself. "And what good would that do?"

"None for me, that's for sure. I'd have your cop buddies jumping all over me. But it would make me feel a hell of a lot better."

I stood my ground and stared him straight in the eye. "I didn't hit her, Owen. She made it up. And as for the argument, that was down to Willow."

This wasn't going well. He seemed determined to cast me in the role of villain, no matter how much I pleaded my case.

"Let me tell you what happened," I said. "Exactly as it happened." And so I talked him through our confrontation, told him of Willow's scathing attack on my moral integrity. "Not that I blame her," I said.

I held my hands up in a show of acceptance. "Mea culpa. I deserved it. And it brought it home to me just how strongly she felt. She and Donna had become good friends, and Willow took Donna's side. You know that. I can only imagine she wanted to get back at me out of some sort of misguided loyalty to Donna."

"Really? And then killed herself out of remorse? Not very likely, is it?"

"I have no idea why Willow would want to take her own life. But it wouldn't be the first time she'd tried, would it?"

A strangled cry escaped his lips. Slowly shaking his head, he kept his gaze fixed on me, staring at me open-mouthed and wide-eyed. His face sagged, and what little colour there was in his complexion drained away.

"Oh my God. You didn't know." I raised a hand and held it toward him, open-palmed in a show of appeasement. "That was crass of me. I'm so sorry. I thought you knew."

Owen's face creased in a picture of pain. "I don't believe it. You're making it up."

"Why would I?"

"You tell me."

"You don't need to take my word for it."

"Really? I should ask your police buddies, should I? Yeah, right. Like I'd get the truth from them." He pointed an accusatory finger at me. "This is down to you. I don't know what happened between you and Willow. But whatever it was, you drove her to this."

An elderly man with a walking stick shuffled past us from behind me and glanced at Owen. He shook his head and muttered as he moved on.

I waited until he was out of earshot and said, "Owen, please, let's not turn this into a public spectacle. Can't we go inside and talk this over calmly?"

"Believe me, I have plenty to say. But not to you. So, unless you want to add harassment to the complaints against you, I suggest you be on your way, MacGregor."

Turning away, he headed towards the steps.

So far, I'd held my emotions in check. But I was struggling to stay calm. "For God's sake, Owen, I came here to offer my support, not get into a fight. We used to be friends. After all the hassle I went through after my divorce, after all that public humiliation and pain, do you really suppose I'd screw up now and put myself through that again? You can't believe I'd do such a thing. You know me better than that."

He stopped and faced me again.

"What?" He made a sound that was supposed to pass for a laugh, harsh and bitter. "Is that some sort of sick joke? The person I thought I knew was a happily married man, someone who shared my values, someone I could trust, not some queer who got his kicks in sleazy pickup joints."

The blood drained from my face and I stared at him in frozen silence. When I found my voice again, it was hard to keep the ice from it. "Queer?"

He didn't respond. Just eyed me with contempt.

I said, "If you want to hate me for the hurt I caused and for deceiving you, then so be it. I deserve that. But I never had you down as a homophobic bigot."

"Well, now you know." Short and to the point.

I looked him up and down. This was the man who had once been a close friend. In his place, I saw a stranger.

Following the debacle surrounding my divorce, we'd lost touch with each other. More my doing than his. I'd been too ashamed to face any of my old crowd. But he'd not tried to contact me either. And now I knew why.

There was little point in pursuing this argument. Nothing I could say would make any difference. "I understand the local station are appointing a Family Liaison Officer to help you through this," I said. "So I'll leave your welfare in their capable hands." I left him with a curt nod. "Goodbye, Owen."

All thoughts of checking in with Robert Dunn long forgotten, I headed back along the Esplanade. As I moved away from him, Owen called out behind me. "Don't think this is over. I'm going to make you pay for this."

I didn't bother to reply.

CHAPTER ELEVEN

The broken stick sailed through the air and landed between two beech trees about seventy feet away. Rocky was after it in a flash.

"Nice shot," said Nathan.

"Yeah, it should keep him busy for all of five seconds." A moment later, Rocky was back at my feet. He dropped the stick and looked up at me, bright-eyed and eager, drooling tongue hanging loose, ready for more.

It was early morning, and we were wandering through Tinkers Wood. A brief respite before the working day began. The mossy ground was soft underfoot, and distant birdsong vied with the hum of insects hovering nearby. I loved this time of day.

"What is it with dogs and sticks?" I said. "Do they never tire of chasing after them?"

"I've never been able to keep up with one long enough to find out."

"As long as it makes him happy," I said and reached down for the stick.

"And how about you? Are you feeling any better?"

"So so." I hurled the stick ahead of me as we trekked towards a familiar clearing where a fallen tree provided a convenient seat.

The stick missed its mark, ricocheted off an overhanging branch, and landed in a clump of bushes at the side of the clearing.

Nathan had arrived home the previous evening to find me out of sorts. My confrontation with Owen earlier that day had left me deeply depressed. Ever sensitive to my moods, he could tell something was badly wrong. I did my best to deflect his relentless probing, but I was no match for a man of his superior interrogation techniques.

Where he particularly shone was in extracting confessions under pressure - a skill finely honed over many years on the job - and so, in the end, I caved in to his barrage of questions and told him of my meeting with Owen.

Not something he was happy about. I had to endure a rollicking about ignoring his advice, about how my thoughtless, impulsive behaviour had made the situation a thousand times worse, and what a total idiot I was. But he could see how miserable I was and, now he'd calmed down, he was more sympathetic.

Rocky was still scrambling around in the undergrowth as we entered the clearing.

Nathan dropped into place on the fallen trunk. "You should have stayed away," he said. "The guy's not worth the bother. I did warn you."

"I thought I knew him," I said. "I thought he was a friend."

Rocky found his wayward stick, extracted himself from the clawing branches that scraped him and bounded over to us, panting heavily and with several leaves stuck to his fur.

This time, Nathan took up the proffered stick and threw it back along the path we had just taken. "It's inevitable he's going to take Willow at her word. She was his wife. What else is he to do?"

I seated myself beside Nathan and watched Rocky speed away. "I get that," I said. "I'm still pissed he didn't believe me, but I can understand why. Of course he's going to support Willow's claim. It's the homophobia I can't forgive. I never had him down as a bigot."

"Isn't it better to know him for who he really is? If he can't accept you for who you are, he was never much of a friend."

"What saddens me is that he needs a friend right now. I wanted to be there for him, not locked in a battle of blame and prejudice."

"His loss."

Rocky was back, the stick at my feet once more. I picked it up, pretended to throw it across the clearing and, when Rocky sped away, dropped it behind the trunk.

I said, "All those years I stayed in the closet, I thought I was protecting myself."

"You protect yourself from bigots by standing up to them, not hiding away."

"A lesson I learned later in life. But at the time, it seemed the better option."

"All you did was hurt yourself."

"And not just me."

Rocky's search wasn't going too well. He'd already covered most of the clearing before zigzagging back towards us, snuffling the ground. He stopped and eyed me with what I could have sworn was a glint of suspicion in his eyes.

I held up my hands, palms out, towards him. "Sorry, boy. No idea where it is."

Nathan said, "It's best if you keep Owen at a distance from now on." The censure in his words wasn't lost on me. He spoke them in his you-should-have-listened-to-me-in-the-first-place tone of voice.

I said nothing.

Rocky gave up his search and settled down, head on paws, at Nathan's feet. I leaned over and scratched his head. "You do know he'll go to the press?"

"Let him."

"And you do know they'll drag our relationship into it?"

"Not much we can do about that."

A determined fly tried to land on my face. I sent it on its way, buzzing furiously, with the swat of a hand. "And they may claim a conflict of interest," I said.

"There isn't one."

"Willow's assault claim?"

"Willow's malicious assault claim. One without merit."

"That's not how Owen sees it," I said. "He's convinced I assaulted Willow and somehow that led to her death. And he'll persuade the media to see it that way too."

"Can't argue with the facts." He rose to his feet. "Time we were heading back."

I rose and brushed the dead bark from the back of my jeans. "The media aren't interested in facts. They just want a good story. And you heard what Owen said about closing ranks. The press will make something of that too."

Nathan barked out a command to Rocky. "Heel, boy."

We headed on our way back home with Rocky trotting dutifully at Nathan's heel.

Nathan said, "Media speculation is just that, speculation. There's little we can do about it. So what's the point of agonising about it before it's happened? We just have to get on with our work the best we can."

"And they're going to drag up all that stuff about my divorce again. Anything to add a bit of spice to their tale. Remember the last time they made me flavour of the month? I'm still living down the repercussions of that. I can see it now," I said, spreading my hands in front of me. "Distraught woman found dead after assault by notorious media presenter."

"Hey, come on. Don't get ahead of yourself." Nathan slipped an arm around my waist. "I know it can be a pain, Mikey. But we'll get through it."

I wrapped my arm around him. "It's you I'm worried about. Not me. I've been hit by the press so often I'm beginning to think it's normal."

"We're in this together."

We reached the back gate of Woodside Cottage. Nathan opened it and led the way up the garden path.

As Nathan unlocked the cottage door and stepped inside, I said, "Do you ever regret us getting back together?"

He spun around and shot me a look that showed his displeasure. "How can you even ask?"

"I just wonder sometimes."

"Well, quit wondering. I thought we were over all that."

Rocky padded across the living room floor and into the kitchen and, a moment later, he was lapping water.

Nathan glanced at his watch. "And if we don't hurry, we'll be late."

"We? You want me at the station?"

"I've called a meeting to take stock of where we are with the investigation. And I'm hoping we might have the interim autopsy report." He hurried for the stairs, back in action man mode.

I suspected that mornings like these, the chance to recharge and enjoy some time out from the pressures of work, would soon be few and far between. And despite Nathan's almost casual dismissal of unwarranted media attention, I didn't share his confidence that all would be well.

The storm clouds were gathering.

CHAPTER TWELVE

The mood in the room was sombre.

We were in Nathan's office at the local station. Nathan sat facing Lynch and me from the other side of his desk, the autopsy report open in front of him.

The repercussions of a press leak still worried me but, for the moment, they were the least of my worries. Right now, we had more pressing concerns. We had a murder on our hands.

"There's no doubt about it?" Lynch asked.

Nathan tapped the file. "Most of the injuries are consistent with a fall. We already know that. But there are anomalies that don't fit with the suicide scenario."

He looked down at the report. "Some of the wounds to the scalp were embedded with flakes of blue paint. That's inconsistent with forensic evidence gathered at the scene of death."

"What of the wounds themselves?" I said.

"Lacerations rather than incisions," said Nathan. "Though obviously some of those injuries were sustained in the fall."

"So, she was hit with a blunt object," I said. "One that left behind some of its paintwork?"

"That's the theory we now need to work with," said Nathan. "She was killed either on the clifftop or elsewhere and then thrown from the cliff to make her death look like suicide."

Lynch said, "Seems certain then."

"There's always room for doubt," said Nathan. "But it's looking more likely that we're dealing with a murder here."

All three of us fell silent as we considered the implications of this.

Nathan was the first to speak. "It's even more imperative now that we try to move this on as quickly as possible."

Lynch said, "Could I look at the report?"

Nathan handed it over, and Lynch flipped through it, running his finger down each page. He stopped at a particular point and said, "According to this, livor mortis was consistent with the position of the body at the scene. Doesn't that suggest she died where she was found?"

"Not necessarily," I said. "Stagnant blood settles in the lower parts of the body soon after death. But it doesn't become fixed for about four to six hours. What it does suggest is that, if death took place elsewhere, the body must have been moved and thrown over the cliff within that time frame."

"So, any time that morning," said Nathan.

"Which doesn't help us any," I added. "We know she was alive early that morning when the Sarge here dropped her off. So she could have been killed any time between then and when she was found."

Nathan said, "So far, we don't have much to go on."

"We should interview Bryan Yates," I said. "See if we can learn any more about the disturbance he reported."

"Bryan Yates?" Nathan sounded puzzled.

"I took a look around the cliff top the other day and bumped into him. He has a smallholding up there."

"Bumped into?" Nathan voiced the term 'bumped' as if it was a dirty word.

"That's right," I said, ignoring the implied criticism. The last thing I needed was a rebuke for interfering. "I was checking out the terrain along the edge of the cliff."

Fortunately, he let it pass. "Go on."

"There was some sort of incident up there. Yates thought he had an intruder in one of the outbuildings. The Sarge here investigated it."

"You think there's a connection?" Nathan asked.

"Given the timing, it's a possibility," I said. "It was earlier that day, a few hours before they found the body. And it's the nearest place to where Willow went over the cliff."

"Yates and his wife have already been questioned as part of a general local sweep," said Lynch. "I see little point in singling him out for special attention because of a stupid mistake."

A frown from Nathan. "Mistake?"

"You remember that break-in he had a few years back?" This was directed at Nathan.

Nathan confirmed that he did.

Lynch said, "I've known Bryan for years. He was never an outgoing sort of guy. But he was no wimp either. That episode changed him, though. It turned him into a nervous wreck. These days, he'd jump at the sight of his own shadow."

Nathan nodded. "You think it was a false alarm?"

"I'm sure of it. And I'm sure he knows it too. He probably feels foolish about calling us out. There was no sign of either a break-in or any kind of intrusion."

Nathan picked up a pen and tapped it on the desk, a sure sign he was thinking over his options.

He said, "We'll bring him in, anyway. It can't do any harm. Arrange a suitable time with Mikey."

Lynch acquiesced, though reluctantly. He pulled a face, obviously not happy about it.

"Where are we with the rest of the investigation?" said Nathan.

Lynch said, "We're conducting house-to-house enquiries as usual, and stop-and-question in the area where Willow was last seen." He sounded despondent. "We're not having much luck out on the streets. It's like Willow vanished where she stood when I dropped her off."

I said, "The owner of the garage on Salem Row saw her cross the road and head around the corner away from the Fairview."

Judging by Nathan's tight-lipped expression, it was obvious he thought I'd been making my own unofficial enquiries. I offered a hasty explanation. "He recognised me and stopped me as I was passing by. He used to watch my TV show." There were times having a public profile had unexpected advantages.

Lynch interrupted. "Carl Tanner. I've already spoken with him. That's where I dropped Willow, outside his garage. He must have been one of the last to see her alive. So he was of particular interest."

"Do we need to look at him more closely?" Nathan asked.

"I don't think so," said Lynch. "I know they chatted for a while - they were friends back in the old days - but it was nothing of significance. Just small talk. Nothing that could help us."

I butted in. "He told me her old friend, Amelia Cole, ran a newsagents just around that corner on the Esplanade."

"She's already been interviewed along with all the other shopkeepers on that stretch of road," said Lynch. "We weren't able to get any leads there either. None of them recall seeing Willow that morning."

Given Amelia Cole's reluctance to talk to me earlier, I was about to suggest we re-interview her anyway, but Nathan beat me to it. He said, "Let's get her in. She was close to Willow at one time. We may get some useful background information."

That put me in the clear. No need to confess I'd spoken to her already.

Lynch agreed to set up an interview and added, "The only other person of significance is Willow's sister over in Colton Drey. We've already interviewed her. She's not seen Willow for some time. She didn't even know Willow was back in Elders Edge. They weren't close."

"You surprise me," I said. "She visited Willow in London a couple of times. I met her there. They seemed on good enough terms."

"That's not the impression I got," said Lynch.

Nathan grunted. "Something else to follow up." He pulled a typed sheet from the file. "And this guest list. Where are we with that?"

Lynch was more upbeat when he replied. "We're getting plenty of feedback there. Willow was known to many of the guests."

I interjected. "Most of them were from Willow's past. Before she moved away. I know she stayed in touch with Karen, but was there anyone else she was still close to?"

"Not that I'm aware of," said Lynch. "She did put herself around at the reception, though. And I saw her get into several arguments."

"She was quarrelling with Ralph Ferguson not long before we left." I directed this statement to Nathan. "And she looked very much the worse for wear."

Nathan said, "Most of those on the list were locals. So let's get some interviews set up as soon as possible. Anyone who spoke to or argued with Willow during her stay."

Lynch confirmed that enquiries were well underway. And some interviews had already been set up.

Nathan continued. "It's to our advantage that some of the guys from the local station were at the reception. Let's see if any of them saw anything suspicious. And make a note of those guests we know had any sort of communication with her. We'll pay particular attention to those."

He was just about to add something more when a sharp rap at the door interrupted us.

It opened, and a smiling woman in a formal grey suit entered. She was one of those no-nonsense types, face clean of makeup, dark-blonde hair scraped back in a bun, brisk straightforward manner.

She said, "May I join you, gentlemen?"

Nathan signalled her in. "Grab a seat, Sharon."

As she smoothed her skirt and lowered herself onto the remaining empty chair at the side of the desk, Nathan introduced her to me as Sharon Worth, explaining that she had been assigned to Owen as his Family Liaison Officer and had just been over to the Fairview to break the bad news to him. "Mikey's our profiler," he said. "He's here to to give us the benefit of his expertise."

She acknowledged this with a welcoming smile. "I'm an admirer of yours," she said. "I was working on the Carson case in London when you broke it open. Nice work."

My face flushed. It was always a pleasure to meet someone who appreciated my work instead of thinking it on a par with medieval witchcraft.

Before I could thank her, Nathan interrupted and asked how she had fared at the Fairview with Owen.

Sharon's smile faded. "Strangely enough, once he'd got over the initial shock, he seemed almost relieved to learn it wasn't suicide. Personally, I would have thought murder far harder to cope with."

"It's understandable to some extent," I said. "Those closest to a suicide often carry a burden of extreme guilt, a belief that somehow it was their fault, that they could have prevented it." In this case, though, Owen had already assuaged himself of most of that guilt by transferring blame to me. I kept that to myself. "Owen must be going through an emotional mix of feelings right now. But once he's had time to take it in, it will hit him hard."

Sharon agreed. "I asked if there was anyone we could get in touch with. But he said not. His son is staying with his parents in London, and there's no other family. At least no one he's close to."

Nathan grunted an acknowledgement.

Sharon said, "Owen brought up the issue of the assault complaint. I did my best to assure him the matter had been properly handled, but it was a difficult conversation." With an apologetic look my way, she added, "I think he now accepts there was no case to answer."

"I'd like to know who told him," I said.

"Owen gave me a name," she said. "It was one of the guests at the reception. Ralph Ferguson."

That was a surprise. I said, "He'd be the last one I'd expect her to confide in. In fact, they argued at the reception."

Nathan butted in. "Let's make him a priority," he said to Lynch. "Get him in as soon as possible. We may learn something new there."

"He raised another concern too," said Sharon. "About his wife's possessions. Not all of them were returned to him."

"Did you check the inventory?" asked Nathan.

Sharon confirmed she had. "All the items found at the scene and on the body are accounted for. But her mobile is missing. And he's particularly concerned about a gold locket. One she wore on a chain around her neck. It was an anniversary present, and she was never without it."

Lynch said, "They were probably lost when she was attacked."

"That's what I told him," she said.

I interjected. "The mobile, maybe. But she was wearing a coat when we found her. The locket could only have been removed deliberately. I don't suppose it could have been a robbery gone wrong?"

Nathan dismissed the idea. "Hardly likely. Her purse and bag were among her returned possessions. Including cash and credit cards."

"Something else to puzzle over," I said.

Nathan closed the file in front of him, signalling the end of the meeting. "We'll leave it there for the moment," he said.

He reminded Lynch to let him have details of any interviews he set up and called the meeting to a close.

There were a lot of missing answers, and I still had misgivings about my off-the-record conversation with Amelia Cole; I was sure we could learn more from her. But at least we were moving in the right direction.

CHAPTER THIRTEEN

I rolled over, punched the pillow, and tried to settle down to sleep again. No such luck. My mind was racing and sleep wouldn't come.

The luminous face of the clock on the bedside table glared at me. Five-thirty. I turned onto my other side, eased myself up against Nathan's slumbering form, wrapped an arm around him, and closed my eyes.

And opened them again.

Early morning light was creeping in around the edges of the curtains and, outside, the dawn chorus was starting up in earnest.

I turned onto my back and stared up at the ceiling.

A groan from the other side of the bed. Nathan stirred and said, "Are you ever going to sleep?"

"Sorry, I didn't mean to wake you."

"You've been tossing and turning all night."

"I have a lot on my mind."

He grunted, sat up, and switched on his bedside lamp. "Okay," he said, "let's hear it."

I pushed myself up to a sitting position and leaned back against the headboard. "I don't want to interrupt your sleep."

"Too late for that. So come on, what's keeping you awake?"

"You need to ask? Where do I begin? The wife of someone I thought a close friend had been murdered. Not only does he hold me in some way responsible, but turns out he's a homophobic bigot who despises me, anyway. And, to top it all, I'm about to have my name splashed across the tabloids again, accused of assault. That's enough to be going on with, isn't it?"

"You don't wonder why Owen is so keen to throw the blame onto you?"

"That should be obvious. I'm gay. I'm a dissolute degenerate beyond redemption. And, clearly, that makes me capable of all sorts of despicable deviant behaviour, including murder."

He squeezed my arm. "Let's get serious for a moment. Does it not occur to you it might be a smokescreen?"

"For what?"

"To deflect attention from himself."

"You're surely not suggesting he killed her?"

"You know as well as I do the spouse is always top of the list."

I pulled my knees up to my chest and wrapped my arms around my legs while I considered this. "When it's someone you know, it's not always easy to be objective. And, okay, of course he's bound to be hot favourite, but I can't see it somehow."

"Willow knew several of the guests at the wedding. But, as far as we're aware, except for you and Karen, she lost touch with them all years ago. As the murderer is usually someone close to the victim, Owen seems to be our only option. Especially as he knew where she would be."

"You don't really think it was Owen, do you?"

"I think it more likely to be a local. To have killed Willow and disposed of her body in the way they did, and in such a short span of time, without being discovered suggests someone with knowledge of the local area. But even so, Owen is still a contender. I'd be more inclined to let him off the hook once his alibi pans out."

"He called the Fairview from Liverpool Street Station in London. Or so he claims. Can't you trace his calls to there?"

"We're carrying out all the usual checks to confirm his whereabouts. But, given the time frame, he would have been able to murder his wife and make it back to London, anyway."

"I still don't get it. Murder? I was just getting used to the idea of suicide."

"Which is what we were all supposed to think."

Nathan swung his legs over the side of the bed and pushed himself to his feet.

"Where are you off to?" I said.

"Sleep's out of the question so I might as well get up." He grabbed a pair of joggers from the hook on the back of the door, sat on the edge of the bed, and pulled them on.

"That makes two of us," I said and climbed out of bed. I struggled into a pair of jeans I'd left over the back of the bedroom chair, chose a fresh sweatshirt from the chest of drawers, and pulled it on as I followed Nathan downstairs.

Rocky greeted us in his usual way; leaping around us, his wagging tail whipping our legs. I negotiated my way around him and made it to the kitchen. Meanwhile, Nathan filled a bowl with biscuits, put it on the kitchen floor and followed it with a bowl of water.

Rocky gulped down his food in one go and finished off the water with a few laps. Fed and watered and seemingly satisfied, he licked his chops and trotted over to the back door, ready to be let out for his morning constitutional.

I paused in the act of filling the kettle at the kitchen tap, and said, "I still don't understand how Ralph Ferguson got involved. Why would Willow spread her lies to him? Why Ralph, of all people? He used to be a good friend."

"Maybe that's why. If she was out to hurt you, turning friends against you would be the best way to do it."

With the kettle on the boil, I spooned some coffee into a jug and grabbed a couple of mugs from the wall cupboard.

Responding to Rocky's barking, Nathan went over to the back door, let him out, and returned to the kitchen.

"I can't understand why Ralph would tell Owen," I said, "and not discuss it with me first." I poured out our coffees and handed a mug to Nathan.

He said, "I have to admit, I've never thought of Ralph as the public-spirited kind."

We carried our drinks through to the living room and settled ourselves on the couch.

"I sent a couple of my men up to Yates's farm to look around," said Nathan. "Nothing out of the ordinary."

"They checked everywhere?"

"All the outbuildings. I asked them to pay particular attention to the shed where Yates heard the disturbance. But nothing. If anyone had been hiding in there, they sure didn't leave any traces."

"Strange. You'd expect to find some signs of activity. Maybe the Sarge was right after all. Maybe Yates was just spooked and imagined it." An afterthought struck me. "And they did check for a possible murder weapon? He must have several tools and pieces of equipment up there that would match the forensic analysis."

He paused in the act of raising his mug to his mouth and frowned. "Mikey!" His tone was reproachful.

"Sorry. Of course they did. I'm being a dick."

We sat in silence for a few moments, drinking our coffees.

I said, "I don't suppose there's any chance of searching the house?"

Nathan drained his mug, put it on the occasional table in front of us with a heavy hand, and frowned.

"And why would we do that?" He waited for a response and when I didn't reply, he said, "Yates isn't in the frame for anything. We have no just cause to search his house."

"I got the feeling something wasn't right."

He spread his arm across the back of the couch, and said, "Look, Mikey, much as I respect your insights, we can hardly treat Yates as a potential suspect in a murder investigation based on your instinctive reaction to an off-the-record conversation." He picked up his mug again. "Lecture over, okay?" A half-smile played across his lips.

I grimaced and said, "Okay, I hear you. I thought it strange though that he saw nothing out of the ordinary."

Nathan rose to his feet. "The farm is several hundred yards from the edge of the cliff," he said. "And the outbuildings obstruct the view from the house and yard. So it's not surprising he saw nothing." He made his way into the kitchen.

"I guess." I finished my drink, headed after him, and dropped my mug onto the drainer.

Nathan swilled both mugs under the tap and put them in the dishwasher. "We have an interview set up with Yates tomorrow. You'll have a chance to work your magic then."

"Don't ever use that word in front of Lynch," I said. "He already has me down as some sort of witch doctor."

He grinned. "Not to worry. Richard will be back in a few days. He, at least, is beginning to see some merit in your methods."

"Poor guy's going to be thrown in at the deep end. The honeymoon really will be over."

"I'm sure he'll cope. He usually does." He glanced up at the clock on the kitchen wall. "And in the meantime, I'm already up to my neck in it. Maybe I should make an early start and get over to the station." He made as if to head for the stairs.

I stepped in front of him, barring his way, and pressed a hand against his bare chest. "Not so fast." I pushed him up against the kitchen worktop. "If you will drag me out of bed at this ungodly hour, I intend to make the most of it."

"And whose fault is it we're up at this ungodly hour?"

"Guilty as charged." I leaned against him, mouth close to his ear, and murmured, "So why don't I find some way to make it up to you?" I lowered my head and pressed my lips to the side of his neck. "No rush to get to work, is there?"

"I'm not so sure about that," he said, a half-smile playing across his lips. His breathing was ragged. "Duty calls after all." The gleam in his eyes gave the lie to his words.

"Duty can wait," I said and licked his ear. "I have more urgent needs."

He slipped an arm around my waist and pulled me closer. His body was hot and hard against mine, chest rising and falling, his breath warm against my cheek. "I should warn you, Mr MacGregor," he said, "that interfering with a police officer in the execution of his duty is a punishable offence."

"Is that so?" I whispered. "And what sort of punishment did you have in mind?" I slid a hand down his chest, running my fingers through the thick mat of hair.

"I may have to detain you at my pleasure while I think that one through."

"Tell you what," I said, "why don't we go upstairs and I'll help you shower while you think it over. Maybe something will come up. In fact…" I ran my hand down past his waist until I found what I was looking for. "… something seems to be coming up already." Through the fabric of his joggers, I squeezed the thick penis. Already swollen, it twitched and stiffened some more under my touch.

Nathan pulled my hand away. "Upstairs. Now." His breathing was laboured.

I didn't need telling twice. "Whatever you say, Chief."

It was a race to see who got there first.

Even now, after all these months of settled domesticity, there were times like this when the usual slow considered pace of our lovemaking gave way to something raw and untamed, a wild urgent need that demanded immediate release.

Times like now.

Outside the back door, Rocky barked to be let back in.

Rocky would have to wait.

CHAPTER FOURTEEN

I didn't place him immediately. He was standing on the forecourt of the local police station with his back to me as I hurried across the car park. Only as I reached the main entrance and he turned to face me did I recognise him.

My throat tightened, and there was a sinking feeling in my stomach.

Jeff Stokes. Sleazebag reporter from the Charwell Sentinel. His mouth twisted into a pitiful impression of a smile. "Think of the devil and he appears," he said.

It was the afternoon of the following day. The interview with Bryan Yates was due to start in thirty minutes, and I had arranged to meet Nathan beforehand. The last thing I needed was a confrontation with this lowlife, but I wasn't about to let him get the better of me either.

"You took the words right out of my mouth," I said. "You must have read my mind."

A year ago, my father's untimely death had brought me back to Elders Edge and into the spotlight. My status as a minor public figure had been a godsend to Stokes who had done everything he could to sully my reputation and cast me in the role of prodigal son gone bad. And I wouldn't forget it anytime soon.

"I heard you'd got yourself into a spot of bother," he said. "An assault, wasn't it?"

"You heard wrong."

"Just looking for the facts," Stokes said.

"You're looking for facts?" I widened my eyes in mock surprise. "Well, that makes a pleasant change."

That sardonic grin again. "Do I hear a hint of bitterness in your tone?"

"What you hear is contempt."

Stokes turned to face me fully and took up a position between me and the door. "Assault is a serious offence, Mr MacGregor. I'm giving you an opportunity to defend yourself. Did she provoke you? Is that why you hit her?"

The heat rose in my face. "You had me fooled there for a moment. I thought you said you were looking for facts."

"Mr Brookes was very forthcoming. I had an interesting chat with him the other day over at the Fairview."

"There you go again, confusing facts with secondhand tittle-tattle."

"He wasn't my only source."

Given that Ferguson had passed on details of Willow's claim to Owen, I half-suspected that maybe he was Stokes's other source. I said, "I suggest you check your sources a little more carefully. Ralph Ferguson isn't the most reliable of people."

The quick flash of recognition in Stokes's eyes told me I was right.

"You know we never reveal our sources," he said.

"And I don't comment on unsubstantiated claims. So I think we're done here."

I skirted around him, making towards the door, but he stepped in front of me again and blocked my progress.

"I'm just doing my job," he said.

"And since when did that include harassment? I already told you, I have nothing to say."

Behind Stokes, the door opened, and Nathan appeared in the doorway. "When you're ready, Mikey." I guess he must have seen what was keeping me and come to the rescue.

"As soon as Mr Stokes gets out of my way."

Stokes stepped to one side and held up his hands in a conciliatory gesture. "Just trying to get a story. A local murder is big news. Maybe you'd like to say something, Chief."

"You already have the official statement."

"Sure. A carefully prepared and worded handout that tells me precisely nothing."

Nathan went into professional mode. "It tells you everything you need to know about the current investigation."

"This is a human interest story, Chief. I need something more. Mr MacGregor here is under suspicion of assaulting the victim. Anything to say about that?"

A touch of ice crept into Nathan's voice. "Any suspicion attached to Mr MacGregor is without foundation. I suggest you remember that, Mr Stokes."

Stokes persisted. He was clearly enjoying this. "Doesn't it make his involvement in the case inappropriate?"

I could feel my blood pressure rising, but I stayed silent. Nathan was acting in his official role, and I left him to it. Even though I could have cheerfully driven a fist into Stokes's smug face.

"Mr MacGregor is an experienced member of our team whose expertise is invaluable," said Nathan. "The only inappropriate action would be to remove him on the basis of ill-founded rumour and gossip."

Stokes wasn't to be put off. "I understand you're in a sexual relationship with Mr MacGregor. Is that so?"

Nathan was a past master at keeping his emotions in check. But I had learned to read him well. The tightening of his jaw and icy tone betrayed his real feelings. He was growing increasingly angry.

He said, "It's no secret that Mr MacGregor and I are in a committed relationship and share a home. Though I'm at a loss to understand why that should be of interest to you."

"It could lead to complaints of personal bias. That maybe you're prepared to cover up for Mr MacGregor."

"I warn you, Mr Stokes, that any such accusations will result in my seeking legal redress. My professional working relationship with Mr MacGregor is the only one that need concern you here."

Stokes smirked. "I was looking for the personal angle."

"This is a police investigation," said Nathan. "There is no personal angle." He stepped back and held the door open to let me pass. "And now, if you'll excuse us, we have work to do."

Stokes shrugged and said, "At least I gave you a chance." He turned on his heel and made his way back across the car park.

I followed Nathan inside. "I detest that guy," I said. "You can almost see the slime dripping off him."

Nathan grunted. He was still mad.

As we headed towards the smaller meeting room, I said, "You do know he'll stir things up? It's what he does."

"Don't worry; I know the type. But we can't let some oink from the gutter press dictate how we conduct our investigations."

Nathan was used to speaking with the media. He was confident and sure in his dealings with them. But this was different. This time, his reputation was at stake, and he was open to personal attack. I knew what it was like to suffer at the hands of a vindictive press and could only hope he was prepared for what lay ahead.

We reached the meeting room, and I opened the door and stood aside to let him through.

As I followed him in, I whispered, "Don't say I didn't warn you."

CHAPTER FIFTEEN

It wasn't the best of starts to an interview. Lynch griped about it being a waste of time, and Nathan was keeping what I presumed was a diplomatic silence. Seems I was the only one who saw some point to it. And so - for once - I kept my mouth shut.

We sat around the desk and watched Sgt Miles Barber on the monitor screen. He was seated at the desk in the main interview room going through the case file, waiting for Bryan Yates to be shown in.

We didn't have long to wait.

A uniformed constable ushered Yates into the interview room and left again, closing the door behind him.

Yates was scowling; his mouth pinched, his eyes narrowed. Barber offered him a chair and, as he seated himself on the other side of the desk, he complained about the inconvenience he was being caused.

"Let's try to keep this short and to the point then," said Barber.

Yates wasn't going to let it go. "You're interviewing everyone in town, are you? Or is it just me that's being picked on?"

Barber folded his arms, leaned back in his chair, and faced Yates full on. "Not only is your home in near proximity to the crime scene - the nearest, in fact - but you also reported some unusual activity at around the time the murder may have taken place. Obviously, that's going to be something we're interested in. I'm sure you understand that."

Yates nodded, a reluctant acknowledgement.

"Fine," said Barber and opened the file in front of him. He picked up a pen and said, "So let's go over it again, shall we?"

In a sour monotone, Yates recounted the disturbance he'd reported to the police, just as he had told it to me. He tried to make light of it, admitting he may have overreacted and got it wrong. And all the time complaining about being implicated in a murder.

"Hope you're not saying it's owt to do with me," he said. "I've never done a bad thing in my life, always lived on the right side of the law. Never been mixed up in anything like this."

"Methinks he doth protest too much," I muttered.

"What's that?" said Nathan.

"Nothing. Just thinking out loud."

Barber said, "And as a law-abiding citizen, I'm sure you want to do all you can to help in what is, after all, a very serious matter. The victim was known to you, wasn't she?"

"Long time ago." Suddenly agitated, he added, "I've not seen her recently though if that's what you're saying."

Barber didn't comment but scribbled a note on the file.

"You understand that?" said Yates.

"I hear you."

Barber changed the topic and asked Yates about his movements later that day, whether he had seen or heard anything suspicious or out of the ordinary within the immediate vicinity of the farm. Yates continued to answer in the same defensive manner, making it clear he had seen and heard nothing.

With no more to gain, Barber brought the interview to a close and escorted Yates out of the room.

Lynch slapped his leg. "Well, that was a waste of time. I said it would be. We didn't learn anything new."

I swivelled around to face them both. "You might not have, but I did. At least I now know he's lying."

"About what?" Lynch sounded exasperated.

"I don't know. But he's lying about something."

They both looked at me blankly, waiting for an explanation.

I leaned forward and spread my hands. "Look, in an investigation like this, we ordinarily have a clear idea about the suspect's involvement."

Lynch said, "Yates isn't a suspect."

"I'm speaking hypothetically," I said, dismissing Lynch's comment with a flick of the hand. "We usually have some idea of the direction we want to move in and those specific points where we need to apply some pressure. We don't have that here."

Lynch again. "Doesn't that suggest he has nothing to answer for?"

"It means we don't know for sure. But one thing I am sure of is that he's lying about something."

Nathan this time. "You want to talk us through that?"

Unlike Lynch, at least Nathan was prepared to listen.

I said, "Do you ever wonder why we are all either left or right-handed? I mean, why we all have a dominant hand?"

That seemed to throw them.

Nathan said, "Can't say I have. Why?" He sounded puzzled.

"If someone throws a punch at your face, what are you going to do?" I said. "Raise a hand to defend yourself, right?"

"Sure."

"Which hand?"

"My right hand. Goes without saying."

"Exactly. Your dominant hand. And that's the point. You may need to react in a split second, and your mind doesn't have time to pause and make a choice. It's an inbuilt defence mechanism. Your body bypasses your mind and reacts without thinking."

Lynch said, "What does this have to do with whether or not Yates is lying?"

"Simple," I said. "There are times our bodies make decisions without our being consciously aware of it. An automatic reaction. And when we lie, our bodies contradict our words by leaking out the deception."

They both stared at me blankly.

"Yates is right-handed. And yet every time he claimed innocence, he raised his left hand to punctuate and emphasise his words, his non-dominant hand."

Nathan said, "And that tells you he's lying?"

"Lying is a conscious decision. But our bodies never lie. And subconsciously using our non-dominant hand when telling a lie gives the game away."

Nathan was nodding now.

"And it's not the only sign. Let's go back over what just happened. For starters, Yates knew Willow and yet shows little concern for what happened to her."

Lynch interrupted. "They hadn't seen each other for years."

"Okay," I said, "but neither was she a total stranger. That makes a difference. It makes it personal. You would have expected him to show some concern for what happened to her, a willingness to help. Instead, what we got was resentment."

Nathan's turn again. "You said 'for starters'."

"A few things. Apart from his general attitude. His explanation to Sgt Barber was word for word as he told it to me. As if he'd rehearsed it."

Nathan nodded again, and I felt I might be getting somewhere at last.

I continued, "Two other pointers. The first is the guilt trip approach. The suggestion that he was being picked out for special attention. Under suspicion. It's an evasive tactic designed to avoid the question and put the questioner on the defensive."

"And the other?" said Nathan.

"All that stuff about being an upright citizen. It's a protest statement. Another way of deflecting focus from the case and, at the same time, claiming innocence based on past behaviour."

They were both nodding now.

I pushed home my case. "Attitude and statement structure are two of the ways we can spot if someone is lying. Individually, they may not mean much, but when you see a cluster of indicators, it's a sure sign that something's not right."

Nathan said, "If he is lying, it could, of course, be about something else."

Lynch chimed in at this point. "Something else we've not thought of. If Yates was up to no good, why involve the police? It doesn't make sense."

"I can't answer that. But I'm still convinced that Yates is lying about something."

Nathan picked up a pen, leaned back in his chair and stared into space while tapping his pen on the desk. He dropped it again and said, "For the moment, I think we have to accept there's not much else we can do."

I opened my mouth to protest, but he held up a restraining hand and cut me off. "I fully accept your analysis, Mikey. But without solid evidence to the contrary, we have no way of refuting Yates's statement."

Lynch took up the argument. "And we made a thorough search of the farm buildings and found nothing of any note."

Nathan again. "And Andrew is right. Why involve the police if you have something to hide? I don't doubt that he's keeping something back, but I suspect it has nothing to do with our investigation. All we can do at the moment is keep our ears to the ground."

So that was it. I knew when I was beat.

Back to square one.

CHAPTER SIXTEEN

It was another one of those cold, bright mornings. Ideal running weather. This morning, I had Lynch for company, and we were jogging around the edge of town towards the far side of Tinkers Wood.

After Yates's interview the previous day, the Sarge had asked if he could join me on my daily run, claiming the need to get back into shape.

By the way he was puffing and panting, I figured that would take some time.

"Let's stop for a breather," I said, grinning. "You sound like you could use one."

He nodded, too winded to speak, slowed to a halt, and took in some deep breaths.

He wiped his brow with the back of a hand. His bald head gleamed, and trickles of sweat ran down the sides of his face. "I'm in worse shape than I realised," he said.

No argument from me there, but I thought it politic not to say so. If he was thinking of doing this on a regular basis though, I would need to teach him some breathing techniques.

A stone wall bordered the railway embankment to our left. Lynch leaned against it while he caught his breath. He pulled up his sweatshirt by the hem and wiped his face with it.

"It's not like I couldn't use the exercise," Lynch said, "but it wasn't the only reason I came along this morning. I had an ulterior motive."

"Yes?" I continued running on the spot while he spoke.

Down below, a goods train chugged past. Three blasts of its whistle, short and shrill, reached up to us. Lynch waited until it had passed before answering. "It was after yesterday's interview," he said. "I could have been more supportive. I don't want you thinking I dismissed your input out of hand."

I laughed and said, "Please don't say you put yourself through all this physical exertion just to tell me that."

"I thought maybe I owed you an apology."

"No way. I'm used to having my methods questioned. It wouldn't be the first time."

He pushed himself away from the wall and eased his leg muscles with some knee raises, ready to move on again. "I guess I'm one of those old-fashioned cops. I like to see what I'm dealing with."

I slapped him on the back. "No worries," I said. "Don't give it another thought."

As we moved on, I set a slower pace so we could talk on the way. "It's one more tool in our arsenal. Whatever gets the job done, eh?"

"Still seems like magic to me," he said. "What sort of things do you look for?"

He seemed genuinely interested, so I was happy to go into detail.

"It's a combination of things. There are the physical tells, of course, the clues we get from body language. But there are verbal indicators, too. Such as speech-statement structure, verbal leaks, vocal quality and attitude."

"I don't begin to understand, but you obviously know what you're talking about."

Even if he didn't understand, at least he was willing to listen.

"When you've done this sort of work as long as I have," I said, "it becomes second nature, difficult to put into words. And it's not an exact science, but I don't doubt that Yates was lying. You saw for yourself how hostile he was."

"He always was a miserable bastard."

Lynch was panting heavily again, forcing his words out between gasps.

I slowed, stopped, and turned to face him. "Another breather?"

Still gasping, he nodded, leaned forward, hands on thighs and drew in several large gulps of air. He straightened up and said, "I think I'm done."

"Let's call it a day then." I nodded towards a spot on the other side of the road where a path ran into the woods. "We can take a shortcut through to the High Street. Just a gentle stroll."

"Sounds good to me. But let me get my breath back first." He leaned against the trunk of an elm at the side of the path and wiped his face with an arm.

I said, "Have you known Yates long?"

"I was born and raised in these parts. Over in Charwell. And we were of an age. In small communities like this, you get to know everyone."

"He's a friend?"

"I wouldn't say that. He was just one of the crowd I went around with. But he was the quiet one. Kept to the fringes. Bit of a complainer, though. Even then."

"I guess you must have known Willow and her friends too. You were all about the same age."

"There weren't many places where young people could socialise back then - not that things are much better these days - so we all tended to use the same places; a couple of popular bars and the Vortex Nightclub in Charwell. So, yes, I'd see them around a lot." He straightened up. "Ready to go?"

I nodded, and we headed over to the woodland path.

Lynch shot me a quizzical look as we moved on. "I'm surprised our paths never crossed back then. We must have moved in the same circles."

"I was never one for the nightclub scene in those days. Not really my thing. And I moved to London in my late teens." A sudden thought struck me. "Do you know Ralph Ferguson? He was part of that crowd too."

"Sure. Ralph's my brother-in-law. I married his sister."

"I didn't know that. Small world. He and I were good friends before I moved away."

"So he tells me."

"You know it was Ralph who told Owen about Willow's sexual assault complaint?"

Lynch grunted and said, "No, I didn't. But I'm not surprised."

"Why do you say that?"

"He was jealous of you."

"Jealous?"

"You were the local boy made good. You'd made a name for yourself. Your TV and radio shows were popular."

"Why would he be jealous of that?"

"He was the one with all the big ideas. Dreams of success. And where did he end up? A not very successful salesman for a local insurance company. You left him behind in your wake and he resents it."

"Wow. I had no idea. I thought he seemed distant at Richard and Karen's reception."

"Any mention of your name and he'd make some crack about luck winning out over talent. He was bitter about it."

"Jeez, that's sad."

"His problem, not yours."

We walked on in silence for a while. The High Street was not yet in sight, but the sounds of traffic from that direction filtered through to us.

Lynch's mobile rang.

"That's the station," he said. He dipped into the pocket of his joggers and dug out his phone.

"I asked them to get back to me if there were any developments. Let's hope they have something," he said and answered the call.

He stopped abruptly, took me by the arm and brought me to a sudden halt.

"Where?" He barked the question into his phone, his voice tense.

A moment's silence and he finished his call and pocketed the phone.

"We need to get over to the Fairview now."

He set off at a pace, hurrying towards the High Street, his fatigue no longer evident.

I took off after him. "What happened?"

He called back over his shoulder, "It's Owen Brookes. He's been attacked and injured."

A moment later, I had overtaken him and was hot-footing it to the Fairview.

CHAPTER SEVENTEEN

I was several minutes in front of Lynch. By the time he came panting in behind me, I was in the Fairview's reception, sizing up the situation and trying to find out what happened.

Owen's Family Liaison Officer, Sharon Worth, was already there. She had arranged a meeting with Owen to update him on the current position with the investigation and had found him nursing some cuts and bruises in the company of Robert Dunn.

Owen was perched on a wooden dining chair by the reception desk, holding a bloody handkerchief to his head. Robert Dunn was hovering nearby, wringing his hands, making sympathetic clucking noises, and looking thoroughly out of his depth.

Sharon had taken control and was trying to persuade Owen to have his injury checked out.

"As far as I can tell, it's a superficial scrape," she said, "but I'd like you to get it looked at to be on the safe side."

Owen dismissed her advice with the wave of a hand. "It's just a graze. Nothing to make a fuss about." His voice trembled.

"Is someone going to tell me what happened," said Lynch, taking charge. He was still gasping.

"I'll leave you to it," said Dunn and scuttled away, clearly not wishing to be involved.

"Looks like a mugging," said Sharon. "I was getting some details."

We all turned our attention to Owen, waiting for an explanation. I stood back from the others, preferring not to engage too closely with

Owen. This was my first encounter with him since our confrontation a few days earlier, and I wasn't feeling well-disposed towards him. His lack of response to my presence suggested the feeling was mutual.

After casting an uneasy glance my way, he pulled his jacket around him and slumped down in his chair, shoulders hunched. Directing his words to Lynch and Sharon, he said, "I needed some air. And time to think. It's not as if I can sit in my room all day." He was on the defensive. "There aren't many people about at that time of day, so I headed out to the woods. He must have followed me."

Sharon took a notebook and pen from her breast pocket and scribbled in it as Owen recounted his ordeal.

"He came up from behind," he said. "I felt his boot in my back. Next thing I know, I'm on the floor, and he's standing over me with a knife."

"How did you get the injury?" asked Lynch.

I said, "You didn't fight back, did you?"

Owen glanced up at me, opened his mouth to speak and closed it again. With a quick shake of the head, he turned away, unable to keep eye contact. When he replied, it was Lynch he addressed. He said, "I hit my head on a tree root when I went down."

"You sure you don't need that seeing to?" Lynch said.

"I swear, it's nothing. I'm just shaken." He took the handkerchief from his head and checked it. "See. It's stopped bleeding." He held the handkerchief up for inspection. "Really, it's nothing."

Sharon stopped scribbling, and she and Lynch exchanged a look of shared scepticism.

Pen poised, Sharon said. "What did he take?"

"The usual stuff. Wallet and phone."

I said, "Anything else of value?"

He didn't answer. Just another quick shake of the head. Again, he avoided eye contact, keeping his head lowered, and looked down at the floor instead.

Sharon said, "What was in your wallet?"

"A few quid, some spare change, and a couple of store cards," said Owen. "My mugger is going to be disappointed. The credit cards were locked away in my room."

"Make sure you report the phone theft to your network provider," said Sharon. "And ask them for the ID number. We'll need that." She went back to her note-taking.

"It was pay as you go. So all I've lost is some credit and a few family photos."

Lynch said, "Did you get a good look at him?"

"I was too preoccupied to check him out." There was a touch of sarcasm in his tone. "And it was over in a flash, anyway." He added, "I spotted him first on the Esplanade, but he was wearing a hood and had a scarf across the lower half of his face."

Sharon said, "And that didn't make you suspicious?"

"Why would it?" said Owen. "It's chilly out there this morning. Especially on the seafront. I presumed he was wrapped up against the cold."

Lynch said, "The more you can remember, the more we have to go on, the more likely we are to catch him."

He snorted. "Good luck with that, Sergeant. I wish I shared your confidence." He dabbed at his forehead with the handkerchief, checked it for signs of blood, screwed it into a ball and shoved it into his jacket pocket. "It was over in minutes, anyway. He only said a few words, and I have no idea what he looked like."

"It's always best to stay positive, Sir." Lynch sounded strained.

Owen said, "I'm finding it difficult to stay positive about anything right now."

Lynch grunted and said, "We'll need to take a formal statement from you. If you could come down to the station?"

Owen cried off. "Can we do it another time? I'm not sure I'm up to it right now."

Lynch agreed to take a statement later and arranged to see Owen at the station the following day.

Sharon pocketed her notebook and pen. "I'll see you in the morning as usual," she said. "I'll let you know if there are any developments then."

She suggested Owen might be more comfortable over on the other side of the lobby, where a recessed area held a couch and a couple of matching sagging armchairs.

He agreed, and she walked him over there.

Once they were out of the way, Dunn appeared from wherever he had been skulking. "Just as well we don't have any visitors yet," he said. "I'd hate to think what sort of impression they'd get of this place."

I assured him that rampant crime wasn't one of Elders Edge's usual characteristics.

He took charge of the chair Owen had been sitting on and carried it back to the dining room.

I waited until he was out of earshot and said to Lynch, "Seems odd that some mugger would follow Owen all the way from the Esplanade."

"It's not the best of weathers out there at the moment," said Lynch. "There was no one else around and I guess he saw another person out on their own as an easy target."

"And by the same token, it's not the best of weathers for some mugger to be hanging around in."

Lynch frowned. "You're not suggesting Brookes was deliberately targeted?"

Sharon caught the tail end of our conversation as she returned. She raised her own objections. "We've had a couple of similar incidents recently. It looks like he was just in the wrong place at the wrong time." She took a quick backward glance in Owen's direction, lowered her voice, and said, "Not one of the most cooperative types I've ever come across."

Lynch added his criticism. "You have to wonder if it's worth the bother sometimes." Addressing me, he added, "I couldn't help noticing how he ignored you."

"Yep, seems I'm still the bad guy here," I said. "But at least he didn't threaten to thump me this time."

Still speaking in hushed tones, Sharon said, "I don't think that's something you need worry about. If anything, he's embarrassed."

"Embarrassed?"

"He overreacted. He knows that. We've talked it through a few times and he accepts the charge against you was without merit. Too many details didn't add up. His reaction was understandable in the circumstances; he was in shock. But he's thinking rationally now, and he's coming to terms with the inevitable. And he confessed it wouldn't be out of character for his wife to make such a claim."

"Anyone who knew her could have told you that. She had a mean streak. And God help you if you got on her wrong side."

After another quick glance in Owen's direction, Sharon leaned towards me and added, "To be frank, the more I learn about that woman, the more I'm inclined to think the worst of her. Brookes was trying to play it down, of course. Make excuses for her. But you can't blame him for that. She was his wife, after all."

His support for a miscreant wife was the least of my concerns. I could forgive him that. But his homophobia was a different matter.

Before I could respond to Sharon, Owen left his seat in the lounge area and made for the stairs. We fell silent as he passed us by.

"I'm going up to my room," he said. "I've had enough excitement for one day."

We watched after him as he climbed the stairs, and Sharon said, "Maybe we're being harsh. The poor guy must be going through hell."

"Perhaps he'll be in a better mood tomorrow," said Lynch.

"I'll be calling on him in the morning anyway," said Sharon, "so I may as well take his statement then. It'll save him the bother of a trip to the station if he's still feeling out of sorts."

We called it a day and were about to leave when the outer door opened. It was Nathan. He made his way towards us, his face creased with concern. "I heard what happened. Is Brookes okay?"

"Just a minor cut," said Sharon, "but I think he's more shaken than he's letting on."

Lynch brought him up to date with developments.

"We're taking a statement from Brookes tomorrow. We thought we should let him get some rest today. We were about to go on our way."

Nathan agreed it was probably best to let it lie for the moment, and we all left the Fairview together.

We parted company on the Esplanade at the bottom of the terrace steps, Sharon and Lynch going their separate ways, and Nathan and I heading for home. As we made our way to the car, I said, "You think there could be a connection between this and Willow's murder? Lynch and Sharon Worth think not."

"Could be a coincidence. There have been several similar incidents recently. But I don't like coincidences. They make me suspicious."

"I've been racking my brains to work out what the connection could be. But nothing comes to mind." I shrugged. "Maybe we're just being paranoid and it's a simple mugging after all."

"Better to be paranoid and keep an open mind than to dismiss other possibilities out of hand."

"It's like something is going on all around you, just out of sight. You get the odd glimpse but can't quite put it all together, can't quite work out what it is."

"Which is why we have to keep everything in the mix. And in the end, it will all fall into place."

I hoped so.

But right now, nothing was making sense.

CHAPTER EIGHTEEN

"I'm not sure I'll be much help," I said. "It's not as if he's very forthcoming when I'm around."

Sharon said, "Not to worry. I'll do the talking. Just steer me in the right direction when I need it."

It was the morning of the following day and Sharon Worth was driving us over to the Fairview for her regular update with Owen and to take his statement about the mugging. Our key concern, though, was to build a more detailed picture of Willow's background.

"There's not much I can tell him at the moment," she said. "We're not making any headway on either the murder or the mugging. But at least we may get some useful information from him."

"Let's hope he chooses to be more cooperative this time."

Sharon gave me a sideways glance. "I hear you used to be good friends."

"Used to be. Past tense."

"Must have been a shock to be told you'd assaulted his wife."

"Can't say I was too happy about it either."

"He knows he overreacted. Understandable in the circumstances. But he regrets it now."

"He should try telling me that himself."

"He's probably too embarrassed. I'm confident it would help if you two got together, talked it through."

Yeah, right. Nothing I'd like more than a cosy chat with a bigot.

I said, "I'm sure Owen appreciates we have a job to do, so let's just stick to business shall we."

She took the hint and dropped the subject.

Nathan shared my view that Willow's killer was most likely someone she knew, someone who was part of the local community and intimately aware of her movements. Trouble was, we hadn't been able to establish any recent contact between Willow and her old friends and acquaintances in Elders Edge other than the cursory contact at Richard and Karen's wedding. Certainly, nothing that could have led to her murder.

That's where I came in.

It was time to spread the net wider.

I had once been close enough to Owen to learn details of his and Willow's personal lives, details that could help the investigation; their other friendships, problems with colleagues at work, Willow's lack of communication with her parents, her relationship with her sister, anything that could link her in a potentially harmful way to others in her old home town.

Given our strained relationship, Owen was unlikely to give me his full cooperation. But, over the last couple of days, Sharon had established a sympathetic bond with him and so, at Nathan's suggestion, we were to question Owen together with Sharon taking the lead.

Owen was waiting in the recessed seating area at the other side of the Fairview's reception. He rose from his chair at the sound of the door opening and turned with a smile, expecting to see Sharon alone. The smile faded when he saw me, and his cheeks flushed.

Robert Dunn was leaning over the reception desk, reading through the morning post. I signalled a greeting as we crossed the floor and earned a raised hand in response.

As we approached, Owen stiffened. "I wasn't expecting to see you," he said.

I offered him an understanding nod and a sympathetic tone, an attempt to bring him onside and make him more amenable to questioning. "I'm here to help if I can, Owen."

He seemed unsure, his brow creased.

"I know we have some unresolved personal issues," I said, "but I suggest it's to our mutual benefit to put them aside. We have a shared interest in solving Willow's murder. And I'd like to help. I hope you'll allow me that."

"Yes, of course," he said. But the stiffness remained.

Sharon explained our need for a more detailed examination of Willow's background and personal relationships. She suggested it may take a little longer than usual and we should make ourselves comfortable.

She tried to put Owen at his ease. "Shall I order us some coffee before we start?"

Owen declined the offer and seated himself on the couch. Sharon followed suit.

I dropped into the armchair opposite. "It's part of my remit to build up a profile of Willow," I said. "Anything that can help form a picture of her as a person, including recent activity and contacts. The more information we have, the more able we are to draw up a list of potential suspects."

"I thought you'd already made your mind up about that," said Owen.

Sharon and I exchanged puzzled glances.

"I've been asked for an alibi," he said, "a breakdown of my movements during the time Willow was here? As if I'm the one under suspicion."

Sharon tried to reassure him it was normal procedure. "It's part of the process of elimination," she said. "We wouldn't be doing our jobs if we didn't check your alibi. There really is nothing to worry about."

I backed her up. "Most murders are committed by the spouse. It's inevitable you'd be checked out."

"Maybe," he said. "But that doesn't make it any easier to deal with. Bad enough that I lose my wife, but to be suspected of her murder..." He shook his head. "And now this intrusion into our private lives. I'm not sure I see the point."

"It's more important than ever right now," I said.

"I don't see why."

"Then allow me to explain." I settled myself back in the chair. "If we define murder in terms of the relationship between murderer and victim, there are three broad categories; murder by spouse - and I'm sure you'd prefer us to rule that out, murder by someone known to the victim, and stranger murder. Most stranger murders involve sexual assault or rape. And, thank God, there was no sign of that. Strangers who kill for the pleasure of it or under compulsion - psychopaths, in other words - are rare."

"So that leaves someone who knew her," said Sharon.

"But isn't it more likely to have been someone local?" Owen said. "The circumstances suggest that. Someone who knew the area."

"Exactly. Which is why it's necessary to delve so deeply into Willow's background. We have to dig out those old local relationships that still have a meaningful impact all these years later. As you so rightly say, everything points to Willow being targeted by someone who knew her, someone who lives locally. And she was killed for a reason, a pre-established reason. It's the only thing that makes sense. We need to find out who, what and why."

Owen fell silent and stared down at the floor. "I'm not sure what I can tell you that I've not already passed on to the police. Other than you, Karen was the only other person Willow still knew from the old days."

I had already briefed Sharon on some possible leads and so she started with a question about Willow's relationships with her family. "I understand Willow was estranged from her parents. What can you tell us about that?"

Owen shot a glance in my direction. He must have known the information came from me. To Sharon, he said, "Willow's parents lived in London, but I never knew them. When I first met Willow, she'd already distanced herself from them. I never really understood why. I believe they were very controlling when she was a child and she was happy to break away from them when she could support herself."

"And her sister?" said Sharon.

Owen wasn't so ready to answer this time. He stammered and said abruptly, "They're not close." Something about his reaction told me there was more to it.

"I seem to remember Laurel and her husband were regular visitors," I said.

A lengthy pause. "We lost touch after a while."

This was something I needed to follow up.

"What about Willow's previous partner?" I said. "What happened there?"

"His name was David Masters," said Owen. "And that's all I know about him. Except that he died in a car accident. Willow never spoke about him. And I didn't like to push her. It was a painful time in her life."

"It's not a name I recall from the past," I said. "Was he someone she met in London?"

"I think so," he said. "But I can't be certain."

Something else for me to follow up.

Sharon prompted him for information about Willow's other connections; old school friends, casual acquaintances, colleagues at the accountancy firm where she had worked as a business development manager. But she learned little of any use.

Owen was being deliberately vague about Willow's other relationships, or she really had kept him in the dark about her past. Either way, it was odd. Did one of them have something to hide?

It was only when Sharon asked him how his son was faring during his absence that Owen became more upbeat. After explaining that Simon was happy in the care of his grandparents for the time being, he told her how well he was getting on at school, how good his grades were, and that he was showing an interest in engineering and had a real aptitude for it. He was clearly proud of his son and took pleasure in talking about him. I could only hope the boy didn't take on his father's bigoted views.

While Sharon and Owen were still in conversation, the outer door opened and Lynch came in accompanied by a constable. Sharon and I both rose to meet him as he crossed towards us. He didn't waste any time with a greeting. "We need you to come down to the station, Mr Brookes."

Owen glanced at his watch. "It's coming up to lunchtime," he said. "Can't this wait."

"I'm afraid not. We have some more questions we need to ask." He seemed determined.

Owen hesitated. "It really isn't convenient right now."

"I'm afraid it won't wait, Sir. There are some issues that need to be resolved. I must insist."

Owen was just as insistent. "Sorry, but I've said all I'm going to say."

Lynch's face darkened. "In that case, you leave me no choice." He adopted a more formal tone. "Owen Brookes, I am arresting you on suspicion of the murder of Willow Brookes."

I stood in stunned silence as Lynch reminded Owen of his rights and said, "We have a car waiting outside, Sir. If you'd like to accompany us."

Sharon said nothing.

I found my voice. "What the hell?"

Behind us, the outer door opened, and a voice said, "Owen, what are you doing here?"

We all swung around.

It was Karen. Richard was coming through the door behind her, carrying two suitcases.

Karen looked around and said, "Is Willow with you?"

No one spoke.

Karen's expression of curiosity faded to one of concern. "Is someone going to tell me what's happening here?"

CHAPTER NINETEEN

"Of course I haven't been checking the bloody news. I was on honeymoon." Karen stood, hands on hips, and glared at me. "Why didn't you call me?"

"For that very reason," I said. "You were on honeymoon."

We were in Karen and Richard's private quarters at the back of the Fairview. Richard was hovering in the background, shuffling from one foot to the other, a despairing look on his face.

Once Owen had been escorted away and Sharon had also left for the station, Karen had ushered us through to her living room and demanded an explanation. I'd just finished bringing her up to speed on recent events and asked why she hadn't been checking the news.

Karen sank onto the couch behind her. "I can't believe it," she said.

Richard and I followed her lead and sat down. He seated himself at her side and squeezed her thigh in a show of sympathy. I dropped into the facing armchair.

"Why did they take Owen away?" she asked.

"I wish I knew. But I'm about to find out." I delved into the pocket of my jeans, dug out my mobile, and speed dialled Nathan. He had some explaining to do.

The call went to voice-mail.

I ended it.

"Nathan's not answering."

Richard said, "I'll go over to the station later. See if I can find out what's happening."

"I'm sure there's no need for that," said Karen.

"Looks like you're going to be thrown in at the deep end," I said.

He shrugged. "Goes with the territory."

Karen said, "Surely they can't think Owen did it?"

"Obviously they do," I said. "Why else would they arrest him?" I flopped back in my chair. "I'm in total shock. It came out of nowhere."

"Arrest him?" Karen looked dazed. "I've known them both for years," she said. "And I know he would never have harmed her."

"I'll see if I can get some info from the station." I tapped the number into my mobile.

Miles Barber took the call, and I soon had my answer. "His alibi didn't stand up," said Miles. "Seems he lied about his whereabouts during the time his wife was over in these parts. The Chief's interviewing him."

At least that explained why I couldn't get hold of Nathan. "Would you ask the Chief to call me when he's through," I said.

I thanked Miles, finished the call, and passed on the details of my conversation to Karen and Richard.

"I knew they were having problems," said Karen, "but nothing that couldn't be worked out."

"Were they?" I said. "I didn't know that. I knew they could both be volatile - I witnessed many a row - but they seemed reasonably well settled."

"It was long after I came back here. But we stayed in touch by phone."

"What was the problem?" I asked.

"Willow was suffering from depression and Owen was finding it hard to cope. Did you know she was bipolar?"

"I didn't. But I do now."

"It's not something she liked to share, but she confided in me when she was going through a rough patch."

Richard butted in. "You all had your relationship problems back then. If that's what London life does to you, I'm glad I stayed a small-town boy."

Karen patted his leg. "And we're all the better for it, hon."

I said, "I've been trying to figure out if there was anything in Willow's past that could account for her murder. I hope I didn't get it wrong."

"I still don't believe it," said Karen. "Owen's not the type."

I knew from experience there was no such thing as a 'type'. Some of the most amiable, well-respected people turned out to be murderers. Even so, I hated to think I could have been mistaken about Owen all this time.

"Willow was part of our crowd back in the day," I said, "but I didn't have much to do with her. Even then, we never hit it off."

Karen said, "I wasn't close to her before we all split up and went our separate ways. We formed more of a friendship when she moved to London. You and Nathan were my closest friends in those days."

Richard interrupted again. "I'll leave you two to talk while I go and unpack."

Karen squeezed his arm and smiled up at him as he raised himself from the couch and went into the bedroom.

Once he was gone, I said, "I should be asking you how you enjoyed the honeymoon, not debating whether or not Owen killed his wife. I'm sorry you had to come back to this."

"Have to admit, it's not one of the smoothest transitions into married life, but it can't be helped." She added, "I'm trying to remember who Willow went around with back then. Amelia Cole was probably her closest friend."

"I've already spoken to her. She wasn't very helpful. I got the impression their friendship ended abruptly."

"I'd moved away by then. But I suppose we all go our separate ways, eventually."

We were talking some more about the old days when Richard came out of the bedroom. He was wearing his uniform. "I'll go down to the station and check on the current state of play," he said.

Karen didn't look too pleased. "You're supposed to be on holiday."

"I'm going to get involved in the investigation anyway," he said. "I might as well get up to date first."

They were still arguing about it when we were interrupted by a knock at the door.

It was Nathan.

He looked Richard up and down. "You're eager to get back to work," he said.

"I was on my way to the station for a briefing," said Richard.

Karen said, "Well now you don't need to so you can get out of that uniform."

I said, "We're all in shock here. What the hell's going on?" I didn't give him chance to answer. "If you knew this was going to happen, why didn't you call me?"

"I'm here now, aren't I?"

"You could have warned me in advance."

"I didn't want you giving the game away," he said.

I protested. "I wouldn't have said anything."

His expression changed to one I was familiar with. It was his who-do-you-think-you're-fooling look.

I was about to respond but bit back my words. Now wasn't the time for an argument. "So are you going to tell us what happened?"

Nathan sank into the armchair at my side. "He lied about his whereabouts. Simple as that. He claims to have been at home or at work while Willow was away."

"So where was he?" I said.

"We're still trying to find out. What we do know is that he handed his son into the care of his parents and told them he had to leave town for a couple of days."

I said, "The implication being that he followed Willow here and killed her, presumably?"

"Why go to such lengths?" said Richard. "If he wanted to kill her, why not make it easy on himself and do the deed at home. It doesn't make sense."

I said, "It's not about making it easy for himself. It's about making it harder for the investigation. The further away from his home ground, the less likely it is that suspicion falls on him."

"You don't really think he did it, do you?" said Karen.

"I was speaking hypothetically," I said.

Richard said, "But he must have known his alibi would be checked."

I said, "I don't think it occurred to him for a moment. He made it plain earlier how annoyed he was at being asked for an alibi. More than likely, he thought he'd be in the clear because Willow was killed so far from home."

Nathan interrupted our debate. "Until we do find out where he was, we're keeping him in custody."

"How will this affect the investigation?" said Richard. "Will it change the focus?"

"Absolutely not," said Nathan. "It's just one more avenue to explore."

"So we're still going ahead with the interviews we've set up?" I asked.

"Of course," said Nathan. "And you'll be pleased to know we're interviewing your old friend, Ralph Ferguson, tomorrow."

In other circumstances, I would have been pleased to hear that. I would have seen it as a step forward, a chance to unravel more of the mystery.

But now everything had changed.

I was having a hard time believing Owen could be our guy. I had known him long enough to realise that this pattern of behaviour was out of character. But for reasons best known to him, he had lied, and I had to accept that I may be mistaken.

Had I been looking in all the wrong places? Trying all this time to find connections where there weren't any?

I hoped not.

CHAPTER TWENTY

Ralph Ferguson's interview was of particular interest, one I'd looked forward to. As much to satisfy my curiosity on a personal level as anything else. This was a man I had once counted among my friends and yet he had sought to harm me, to sully my reputation.

And I wanted some answers.

Which is why, the following day, I was back in the smaller meeting room down at the station with Nathan, Richard and Lynch.

Richard had insisted on returning to work immediately and Karen had eventually capitulated, giving in with good grace. As she herself had pointed out, he was returning to help investigate the murder of someone she counted among her friends, hardly something she could complain about.

In other circumstances, Richard's return would have allowed Lynch to go back to his posting in Charwell. But in anticipation of the increased workload brought about by the investigation, Nathan had arranged for Lynch to stay on and see it through.

We sat in front of the monitor screen, watching an image of the interview room, and waited for Miles Barber and Ralph to appear.

Despite my desire to gain some insight into what I perceived as Ralph's public display of ill-will towards me, I was less enthusiastic about the chances of this interview furthering the investigation. Lynch was already complaining about it being a waste of valuable time, claiming our focus should be on Owen.

I hoped he was wrong.

When Ralph finally entered the interview room, escorted by Barber, I was struck by how nervous he was. In these circumstances, a certain level of nervousness is inevitable. But there are limits. As he seated himself on the opposite side of the desk from Barber, his hands were shaking.

He wore a shirt and tie under a lightweight summer jacket but, despite the cool weather, he was sweating and, several times, dabbed at his forehead with a tissue before seating himself.

Once seated, he clasped his hands together, sat with them in his lap, and stared at Barber stony-faced, waiting for the interview to start.

Nathan said, "Is he always this edgy?"

So I wasn't the only one who had noticed.

Barber opened the file on the desk before him and began the interview by asking for and recording Ferguson's name and noting the date, time and place.

He also reminded Ferguson of the reason for the interview and asked him about his conversation with Willow. "I understand you had an argument?"

"An argument?"

A delaying tactic if ever I heard one.

Barber looked up from his file. "We've interviewed several people, most of whom saw you in a heated argument with Willow Brookes."

"With Willow Brookes?"

Again, that delaying tactic. Throwing back the question to buy enough time to consider a response. What was he hiding?

"Ah, yes, I remember now. She'd been drinking heavily and was clearly in a difficult mood, argumentative. Some child bumped into her, and she overreacted. Used inappropriate language. Not something a child should hear. I told her to be more careful about how she spoke to people."

"And that prompted an argument between the two of you?"

"More like a stream of abuse. I should have known better than to waste my time. She and I never were on the best of terms."

Barber leaned back and folded his arms, his forehead creased in a frown. "Now this puzzles me. You say you weren't on the best of terms. And yet she chose to confide in you. It was you who told her husband about her assault claim, wasn't it?"

Ferguson stared at Barber, swallowed, and twisted the ring on his finger around and around.

"Wasn't it?" Barber repeated.

"I believe it was, yes."

"And yet you'd argued. Quite violently from the sound of it. Strange that she should have chosen you to confide in."

"If I remember correctly, it was earlier that afternoon."

"From a woman you'd never been on the best of terms with?"

Ferguson squirmed in his seat. He adjusted the knot on his tie and ran a finger around the inside of his collar before answering. "You have to remember," he said, "it was a celebration. Lots of wine and spirits. People let their guard down in such circumstances, say things they wouldn't otherwise, say things they don't mean." He laughed, a sharp stilted sound, and said, "I'd had a few myself. So I'm sorry if I'm vague on the details. But I can't remember exactly how it went down."

I leaned towards the microphone and pressed the switch. "Ask him why he contacted the press?"

Lynch said, "I'm not sure that's pertinent to the investigation."

"Everything's pertinent," I said.

Barber raised a hand and touched his earpiece in acknowledgement. "If you were so uncertain about what you discussed, why did you feel it necessary to involve the media?"

Ferguson responded with a sharp intake of breath and adjusted his tie again. He recovered himself, pulled himself upright, and in a pompous tone, said, "I saw it as a public duty."

Barber stared back at Ferguson without speaking. It was an old trick designed to elicit more from the respondent.

It worked.

"Men like MacGregor think they can get away with anything. They think just because they've made something of a name for themselves, they can do as they please. They need to know there are consequences for their actions." As he spoke, his mouth twisted into a sneer. "They're nothing special. Even if they think they are."

I said, "I don't suppose I'll be getting fan mail from him any time soon."

Richard said, "You're not one of his favourite people, that's for sure."

Nathan grunted.

"It's as I thought," Lynch said, "he resents your success."

Barber changed tack. "Are you able to confirm your whereabouts on…" He looked down at his file "…Sunday, the eighth of April." He looked up again. "That's the day after the wedding reception."

Ferguson sounded more confident when he replied. "I was visiting my children."

"Visiting?"

"My wife and I are separated. The children live with their mother over in Cheltenham. I drove over there early Sunday morning."

"And your wife can verify when you arrived?"

"Of course she can." Ferguson sounded indignant. "I took the kids out for the day and dropped them back off at their mother's that evening before driving back home. She'll be able to tell you what time I left too."

There was a marked change in his attitude now his interaction with Willow was no longer the subject of scrutiny. He was more self-assured. And the nervous tics had disappeared. I could only surmise that his alibi would stand up. And that would absolve him of any direct involvement in Willow's murder.

But something wasn't right.

Was there some truth to what Lynch had told me? Was Ferguson really so jealous of my success that he would try to ruin my reputation? Is that why he was so nervous?

Nathan interrupted my thoughts. He leaned towards the mike, pressed the switch, and said, "I'm not too happy about this one. I want his wife's details - name and address - and tell him we need to know his future whereabouts in case we want to speak with him again."

I was glad to know Nathan had his misgivings too, and I wasn't just being paranoid.

Barber acknowledged his Chief's request with the usual touch of the earphone and asked Ferguson for the details.

"Why would you want to see me again? Don't you believe me? I have nothing to hide." The nervousness was back, wrapped up in the protestations.

Barber reassured Ferguson it was routine. "We're following up on all interviews where there was a connection to Willow Brookes."

Once he'd noted down Ferguson's response, he closed the file and said, "I think we're done here."

He may well have been, but I wasn't.

Now the interview was over, I was able to shake off my earlier doubts about Ralph Ferguson's tie to Willow's murder.

It seemed clear to me that his dubious claim to a public-spirited need to out me the way he did was personal, nothing more than a cover for envious malice. But his account of the conversation with Willow was a different matter. It didn't ring true. And he seemed to be on shakier ground when talking of it, less certain, discomposed. But if Willow hadn't told him of her fabricated assault claim, who had?

There was more to this than meets the eye, and I intended to find out what it was.

CHAPTER TWENTY-ONE

Lynch was still grumbling as the meeting broke up. He had moaned throughout the following debriefing, complaining that the whole thing had been a waste of time. He refused to accept the merit of interviewing Ferguson, convinced that Owen must be our man.

As Richard followed him out of the door, making sympathetic noises, Nathan motioned me to stay behind. Once they were out of the way, he sank into his chair with a sigh.

I jumped in with my own take on the interview before Nathan could say anything. "You saw how nervous Ferguson was and how vague he was about his argument with Willow. Don't tell me that's the behaviour of an innocent man."

Nathan rubbed the back of his neck and twisted his head from side to side. A sure sign he was stressed. "It's not me you need to convince," he said. "You saw how those two reacted."

"You're the boss," I said. "It's your call." I went and stood behind him and kneaded his shoulders. The muscles around the neck were tight, and I dug my fingers in deep, trying to loosen the muscle fibre.

"Doesn't make it any less of an uphill battle," he said and leaned his head forward. "I need to keep these guys on board."

"Ferguson is lying about something."

"Sure, but there's no hard evidence to connect him to Willow's murder."

"And Owen?"

"Brookes is still playing hardball. He claims he changed his plans after dropping his son off at his parents."

"Maybe he did."

"Then why leave his son with them? And he's being vague about why he needed to leave town in the first place. Some nonsense about needing some 'me' time and wanting to get away. It doesn't ring true."

"Doesn't make him a murderer." I finished massaging his shoulders and dropped into the chair opposite.

"There's something else." He paused and chewed his lip. "We checked his bank and credit card statements. The day after Willow left for Elders Edge, he used his card at a petrol station in Braintree."

"Braintree?" I made a quick mental calculation. "That's about halfway between here and London."

"Exactly."

The implication was obvious.

"Have you questioned him about it?"

"Same old story. He said he wanted some time to himself and drove around for the day."

The expression of incredulity on my face must have been obvious. He said, "Not very convincing, is it?"

"So you think he's our guy?"

"I prefer to keep an open mind, no matter how difficult that may be, but you can understand why my team aren't overly enthusiastic about looking elsewhere."

"If your team aren't onside with this investigation, if they continue to see Owen as the prime suspect, as the only suspect, they'll lose focus on the investigation as a whole."

Nathan shook his head. "I just need to get them back on track. Make sure they don't lose sight of the whole picture. Maybe I should give them a pep talk."

He raised himself from his chair and said, "Let's go get some air. I feel stifled in here." He rubbed the back of his neck again as he headed for the door.

I followed him into the corridor. "I'm not suggesting it would be a conscious decision," I said. "But no matter how many pep talks you give them, on a subconscious level they won't be as actively engaged as they would otherwise be. They're human beings with the same psychological flaws that all humans are prone to."

He thought this over as we made our way out to the covered walkway at the front of the building and trod the tarmac to the far side of the car park.

I nodded towards the mini-mart next door. "Let's go grab something for lunch. My treat."

Nathan followed me into the shop. I chose a ham and cheese roll from the display cabinet. Nathan grabbed himself a chicken and leek pie, took it over to the counter to be heated, and ordered a couple of cartons of coffee. Whilst we waited for our order to be completed, he drummed his fingers on the countertop.

Once back outside, we crossed over to the wall fronting the station car park, put our coffees on top of it, and unwrapped our food. I said, "Are you keeping him in custody?"

Nathan turned and leaned against the wall. "Not sure. I'm thinking through the options."

"Which are?"

"I can't keep him for more than twenty-four hours without either charging him or applying to the court for an extension." He bit into his pie.

"Tough choice," I said.

Nathan gulped down a mouthful of food. "Quite. And there's no hard evidence to implicate him in his wife's murder. All we have is circumstantial evidence, and that's not enough to charge him. So my only options are to release him on bail pending further enquiries or apply for an extension and put him under pressure in the hopes he'll come clean."

"So which will it be?"

"That's where you come in."

"Me?"

He said, "You know Owen better than anyone. Before I decide, I want your thoughts on this? You think he's capable of murder?"

"You're asking the wrong person the wrong question. I think everyone is capable of murder in certain circumstances."

"But Owen? In these circumstances? Tell me, truthfully, do you think it could be him?"

I stared out across the car park as I chewed on my sandwich and let my thoughts roll back over the years. All those times in the company of Owen and Willow. The arguments. The stony silences. The tantrums. Times with Owen. The angry spats. The quick temper. A roll call of remembered occasions played out in my mind as the memories rolled by.

When I came back to the present, Nathan was staring at me intently.

I said, "Yesterday, Owen talked to Sharon Worth about Simon, his son, about how proud he was of him, about his hopes for the future.

"Owen and Willow fought like cat and dog. I've lost count of the times I witnessed their arguments. It sure as hell wasn't the easiest of relationships. But what I do know is that Owen dotes on his son. And no way would he do anything to harm Simon's wellbeing or cause him distress. So, no, I don't think he can be our murderer."

Nathan accepted my answer with a nod, still chewing on his food.

"Another thing," I said. "Given how volatile their relationship was, it would be easy to imagine Owen acting without thinking, striking out in the heat of the moment. But that's not what happened here.

"If Owen had followed Willow and killed her here, he would have had to plan it in advance. I've known him long enough to make a reasonable assessment of his core character. He's a hothead, quick to lose his temper and just as quick to recover it. The cool detachment he'd need to prepare Willow's murder isn't a typical feature of his personality type. It's just not in him."

Nathan stared into the distance, still thinking over his options.

"I wonder if this has anything to do with Willow's sister," I said.

Nathan came to with a start. "Her sister?" He sounded surprised. "Why do you say that?"

"Something I picked up on when Sharon and I interviewed Owen yesterday." I told him about Owen's reaction to questions about Laurel, about his seeming reluctance to talk about Willow's relationship with her sister.

"She's already been interviewed," said Nathan. "And we already know she and Willow haven't been in touch with each other for some time."

"But Owen may have been. It occurred to me afterwards that perhaps Owen was having an affair with Laurel. It would explain why he might not want to talk about her and why he might take advantage of Willow's absence to get in touch with Laurel. Perhaps they arranged to meet. It would also explain the credit card payment."

Nathan pushed himself away from the wall and paced back and forth while he considered this. "It could also explain why he'd be reluctant to admit to it. It would provide a motive."

"Can I make a suggestion?" I said.

He stopped pacing and faced me. "Go on."

"You know as well as I that people are often unwilling to divulge their personal histories to authorities like the police. But maybe if I was to speak to her. If I explained I was building up a psychological profile of Willow. Laurel may be more willing to open up."

A pause. "Okay, it's worth a shot. And in the meantime, I'll apply for a court order to extend Owen's custody. I'll see if I can get him to open up too."

"Great. In that case, I'll drive over to Colton Drey this afternoon."

I drained my coffee carton, squeezed it into a tight ball, and tossed it into the nearby trashcan.

CHAPTER TWENTY-TWO

I was struck by how alike the two sisters were. The same dark hair, the same pert nose and pale complexion. And even in the brown baggy jumper and green wellingtons, Laurel still carried herself with the same confident poise I had seen in Willow.

She was hosing down the yard in front of her large rambling heap of a house as I climbed out of the Elan on the other side of the road.

I let Rocky out of the car, slipped on his lead, and crossed the road towards her. As I approached, she looked up and greeted me with a smile of recognition.

Rocky pricked up his ears, responding to the barking dogs in the kennels on the far side of the yard. He answered with a low rumbling noise in the back of his throat.

As we reached her, Laurel turned off the hose and said, "I wondered if you might pay me a visit."

"It's been a while," I said. "I wasn't sure if you'd remember me."

She laughed and said, "After all that publicity you drummed up for yourself, how could I forget."

She said it with an open smile. Unlike her sister, she wasn't out to make a cheap dig, and so I returned the smile and said, "Ouch. Some impression that must have made."

"I make my own judgements." She dropped the hose and squatted down to face Rocky. "And who's this?" she said and stroked his head.

I'd brought Rocky along as a way of breaking the ice. It had worked. "This is Rocky. Living with us in retirement."

"Retirement?"

"He's an ex-police dog having a well-deserved rest from active service."

"That explains why he's so well behaved." She stroked him again and then glanced up at me. "This is about Willow, I suppose?"

I nodded. "So you know I'm working on the investigation?"

"Small town gossip. You know how it works." She stood up. "Let's go to the house. It's quieter there." She led the way across the yard. "You know the police have already interviewed me?"

"They have more immediate concerns. They're trying to determine Willow's recent movements. I'm more interested in her past."

As we reached the house, I said, "I understand you didn't know about Willow's visit. This whole thing must have been such a shock. I'm surprised she hadn't tried to contact you."

"Everything about Willow was a shock."

After removing her wellingtons and standing them by the step, she opened the door and led the way into a large square hall. "You can bring Rocky in. I'm used to dogs around the place."

I followed her through to a comfortable living room, where she offered me a chair by the fireside. She slipped on a pair of loafers and sank into a matching flower-patterned fabric-covered armchair facing me. Rocky curled up by my feet.

Laurel said, "I can't imagine my sister was one of your favourite people. Not after the assault claim."

I stiffened. "Small town gossip again?"

"Small town media. I take it you haven't seen the online edition of the Sentinel?"

I groaned. Another pleasure to look forward to. "I hope you know it's not true."

"I believe you. I know what a bitch my sister could be."

"Doesn't sound like she was one of your favourite people either."

She sank back into her chair with a sigh. "Where do I begin? We were at odds with each other for as long as I can remember."

"Sibling rivalry?"

"To start with, maybe. She was four years younger than me. The baby of the family. I guess I was jealous of the attention she got after I'd been an only child for so long."

"She seems to have had a troubled adolescence. I understand there was a suicide attempt."

Laurel snorted. "Willow always was something of an attention seeker."

"You don't sound convinced?"

She pushed herself to her feet and crossed to a drinks cabinet by the window. "If I'm going to have to relive life with Willow, I need something strong to get me through it." She took a decanter and glass from the cabinet and poured herself a large scotch. She held the decanter up towards me and offered me a drink, but I declined.

After returning to her seat, she took a large swig from her glass and said, "I'd already married and left home long before Willow's meltdown. My choice of husband put paid to the possibility of staying on good terms with my parents. They detested him. With good cause, as it turns out. But that's another story."

"So you weren't around at the time."

"No. And that suited me just fine. But not for a moment did I think Willow intended to take her life. It was just part of her usual attention-seeking routine."

"There must have been a reason for it."

"Willow was a wild child. Took everything to extremes. And our parents didn't help. Social standing was more important than family. Which is why they moved to London soon afterwards. To avoid the embarrassment. They thought it best for Willow and themselves if they made a complete break and started afresh somewhere else."

"Is that where she met David Masters?"

"I guess so." She drained her glass and carried it over to the drinks cabinet where she refilled it before returning to her seat. As she made herself comfortable again, she said, "The first I knew of David Masters was when we visited Willow in London. And that's when I heard about his accident. It's not something Willow liked to talk about. So I never asked."

"It seems no one knew much about him," I said. "A veritable man of mystery."

Rocky stirred at my feet, and I reached down and petted him.

Laurel said, "It wasn't a name I recognised. If he'd been a local man, I'm sure I would have heard of him Everyone knows everyone in a small place like this." As an afterthought, she added, "If you want to know more, you could try speaking to her co-conspirator from those days, Amelia Cole. They were inseparable."

That name again. Time I had another chat with Amelia. I made a mental note to talk with her later and filed it at the back of my mind.

"One thing that puzzles me," I said. "I get the distinct impression there was bad blood between you and Willow and yet you were happy to visit your sister in London. The times I saw you together, you seemed comfortable enough in each other's company."

Laurel stared at the floor in silence for several seconds before answering. "I stayed in touch with Karen in those days. And when I heard Willow had met and married Owen and settled down, I thought it was time to resolve our differences." She gulped down a mouthful of scotch and said, "Big mistake."

We were now edging towards the main reason for my visit. But how to approach it? If I asked her outright, she may clam up. It may be better to lead her towards it and hope she'd come clean.

I said, "Something went wrong?"

She stared at me, a coldness in her eyes and her mouth set in a hard line. In the distance, a dog barked, setting off a series of answering yelps from other parts of the kennels.

Laurel turned away and said, "I told you my parents didn't approve of my husband. And with good cause. He was a philanderer. I put up with his casual affairs for years, even pretended not to know about them. But the one affair I wasn't prepared to put up with was the final one." She turned to face me again. "The one he had with Willow."

My chest tightened, and I dug my fingers into the arms of the chair. I opened my mouth to speak and closed it again, not sure how to respond.

"Bit of a shock, eh?" She smiled. "It was for me too."

I caught my breath and said, "When was this?"

"A couple of years ago."

I cast my mind back. Two years ago, Owen and I had still been close, and all had seemed well with his world. Whatever dramas had unfolded in his life, he had kept them well hidden.

"Did Owen know?" I said.

"Willow made little attempt to hide it. She was completely off the rails."

"And yet they stayed together?"

"Which is more than Roger and I did."

"He's not around anymore?"

"Too right, he isn't. I made damn sure of that. But Willow was the one I could never forgive."

"And yet Owen forgave her?"

"With good reason. He dotes on that son of theirs. Or, more specifically, Willow's son. If he'd split with Willow, he may well have lost the boy too."

"Difficult choice," I murmured.

"You have to admire him for the choice he made. Life was never the same again. They rowed constantly. I wouldn't have blamed him if he'd walked away or even found solace in an affair himself. But he stuck with it, did everything he could to keep the family together. It can't have been easy."

So much for my theory about Owen's infidelity. His having an affair with Laurel wouldn't have got him completely off the hook of course - as Nathan had reluctantly pointed out, it could have been construed as a motive for murder - but at least it would have explained a few things that perplexed me; his reluctance to come clean about his whereabouts, for instance, and why he would need to pass through Braintree. Seems as if I would now have to seek my answers elsewhere.

Laurel said, "Is he staying in Elders Edge? I'd like to get in touch with him. I'm sure he could use some support right now."

"More than you realise. Right now he has no choice but to stay. He's in police custody."

"What?" She jerked upright, glass still in hand, and spilt some drink on her jeans.

I waited until she had wiped the damp patch with the sleeve of her jumper. I explained the current situation and added, "He's not making things easy for himself."

Laurel's face paled. "You can't believe he killed her?"

I told her I didn't and said, "But it's not an opinion that is universally shared."

I did my best to reassure her I was doing everything possible to help Owen. Even if he wasn't making it easy for me. With little else to say, I brought our meeting to an end, promised to let her know as soon as there were any developments, roused Rocky from his slumber, and took my leave.

On the drive home, I mused over possible arguments I could use to persuade Owen to see sense. So far, I had been loathe to believe he was a murderer, but even I was beginning to have doubts. Could he have followed her to Elders Edge, killed her in such a cold-blooded and calculating way? It wasn't his style. He was a hothead, more likely to act on the spur of the moment. But I had to find out for sure. One way or the other.

And that's when it struck me. How I could use his volatile nature to advantage. Give him an emotional jolt. It would be painful, and he would hate me for doing it. But I was sure it could work.

One final attempt to get at the truth.

It was a risk worth taking.

CHAPTER TWENTY-THREE

The cloying smell of cheap deodorant and the pungent odour of antibacterial spray hung in the steam-laden air despite a nearby air conditioning unit running at full throttle.

Personally, I preferred the heady aroma of the sweat it was meant to mask, but each to their own, I guess.

It was early morning the following day, and Nathan and I were nearing the end of a workout at the local gym. I was using the treadmill, keeping up a steady moderate pace, while Nathan finished a series of chin-ups on the cable crossover machine.

I watched him through the mirrored wall in front of me. A sheen of sweat covered his exposed flesh, the wet t-shirt clinging to his chest against the thick mat of hair, and each time he pulled himself up, the corded muscles in his arms bulged and strained.

My laboured breathing and rising temperature were only partly due to the exertion of running; if anything was sure to make me short of breath and put me on heat, it was the sight of him working those muscles.

The only other people in the place were a rotund middle-aged man in an off-white sweat-soaked tee-shirt and a young woman with tied-back hair attired in pink tee and matching leggings. They worked adjoining treadmills; she wearing earphones and steadily increasing her pace at regular intervals, he at the other side of her, puffing and panting, pounding the rubber with heavy feet and wheezing more audibly each time he increased his pace to match hers.

I suppressed a laugh. Yet another fragile ego desperate to show his superiority. I hoped she finished her stint before the poor guy collapsed from exhaustion.

Nathan dropped from the bar with a grunt and, hands on hips, threw back his head and sucked in a deep lungful of air.

I slowed to a halt, turned off the machine, and went to join him.

He grabbed our towels from where he'd hung them over a rack, tossed one to me, and ran the other over his face.

I slung mine around my shoulders and wiped my neck as I followed him through to the men's locker room.

Before he could sit, I wrapped my arms around him from behind, pressed myself up against him, and buried my face in the crook of his neck.

I moaned. "I wish I could bottle that sexy smell. I'd carry it with me everywhere."

He laughed. "Make the most of it while you can. I'm heading for the showers."

Grumbling, I let him go, and he dropped onto a bench.

"Need any help in there?" I said.

Still grinning, he flicked me on the thigh with the side of his towel. "We both know what sort of help that would be."

"Always eager to please."

"And which of us will explain away your particular kind of help if we're interrupted?"

"Spoilsport. Sometimes you have to take a risk, live on the edge."

Still grinning, he said, "Living with you is all the edge I need, thanks."

After unlacing his trainers and removing them, he pulled off his vest and used it to mop the sweat from the mat of hair on his chest. "I'm still not sure I should let him out," he said. "Much as I hate to say it, the more I learn about him, the more convinced I am he's our man."

The statement came out of nowhere, a total non sequitur to the light-hearted banter that had gone before, and it took me a moment to focus in and make sense of what he was saying.

After telling him of my interview with Laurel Ford the previous afternoon, I had tried - so far unsuccessfully - to persuade him to release Owen on bail. He'd promised to think it through, and it had obviously been on his mind during our workout.

I sat down beside him, kicked off my running shoes and struggled out of the rest of my kit. "Look," I said, "you've not been able to get him to talk, you said yourself you're getting nowhere, so why not let me have a try?" I dropped my gear on the floor by the lockers, headed across the room and into one of the shower cubicles, towel in hand. I slung my towel over the top of the showerhead and turned it on.

Nathan slipped out of his shorts and followed me over to the adjoining cubicle. "You're welcome to interview him down at the station. But I'm not keen on letting him out on bail at the moment. The longer he's confined, the more likely he is to talk."

We showered in silence. Once I'd finished, I grabbed the towel and rubbed my hair with it as I made my way back to the lockers.

As I dried myself, I said, "I find it easier to get the best out of someone in a more relaxed setting. Keeping him in custody will make him more hostile." I had another reason for wanting Owen's release. But it was probably best to keep that to myself for the moment.

Nathan turned off his shower and crossed over to where I was dressing. "I know you may not want to hear this," he said, "but after your discussion with Laurel, I'm thinking he may be our man after all."

He opened his locker, took out his clothes and dropped onto the bench to pull on his underpants.

"If his only reason for staying with Willow was to make sure he didn't lose his son," he continued, "the burden of living with her over the past two years might have become too much for him."

He pulled on a pair of pants, stood up to button them, and then reached into his locker for a shirt. As he put it on, he said, "Sounds like good enough grounds for murder, don't you think?"

So much for trying to get Owen off the hook. If anything, I'd made his situation worse.

I threaded a belt through the loops of my jeans and buckled it. "Isn't that all the more reason to let me have one last chance to speak with him?"

Before he could reply, the door opened, and rotund man staggered in, panting heavily, his face dripping sweat. He dropped onto one of the other benches.

I could have done without the interruption at that particular moment, just as I was trying to persuade Nathan around to my way of thinking. But at least it gave him a chance to think it over.

We both acknowledged the interloper with nods, packed our soiled sportswear in silence, and headed for the door.

Once outside, Nathan said, "I'll not be able to hold Brookes much longer without charging him, anyway. So here's what I'll do." He glanced at his watch. "I'll check in at the station this morning and see if there's been any progress. If not, we'll have one last go. If he refuses to play ball, I'll release him tomorrow on conditional bail. But, to be honest, I don't hold out much hope for a change of attitude. The guy's a stubborn bastard."

I slung the gym bag over my shoulder and fell into step at Nathan's side as we headed on home. "Leave him to me," I said. "I have my methods."

CHAPTER TWENTY-FOUR

Three o'clock. I figured I'd left it long enough. True to his word, Nathan had arranged for Owen's release that morning and, with luck, Owen would be settled back in the Fairview by now.

I drove over there to find Karen and Robert Dunn at the reception desk. Dunn had a travel bag with him and was handing control over to Karen before leaving.

"Not quite the posting you were expecting," I said to him, grinning.

"Let's just say it's been... er... eventful," he said.

Karen shot me a dark look. Probably hoping he wasn't going to ask for danger money.

"Just one more task before you go," I said. "Is Owen back yet? I'd like to see him if he is."

Dunn confirmed he was and called his room.

"I didn't know he was here," Karen said. "So they've released him?"

"Not for long if he doesn't wise up," I said.

Dunn said, "He returned earlier this-" He was interrupted by the phone and spoke into it. "Mr MacGregor is in reception. He's asking to see you."

A pause. Dunn put his hand over the receiver and said, "He wants to know if it's important. He's not up to seeing anyone right now."

I snatched the receiver from Dunn's hand, planted it to my ear, and said, "Get down here now. Or I'll come up there and drag you down."

Owen knew me well enough to know I wasn't joking. Once I'd set my mind on something, I followed it through.

A strained voice said, "What the hell?"

"I mean it, Owen. Get down here." I slammed the phone back in its cradle.

Karen and Dunn stared at me, startled into silence.

Karen opened her mouth to speak but was interrupted by the sound of a door slamming overhead and a bemused-looking Owen descending the stairs.

As Owen reached the last step, I said, "We're going for a drive. There's something you need to see."

"I don't understand," he said.

"You soon will." I nodded farewell to Karen and Dunn and headed away without further explanation.

Owen followed me out of the door and down the steps to where the Elan was parked. "What is this?" he said.

I ignored the question and said, "Get in the car."

I circled round to the driver's side and climbed in. Owen kept his eyes on me as he fastened his seatbelt. His face was creased with concern, but he said nothing. He seemed dazed. That was a good sign. It was time for some shock tactics and keeping him wrong-footed was all part of the plan. I needed to make him feel vulnerable.

I turned the car around, sped along the coast road, and took the climb to the clifftop.

We didn't speak on the way. By now, he would have realised I was in no mood for conversation. At our journey's end, I parked up on the cliff road, directed Owen to get out of the car, and led him over to the steps leading down to the beach.

"Down you go," I said.

He preceded me down the steps, gripping the handrail all the way. Halfway, he faltered, slowed to a halt, and stared down at the rock-strewn beach below. He turned and looked up at me as awareness grew in him. An expression of horror spread across his face. "Mikey? Is this...?"

I barked out an order. "Keep going."

"Mikey, I don't understand. Why are we here?"

"There's something you need to see. Keep going."

Reluctantly, he turned and made his way slowly down to the foot of the steps. From there, I took over and led him across the sand to the rocky outcrop where Willow's body had been found. Far over to our right, the foamy crests of waves broke against the shoreline, leaving behind a widening ribbon of wet sand as the sea receded.

"You see those rocks?" I said. "You see how jagged they are?" I didn't wait for an answer. "When Willow hit them, they ripped through her body, tore it to shreds, and smashed every bone. Her abdomen and chest were ruptured, and sections of her flesh fell away.

"When they eventually moved her, she folded up like a bag of broken spare parts and her head hung loose. Where her face used to be was just a bloody tangled mess."

A terrible wailing scream of rage and despair rent the air and Owen, head thrown back, dropped to the sand, sobbing and gasping. "Why are you doing this?" he howled.

This was the emotional breakthrough I'd aimed for, but the strength of it shook me.

I fell to my knees in front of him, took his head between my hands, and stared into his face. "Because I want them to catch the murdering bastard who did this. I want them to find the disgusting piece of shit who smashed the life out of her and then tossed her over the cliff in such a callous and calculating way. I want them to make him pay. And right now, Owen, you're not helping any."

Still sobbing, he said, "I've done nothing wrong."

I leaned towards him and said, "Listen to me, Owen. In the early stages of an investigation like this, time is of the essence. The sooner action is taken, the more likely the police can find and secure material that might otherwise be lost. They need to interview potential witnesses while events are still fresh in their minds, track down CCTV footage before it's destroyed, gather forensic evidence before it's gone for good. And every day that passes reduces their chances."

"What does any of that have to do with me?"

"Because right now, all that attention is focused on you. You're the prime suspect. And so long as you refuse to cooperate, the investigating team is going to concentrate all its resources on you, interviewing friends and family, neighbours and colleagues, checking your movements, your car, phone calls, ATM withdrawals and receipts. And while all that is going on, time is slipping away. And someone is getting away with Willow's murder."

Owen was still sobbing, quietly now, head lowered, facing the ground. "I shouldn't need to prove my innocence."

"That's not how the real world works. You need to tell them where you were and what you were doing. Once you've established your alibi, they can get on with the job and focus attention where it's needed."

He looked up. "You don't think I did it, do you?"

"I wouldn't be here putting you through this if I thought that. But what I believe doesn't matter right now." I took hold of his arm and squeezed it. "Why won't you tell them?"

He stared me in the face, long and hard, tears streaming down his cheeks, and said, "Because I was scared and ashamed."

I didn't respond. Now was the time to keep silent and let him talk. I settled down on the sand and waited.

"Willow and I hit a rough patch." He took in a deep breath and said, "She was having an affair with her sister's husband."

He paused, waiting for a reaction.

I kept quiet and nodded, encouraging him to continue.

"It had been going on for over a year. When we found out, Laurel never forgave her; it destroyed their relationship once and for all. But I forgave her. For the sake of our family, I wanted to make our marriage work. But it changed Willow, left her even more unstable. I think it was the guilt. You know what she was like. Up one minute, down the next. It wasn't easy to cope with. Just before she came down for the wedding, she went through a bad time, battling her demons. I was surprised she still wanted to go."

I made some sympathetic noises and waited for him to carry on.

He said, "The day she left, I was so relieved. I know that must sound callous, but it was like a great weight had been lifted. And maybe that's why I acted as I did. Because the pressure was off." He paused and swallowed hard. "I did something stupid."

Above us, a seagull wheeled around in a wide-sweeping arc and emitted a long piercing shriek before soaring away over the clifftop.

Owen took a deep breath and said, "I'm a recovering alcoholic."

He waited for a reaction again.

None came.

He went on. "That evening, I took Simon round to my parents and told them I had to leave town for a day or two. It was a lie, of course. I had other plans. On the way home, I stopped off to buy a couple of bottles of whisky, and once I got home, I got slaughtered, drank myself into oblivion."

He screwed his eyes tight shut and his lower lip trembled. When he opened his eyes again, they were filled with fresh tears. "The following morning, I woke up on the sitting room floor in a pool of vomit." He shook his head. "Seven years. I've not touched a drop for seven years and I had to go and fuck up." A strained smile played across his lips. "You must think I'm a real hypocrite after the way I treated you."

Hypocrisy I could deal with; bigotry was a different matter. But perhaps now wasn't the time to call him out on that. "I stopped making those sorts of judgements a long time ago," I said. "Round about the time I discovered I was just as human as everyone else."

He nodded.

"So what then?"

"I got myself cleaned up and called my sponsor. Someone I met through AA. I dropped out of the meetings some years back, but we always stayed in touch. He invited me over. He's not local anymore. He lives in Braintree, so I stopped the night. We had a lot to talk about." That rueful smile again. "I guess I'll be going back to the meetings for a while."

"I guess so. But why didn't you say anything about this? No one would have judged you."

"Yes, they would. Willow's parents would. She cut them out of her life long ago and lost all contact with them. But they resented not seeing Simon. They're sure to learn about Willow. And if they try to get in touch again and find out about my problems, they might try to claim custody and take him away from me."

"I'm not sure you have anything to worry about. You've made a good job of parenthood so far."

"I didn't want to risk it. With everything that's happened; Willow's death and then being accused of her murder. It seemed as if the world was conspiring against me. My head was all over the place, and I was scared I might lose him."

"Understandable. But perhaps it's time now to put things right?"

He nodded, and I rose to my feet and helped him up.

"Back to the station?" I said.

As I turned to move, he put a restraining hand on my arm. "It's not the only thing I need to put right. There's something we need to clear up between us. What I said. You know. The other day?"

"Let's not go there," I said. "The only thing that need concern us is the investigation."

"Please, Mikey, I need to do this," he said, holding onto my arm. "I don't want you thinking I'm that sort of person."

I snorted. "I'm not sure what else I'm supposed to think."

"I've been trying to find a way to apologise. What I said was shameful."

"Then why say it?"

"I was angry," he said. "Everything I thought I knew about you was a fiction."

"You had every right to be angry," I said, "but I could have hoped you'd find another way to express it."

"You're not without blame here, Mikey. You lied about who and what you were. Can you wonder that I used it against you? I felt betrayed."

I nodded, unsure what to say.

"What I said. It was a cheap shot and I regret it. I was looking for something to hurt you with. But that's not who I am."

The remorse in his eyes was clear to see, and the hard kernel of resentment and hurt that had built up inside me slowly dissolved. Perhaps it was time to make amends.

"I have regrets too," I said. "You were a good friend when I most needed one and I wish I'd been honest with you. I was a coward."

"I want to understand. Maybe it's something we should talk about."

"That's a conversation for another time. But one we need to have. I guess I have some explaining to do."

"And I know now you didn't hurt Willow. You wouldn't do such a thing. I was just so angry, lashing out. I wasn't thinking straight."

"I don't know why she claimed I did."

"We both know what Willow was capable of. I wasn't blind to her faults. There were times she could be vindictive."

I didn't say anything. This was another of those times when a diplomatic silence was called for.

"Despite everything, we were always such good friends," he said. "I don't want to change that."

"Neither do I. And whatever you're going through right now, I want to be here for you."

"Thank you, Mikey."

"Nothing to thank me for. We're friends. Okay?"

"Okay."

"And I need to make an apology too. I'm sorry I put you through this."

"It was the right call. I screwed up. I should have known better."

"So let's go put it right, shall we?"

He nodded his agreement, and we retraced our path across the beach.

As we mounted the steps back up the cliff face, I fished my mobile out of the pocket of my jeans and called Nathan. "Are you still at the local station?" I asked.

He was.

"Owen and I are on our way over to see you. He has something he wants to tell you."

CHAPTER TWENTY-FIVE

Nathan said, "Your powers of persuasion are obviously better than mine. How did you do it?"

"You can't expect me to give away my trade secrets," I said. Truth be told, I wasn't yet ready to own up to the brutal way I'd forced Owen's cooperation. I still wasn't sure if the ends had justified the means and hoped I hadn't gone too far.

Miles Barber was taking a statement from Owen in another part of the station, and I was in Nathan's office, seated on the other side of his desk, waiting for Owen's return.

In the meantime, I talked Nathan through what I had learned from Owen about the turmoil he'd lived through; everything from his futile attempts to hold his marriage together to his fears of losing his son and his anger at what he saw as my betrayal of our friendship.

"He's in such a bad place," I said.

"Maybe, but I'm still not happy about the anti-gay abuse. God knows you had a difficult enough time coming to terms. He must have known that."

"Which is why he did it. He was angry and was looking to hurt me. And maybe I deserved it. I let him down. And he wasn't the only one I hurt, was he?"

He grunted and changed the subject. "You're sure his story will stand up?"

"No doubt about it."

"Good. Then once we've checked it out, perhaps we can get back on track and stop wasting time on false trails."

"You will go easy on him, won't you?"

"Give me a break, Mikey. I'm not totally insensitive. Of course, I'll go easy on him. But he needs to understand we can't let ourselves be sidetracked. We have to stay focused."

"Sure. And, from now on, I'll do what I can to support him." Now I felt even more guilty about the pressure I'd put Owen under. I had some making up to do. "I'll take him out for dinner. Try to take his mind off things for a while."

Nathan had already made it clear he would be working late and would grab a snack later from the takeaway next door. Not something I was too happy about, but I was getting used to it.

"I hope all this overtime is having results," I said. "Any fresh leads yet?"

"Nothing of value," he said. "We tracked Willow's parents to Wood Green in London. But the father's in the local cemetery and her mother is in a care home suffering from dementia."

"Ouch. I wish Owen had known that. Might have made a difference. And how about this Masters guy?"

During the briefing of my meeting with Laurel Ford, I'd made the point that, despite next to no information about Willow's previous partner, he may have been a local man with local connections. And worthy of a closer look.

"It would help if we had more details," said Nathan, "but, so far, we've drawn a blank. No local info. Nothing on the national database. Even national media archives have come up zero."

"Strange. You'd think there would be some record, somewhere."

He swept a hand across the files piled on his desk. "Well, perhaps something is buried in here. And the sooner I can get back to this lot, the sooner I can knock off for the day."

"Okay, I can take a hint. Don't let me stop you."

I let him get on with his paperwork in silence while I checked emails on my mobile and texted my agent for details of an after-dinner speech I'd been booked for.

I'd just pocketed my mobile when a knock at the door announced Owen's return. Miles Barber ushered him into the room and, once Miles had confirmed he was happy with the statement and returned to his other duties, Nathan waved Owen over to the second chair on the other side of his desk.

Owen seemed even more subdued than usual as he took his seat.

Nathan pushed his files to one side and leaned across the desk towards Owen, his hands clasped before him. He was wearing his official authoritative expression. So I guessed Owen was in for a dressing down.

"This is obviously a very difficult time for you," he said, "and we're mindful of how painful this whole experience must be. But I hope you can appreciate how important it is to have your full cooperation if we're to make any headway."

Owen nodded and shot me a guarded glance. "Mikey's already made that clear," he said. "I'm sorry for any trouble I've caused."

Nathan leaned back, apparently satisfied with Owen's response. "You'll understand that we'll have to verify your statement. But once that's out of the way, we can focus our resources where they're needed."

Owen nodded, his head bowed.

I reached out and squeezed his shoulder. "Why don't we leave them to it and go get something to eat? I'm sure you could use a break."

Still subdued, Owen assented, and once I'd said my goodbyes to Nathan, agreeing to see him at home later, Owen and I made our way out to the car park.

Once we were alone, I tried to apologise again, still painfully aware of the emotional battering I'd put him through. "I didn't mean to hurt you. I hope you know that. I just-."

He interrupted. "You don't have to explain, Mikey. If I hadn't been so pig-headed and obstinate, none of that would have been necessary. And it's not something I want to dwell on. So let's put it aside. Right now, I want some normality. Let's just go eat."

We decided on an Indian at The Ashoka on the High Street - at least, I did, and Owen went along with it - and on the drive over, I tried to put him at ease with some small talk. All to no avail. He wasn't in a talkative mood.

Once we'd made it to the restaurant, settled at a table, and ordered our food, Owen thawed a little. He seemed more relaxed away from the oppressive confines of the police station.

While we munched on some complimentary poppadoms, he told me more about the events that had led up to his recent relapse into drink. "Willow and I hadn't been getting on too well. Not for a long time. I'd thought we could put her affair behind us and move on. But it's almost as if she resented being forgiven. As if she held it against me. I didn't understand."

The pleading look in his eyes told me he was still looking for answers. He needed to make sense of the way his life had unravelled, culminating as it had in this harrowing ordeal. Before I could reply, the arrival of our food interrupted us. A black-suited smiling waiter transferred hot dishes from a trolley to our table: a bowl of chicken madras for me, lamb rogan josh for Owen, and a bowl of pilau rice and a side dish of saag aloo for sharing. The waiter took the trolley away and, as we spooned food onto our plates, I thought over how I could respond to Owen.

I moved the empty serving bowls to one side, sat back in my chair, and focused my attention on him before starting my meal.

"Forgiveness is a strange thing," I said. "We often think of it as being for the benefit of the one we forgive. But, of course, it isn't."

Owen's creased brow told me he didn't understand.

"Forgiveness is about letting go of our negative feeling for the one we forgive. It's for our own benefit, not theirs. A means of coping and finding closure."

"But why couldn't she accept that?"

"Because accepting forgiveness from others isn't enough. Willow needed to forgive herself before she could move on. And forgiving ourselves is so much harder to do."

Even as I unravelled these thoughts in my mind and tried to bring some order to them, to clarify them, I realised how closely they touched upon my own life. How I too needed to own up to my past and come to terms with the hurt I had caused. And to finally let it go.

Owen speared some food with his fork. "I used to be so jealous of you and Donna," he said. "The perfect couple. You had it all."

I laughed. The irony wasn't lost on me. "And I always thought you and Willow were the golden couple. I know you had your rows but, on the whole, you seemed well matched. What a pair of idiots we are. All those years, hiding behind our lies, keeping up a pretence."

"I wish we'd been more honest," he said. "Who knows, we may

have been able to help each other."

"I'm still here for you," I said. "I hope you know that."

Instead of facing up to our problems and finding the moral courage to deal with them openly and honestly, we had both chosen our own furtive and self-destructive means of coping with them; he through drink and me through sex. But while I had finally confronted my past mistakes - albeit by forced exposure rather than choice - he had never had the opportunity to find a way out of the mess his life had become. And now he had to endure the worst defeat of all, losing his wife to a brutal death.

Well, enough was enough.

I was tired of sitting around waiting for results. It was time for action. There were too many secrets in this small, close-knit community. Too many facts hidden behind silence and lies. And I meant to ferret them out. I already had my suspicions about who was hiding the truth and how to make them talk.

And first on that list was Ralph Ferguson.

It was time to pay him a visit.

CHAPTER TWENTY-SIX

The address Ralph Ferguson gave at his interview sounded prestigious. Riverside Mews. It conjured up images of affluent single professionals and mature downsizing middle-class couples living in the isolated splendour of cobbled courtyards behind high-security gates.

In reality, it was anything but. Sited opposite a derelict clothing factory, it was a shabby rundown terrace of small apartments on Charwell's industrial estate at the edge of town.

Not quite what I'd expected for the man who had once boasted that he was going places, the one who had claimed he would be a millionaire by the age of thirty. He'd missed the mark by a year or so.

I knocked at his door.

It was early morning, the day after Owen had given his interview, and I had forgone my usual run, hoping to surprise Ferguson before he left for work.

I was in luck.

He was still in his dressing-gown when he answered the door. And obviously surprised to see me. Unshaven, his dark greasy hair ruffled, he'd clearly just rolled out of bed and wasn't yet ready to start his day.

I didn't let that bother me. With a cheery greeting and a smile, I pushed past him into an untidy living room that stank of stale food. "We need to talk," I said.

"What the hell?" He held onto the edge of the open door and stared at me through bleary eyes.

I looked him up and down. "Not working today?"

"I'm taking the day off." He sounded perplexed.

"Good. We'll have more time to talk." I moved to the door and slammed it shut.

He finally gathered himself together, shaking off the shock of my sudden intrusion. "Who the hell do you think you are? You can't just storm in here as if you own the place."

"And you can't get away with impeding a police investigation," I countered. "But that didn't stop you trying, did it?"

He took a step back. "What?" This time his response was more guarded. "What's that supposed to mean?"

I turned in a full circle, inspecting the room, taking in the cluttered surfaces, the grimy windows, the rust-stained sink piled high with dirty dishes. My nose wrinkled against the smell. "Not much of a place for an Insurance Salesman. Don't they pay you enough?"

"I'm a Financial Consultant."

"Whatever."

I needed to get him mad, the madder the better. If I could keep him stirred up emotionally, mentally off-balance, the more chance there was of his slipping up and saying something in the heat of the moment that he may well have time to reflect on, and so suppress, in a calmer state of mind.

"And what the hell is it to you anyway?" he said. "What is this?"

"Just wondering where it all went wrong. You were so full of yourself back in the day. Remember? All those big ideas? Never came to anything, did they? Is that why you were so jealous?"

"Jealous of what?" The belligerence was back.

"Of me. That's the impression I got. Let's see, what was it you said?" I pressed a finger to my temple and furrowed my brow in a feigned parody of deep thought. "Something about thinking I could do as I please just because I'd made a name for myself. That is what you said, isn't it? That I was nothing special, even if I thought I was? Sounded like jealousy to me."

He stared at me without speaking, hands at his side, clenching and unclenching his fists, unsure of himself. "You were there? At my interview?"

"That's right," I said. "Want to know why?" I didn't wait for an answer. "It's because you were right, I have made a name for myself. And over the years, I've become very good at what I do."

Now was the time to talk up my credentials. He needed to know he was in some serious shit here. That I had skills enough to help discredit him and dig out the truth.

"Thanks to my professional observational methods, I've helped put many a villain behind bars. I read people, you see. People like you. That's why I was there."

I circled him, my gaze fixed on his face as he turned and turned again to keep me before him. "I watch every little move, listen to every word. And each time you tell a lie, I see it and hear it for what it is."

He swallowed hard and said, "I don't see what any of this has to do with me. The police questioned me, I gave a statement, and that's the end of it."

I stopped pacing. "You really believe that? After the lies you told?"

"If you're suggesting Willow's murder had anything to do with me, you're way out of line. I had an alibi. I can prove where I was." His voice rose as he spoke.

"Maybe. But you know something. You lied about your conversation with Willow. And I have to ask myself why you would do that. Did you persuade her to make a complaint against me? Is that it? I can't believe you'd make a false statement just to get at me. Even you wouldn't be that dumb. So what was it? Were you trying to create a diversion? Take the focus away from whatever it is you're seeking to hide?"

Ferguson thrust out his jaw, his face inches from mine. "Fuck you, MacGregor. I don't have to answer to you for anything."

I stood my ground. "I know you're lying about something. Are you covering for someone? Is that it? Because if you are, you need to ask yourself if it's worth it."

"The door's behind you. Get out before I throw you out."

This approach wasn't working. Time to try a different tack. I changed my tone, hoping to sound sympathetic. "I'm trying to do you a favour here, Ferguson, if you did but know it."

"How do you figure that?"

"You have a family, remember?" I tried to persuade him of the consequences of his actions, the risk to his relationship with his children, even the loss of parental rights. "And do you want them to grow up knowing their father's done time? Because if you don't come clean, that's what will happen. I promise you."

The fire went out of his eyes and he stepped away from me.

Maybe I was finally getting through to him.

He cupped the back of his neck with a hand, and shook his head, but said nothing.

I pressed home my argument. "If you're covering for someone, you're not doing yourself any favours. You'll be found out, eventually. And there will be long-term consequences."

When he spoke again, his voice was strained, but the anger was gone. "I've said all I'm going to say."

I was running out of options. Whatever he was hiding, the consequences of exposure were serious enough to keep him quiet. For reasons best known to him, he'd tried to distance himself from the investigation by denying any close prior relationship with Willow. And he'd lied about the exchanges between them at the wedding reception. Minor events in themselves. But a lie was a lie. And whilst I may not know the reason for his continuing deception, of one thing I was certain; he was covering up something that had a direct bearing on Willow's murder.

I tried again. "You're part of this investigation now. We know you're hiding something. And whatever it is, we'll dig it out. Your movements over the past few days will be checked, anyone you've made contact with will be questioned."

He said nothing. Just stared at me.

With a sigh and a shake of the head, I moved over to the door and opened it, ready to leave.

I gave it one last shot. "I'm trying to help you. Give you a chance to make amends."

"And why would you do that?" His tone was defiant, the anger rising again.

"Maybe I feel sorry for you. Maybe I'm giving you a chance to redeem yourself. To do the right thing."

I waited for a response. None came.

Game over. I stepped out into the street and closed the door behind me.

I hadn't got what I'd come for. Though I had only half expected to pressure him into coming clean, anyway. But it had been worth a try. And maybe it hadn't been a complete waste of time. Maybe my visit would give him pause for thought. Despite the aggressive attitude, he had wavered when pushed into reflecting on the consequences. Perhaps once he'd had time to consider his options, he would decide his best interests lay in cooperating with the investigation.

I hoped so.

CHAPTER TWENTY-SEVEN

"How many fucking times do we have to go through this?" Nathan forced himself up from his chair and slammed his fist down on the kitchen table. It shuddered under the blow, rattling the crockery. "What is wrong with you?"

He swept a hand across the table, sending the milk jug and sugar bowl flying across the room. They smashed against the sink unit and fell to the floor in jagged, broken shards, scattering their contents across the tiles.

I pushed away from the table, my chair scraping across the floor. I knew he might not be too pleased, but I hadn't expected this explosion.

I tried to speak, but he cut me off. "You listen to me and listen good." He leaned across the table and pointed a warning finger at me. "Step out of line once more and you're off the case. Is that clear?"

Nathan was taking a half day break, and we were sharing a tuna and avocado salad for lunch.

He'd been quieter than normal that morning, distant and subdued. I'd put it down to his inability to switch off from work. But away from the station, he was usually in a more amenable mood, and so it seemed a good time to tell him about my earlier visit to Ralph Ferguson.

I'd expected the usual angry blah about conducting impromptu interviews without prior consultation - though I had thought I could persuade him my visit was justified - but this was way over the top. The blood drained from my face and all I could do was stare back in shocked silence.

"Don't you ever fucking learn? Did you bother to tell anyone where you were going? Or are you so fucking stupid, you don't stop to think you might be putting yourself in harm's way?"

He didn't give me a chance to respond, just grabbed his keys from the sideboard and charged out of the front door, slamming it behind him.

A moment later, his car engine roared into life before fading into the distance as he sped away.

I sat stunned, wondering where the hell so much anger had come from.

The clock on the mantelpiece ticked away the minutes, breaking the grim silence.

I rose from my chair, skirted the broken crockery, grabbed a dishcloth, fetched a handbrush and shovel from under the sink, cleaned up the mess as best I could, and dropped it into the waste-bin. It was soon followed by the half-eaten remains of our food from the table.

A weak sun had finally broken through the cloud cover and bright sunlight now streamed through the kitchen window, promising a warm afternoon. We had planned to make the most of it and enjoy some time together strolling through Tinkers Wood.

So much for that.

It's not like we didn't have our rows. But this was new. He'd never displayed such destructive behaviour before or run out on me. I tried hard to think what could have caused it and where he might now be.

There was, of course, one person we both turned to in times of need, when we needed a shoulder to cry on or a sympathetic ear. Karen.

I glanced over at the clock. He should be there by now. I dug my mobile out of my pocket and called her.

Trying to sound casual, I said, "I don't suppose Nathan is with you?"

"What's wrong? What have you done?"

How did she do that? How did she always know when I had a problem? There was no point keeping it from her; she would wheedle it out of me, anyway. "We had a bit of a row."

A deep sigh from the other end of the phone. "What now?"

Without going into too much detail, I explained how he had lost his temper following a minor disagreement and left the house in a foul mood.

She agreed it wasn't like him to react as aggressively as he had. "But I suppose he's bound to be feeling oversensitive," she said, "today of all days."

"What's so special about today?"

A pause. "I guess you must have forgotten after all those years apart. It's the anniversary of his father's death."

My hand tightened around my mobile. "I had no idea. I'd completely forgotten." This explained his sombre mood.

"Well, you know now. So you should know where he'll be."

"I know exactly where he'll be. I'll go find him."

I finished the call with a hasty goodbye and hurried out to the Elan. A few minutes later, I pulled over to the kerb behind Nathan's Astra at the front of the church and was soon heading across the courtyard to the graveyard at the rear of the building.

He was standing over at the far end, his back to me, looking down at his father's grave.

The smell of freshly mown grass filled the air as I threaded my way towards him around carved headstones and granite slabs.

He swung around at the sound of my approach, acknowledged me with a curt nod and turned his attention back to the grave. The headstone bore the name 'Jonathan Quarryman' and the simple epitaph 'Served with honour'.

"Karen told me I'd find you here," I said. "I should have known."

He didn't respond immediately. After a few moments, he nodded towards the grave and said, "They say he died a hero."

"And so he did."

"I used to think so."

"He gave his life in the line of duty. Isn't that why you became a policeman too? To honour him?"

"I was just a naïve kid when he died. What would I know?"

I wasn't sure what else to say. Nor did I understand what this was about. I waited in silence for him to speak again. Somewhere in the distance, the thrum of an electric lawn-mower cut through the rustling of leaves and other sounds of nature around us.

"Everyone praised him, said what a hero he was." His gaze fixed on the headstone, he said. "He was out on patrol, alone, when the call came in. He knew what he was facing. There were three of them. Armed. A squad car would have been there in minutes. But he went in, anyway. What was heroic about that? About losing your life for want of using some common sense? I lost my father, and I was angry." At last, he turned to face me. "After all we've been through, to finally find each other again, how do you think I would feel if I lost you because you were too impulsive, too reckless, to think through what you were doing?" He didn't wait for a response. "I know I'm not... you know... I know I don't always say how I feel. But that doesn't mean I don't care."

I took hold of his arm and squeezed it. "You think I don't know that? You don't have to say it. You show it in everything you do."

"I'm sorry I was so angry." He pressed his hand against mine. "But I worry about you."

"You had every right to be angry. What I did was stupid and selfish. I know that now. I'm the one who should be sorry." I slipped an arm around his waist and held him close.

He wrapped his arm around me in response and we stood together like this in quiet harmony.

High overhead, the plaintive cry of a lone bird, winging its way towards the coast, interrupted the chirping of other breeding pairs nesting in nearby bushes.

Nathan turned, pressed his lips to the side of my head, and said, "Sometimes you jump into situations feet first without thinking through the consequences. Promise me you'll think in future."

I squeezed his waist and gave him my promise. "I guess there are times I'm impatient and want to move things on. But I know I don't always stop to think first." I tried a weak smile. "I do listen to you sometimes though."

He returned the smile. "Not often enough."

Perhaps now was a good time to confess my other sins. Not that there ever is a good time. But this was as good as it gets. "While we're on the subject, maybe I should tell you about my other visit."

His arm tautened around me, but he said nothing.

I quickly added, "It was only Amelia Cole. She's hardly a threat. And it was a public place, anyway. It was at her shop."

A pause and he faced me with a pained look in his eyes. "Interviews aren't just to pick up possible leads. You know that. Some of those people are going to be suspects. And if we get it right, one of them could be a murderer."

"I know. I get it."

"Look, Mikey, I'm not saying you shouldn't talk to these people. That's why you're on the team, after all. But we need to make sure we're on the same page here. You have to think of the potential risks."

"I know. And I'm sorry. I get carried away sometimes. I don't always get it right."

"So we have a deal? You'll check with me first in future?"

I agreed. "Deal."

"Okay, end of lecture."

We stood a while longer, looking down at the grave, lost in our own thoughts.

"I know I don't always think before I act," I said. "I just rush in, oblivious to the consequences. But not your dad. He knew what he was walking into and went in, anyway. It was a call of duty. He lost his life answering that call and, okay, maybe it was a bad call, but that doesn't make him any less a man of conviction and courage. Your dad died a hero."

He stared at me, long and hard, nodded and took me by the arm. "Come on," he said. "Let's go home." He slipped an arm around my shoulder, and we walked together towards the path.

CHAPTER TWENTY-EIGHT

I pushed myself up on an elbow, dug my fingers into the thick mat of hair covering his torso, and pressed my throbbing erection against his hard muscular thigh. Leaning over his prostrate body, I lowered my head, circled one of his dark nipples with my tongue, and felt it stiffen under my touch.

Nathan groaned, and the bedsprings complained beneath his writhing form.

We had settled our differences on the way back from the cemetery, Nathan apologising yet again for his burst of temper, me promising not to be such a prat and, once home, we had found a more enjoyable means to consolidate our negotiated peace.

I grinned, raised my head and said, "We should have make-up sex more often. It's almost worth the argument."

"Dear God, no," he replied. "I don't have the stamina for sex that often. We'd be at it several times a day."

"Oh, very funny." I pinched the nipple and earned another long rolling moan in response.

I had learned to read his body well over the months and loved the way he groaned at the grip of my fingers on his nipples, how he melted at the stroke of a hand on the nape of his neck, or my tongue seeking the sensitive spot behind his ears. Such moments marked the gentle, unhurried sex of lovers familiar with each other's bodies and each other's needs.

And, of course, there were the more obvious places too, those places that roused our passions to another level. I ran a hand down over the hirsute chest, down across the flat plane of his stomach, and down again until I found what I was searching for. I wrapped a hand around the thick swollen penis, squeezed hard, ran a thumb over the moist tip of the bulbous head, and earned another drawn-out moan in response.

I released my grasp and turned onto my back. "Of course, if you don't have the stamina, I quite understand."

"Not so fast," He rolled over, swung a leg over my prone body, and pulled himself on top of me. His breath was laboured and warm against my cheek.

I groaned and squirmed beneath him, gripped between his powerful thighs, the full weight of his sweat-dampened body bearing down on me, his racing heart pounding against mine, our swollen cocks pressed together.

"Well if you're sure," I said, gasping for air. "I wouldn't want to overtax you."

"That'll be the day," he said, still breathing heavily, and stretched over to the bedside cabinet, reaching for the tube of lube that lay on its surface.

I turned on my side as he loosened his hold on me, and he ran his hand down my back and over the curve of my ass, his searching fingers setting my flesh on fire.

A moment or so later, a probing lube-slick finger delved between my cheeks, found its mark, and pushed into me.

"Still want to call it off?" he said.

"You know what they say," I said, gasping, "don't start what you don't mean to finish."

"I had a feeling you might say that."

As he rolled back into place, I wrapped my legs around him and pushed up to meet his urgent probing, my need as great as his. I gasped as he entered me, and a raging fire took hold, consuming us in a blaze of heat and lust. And then we were moving together in harmony, my pace matching his, our hands exploring each other's bodies, his lips nuzzling my neck, my fingers digging into the broad muscular back, and, slowly, the measured rhythm increased until we reached a crescendo, and I threw back my head and cried out, caught up in a fiery white-hot explosion.

He matched my cry with one of his own as he slammed into me, thrusting long and hard until he reached his peak and climaxed with a howl.

I whimpered as he pulled out of me and we collapsed together in a smouldering heap, flesh against flesh, arms around each other, his chest rising and falling against mine.

From outside, sounds of spring drifted in through the open window; the chirping of hedge sparrows, the rustle of leaves in the breeze, the creaking limbs of a nearby elm.

We lay together for a while, half dozing, wrapped in each other's embrace.

When he found his voice again, it was to probe me about my visit to Ferguson. Ever the policeman. Ever on duty. "So was it worth it?" he asked.

"I think you just proved that," I murmured and tightened my hold on him. The last thing I wanted right then was to be roused from my drowsy languor.

"Seriously," he said and poked me.

I opened one eye and groaned. "Seriously? Ask me later," I said and closed my eye again.

Responding to a snuffling sound at the bedroom door, he said, "You have to get up, anyway. It's your turn to feed Rocky."

With a deep sigh, I pushed myself into a sitting position and leaned back against the headboard. "How come it's always my turn to feed the dog when I'm trying to relax?"

"Who knows? That's just one of life's eternal mysteries."

I poked him in the chest and rolled off the bed. My jeans and sweatshirt lay where I had discarded them on the floor. I grabbed the jeans and pulled them on, hopping first on one leg and then the other as I struggled into them.

Nathan roused himself and dressed while I headed downstairs preceded by a hungry Rocky. By the time I reached the kitchen, Rocky was already waiting by his feeding mat, padding the floor and wagging his tail in anticipation of a meal.

Nathan bounded down the stairs a moment later and joined us. He wore a fresh pair of grey joggers and a white tee.

As I emptied a can of Pedigree Choice Cuts into Rocky's bowl, I said,

"Not sure about my visit to Ferguson."

"You didn't learn anything new?" He reached for the kettle, filled it under the tap, and put it on to boil while he spooned coffee into a couple of mugs.

I shoved the bowl under Rocky's eager maw and watched him demolish it as I filled another dish with water. "Nothing new," I said and set down the water dish next to the now-empty food bowl. "But I'm convinced he's hiding something." I leaned up against the worktop and folded my arms. "He wavered once or twice as if he was about to come clean but changed his mind."

"Not a very useful visit then." There was a trace of reproach in his tone. A gentle reminder that he hadn't been happy about it. He filled the mugs with boiling water, and said, "Go grab a seat and I'll bring these through."

I went into the sitting room and made myself comfortable on the window box seat from where I could look out over the rear garden.

Nathan followed me through, handed me my coffee, and let Rocky out of the back door before dropping into place beside me.

I said, "If he was that close to changing his mind, he may decide to tell all once he's had time to think about it. So maybe it won't have been a waste of time after all."

"We can but hope," he said and blew on his coffee.

I tasted mine and said, "I've been thinking some more about Willow's ex-partner, David Masters."

"Might help if we knew more about him."

"Still no luck?"

"Not a trace. But let's have your thoughts, anyway."

"Something Owen said. How Willow would never talk about him. His death. I wondered why she would be so evasive."

"It was a distressing experience. Not something she'd want reminding of."

Out in the garden, Rocky was bounding up the path towards us. I left my seat, crossed over to the door and opened it to let him in.

Rocky followed me back across the room and settled himself at Nathan's feet. I seated myself and said, "You'd think Willow would want to talk about it, eventually. Especially to her husband. As a way of putting the past to rest. Finding closure."

"So what do you think?"

I sipped my coffee before answering. "We both know how erratic Willow was. And many is the time Owen complained about her reckless driving."

"You're suggesting she was driving at the time of his death?" He finished his coffee and left the mug on the window sill. "You think she might have been responsible for the accident?"

"It's a possibility." I drained my mug, picked up his empty one from the sill, took them through to the kitchen and put them in the sink. On my way back to him, I said, "The problem is, we just don't know." I dropped into place and leaned back against him as he slipped an arm around my waist. "But it would explain why she was so reluctant to talk about him."

"Was he a local man?"

"Don't know for certain, but the timing would suggest he was."

"So if he had local connections, family maybe, and they held her responsible-"

I interrupted. "I think you get my drift."

"It would be a long time to wait for revenge," he said.

"Maybe. But Willow hasn't been back to Elders Edge in all that time. Not until now. So, someone may have seen her return as an ideal opportunity."

He grunted. "The one person we've been unable to trace, and the only one who could possibly lead us to a suspect with a motive."

"So much of Willow's past seems to have sunk into a black hole," I said. "It's almost like the guy never existed."

"At least it gives us something more tangible to deal with," said Nathan. "Looks like we will have to dig a whole lot deeper."

"Never mind, hon," I said and patted his thigh. "I'm sure you have the stamina for it."

CHAPTER TWENTY-NINE

We were in the kitchen when the call came through, Nathan at the table buttering toast, me placing a dish of Winalot biscuits onto Rocky's feeding mat. It was the station, of course. Who else would call at such an ungodly hour?

Nathan answered it. After several grunts, he said, "Get onto Division, tell them you have my authority, and get a team over there. We're on our way."

He finished the call and said, "That was Richard. Looks like your visit to Ferguson yesterday got some results after all. They found him swinging from the rafters."

I stared at him, my mind whirling. "They found him hanged?"

"Well, I wasn't suggesting he'd found an alternative method of aerobic exercise." He was already reaching for his jacket from the hook on the back of the door.

The sarcasm was another dig at me, his way of reminding me he had disapproved of my visit.

I grabbed my jacket from the back of the door and followed him out to the car. "I hope you don't think this is my doing." Despite my protestations, there was a queasy feeling in the pit of my stomach. I hoped I hadn't gone too far.

"Bit of a coincidence, isn't it?" He unlocked the doors of the Astra with his key fob. "You go see the guy, put the fear of God into him, and two days later he tops himself. I'd say it's a fair bet there's a connection." He climbed into the car.

I opened the passenger door and slid in beside him. As I fastened my seatbelt, I said, "First off, you don't know he topped himself. And secondly, if he did, and it directly resulted from my visit, it can only be because I was right all along; he was mixed up in Willow's murder, and his guilt got the better of him."

He put the Astra into gear and headed out to the main road. "Maybe, but I prefer my suspects alive. It makes interviewing them slightly easier. Unless you're any good with a Ouija board."

I gave up the argument and let him brood in silence for the rest of the journey. There was no talking to him when he was in a sour mood.

As we drew up opposite Ferguson's apartment, Richard stepped out of the open door to greet us. Nathan was first out of the car, asking Richard for details.

I came around from the other side of the Astra to join them as Richard explained the situation to Nathan.

"The postman called it in," he said. "He was on his morning rounds and saw the body through the window."

"Any signs of forced entry," said Nathan.

"The front door was locked from inside," said Richard. "But the back door out into the alley was unlocked. That's how we got in."

Nathan said, "Let's go take a look."

A uniformed constable at the door handed us some paper coveralls, gloves, and slip-over shoe covers. As we donned our extra clothing, Richard nodded towards two plainclothes standing by the window. "Your team are already here, and the medic is on his way. It's tight in there," he said. "The photographer and sketcher have free rein for the moment."

Nathan signalled a greeting to the two guys from his team and followed Richard and me inside.

An exposed wooden crossbeam ran the full length of the apartment at ceiling height. Ferguson hung from its centre at the end of a noose fashioned from a twisted bedsheet. He was suited and booted, hands tied behind his back.

In the cramped confines of the small apartment, it was possible to move around the body only with some difficulty. After an exchange of greetings, the photographer and sketcher ceased working and stood back, allowing us room to manoeuvre.

"Not sure about you, Chief," said Richard, "but I'm thinking this is a setup. It looks like a suicide. But the hands are tied."

I interrupted. "Suicide victims often bind their own hands. It's to prevent a change of heart."

Richard didn't look convinced.

"I'm not saying it is suicide," I said, "but you're going to need a forensic knot specialist to tell you one way or the other."

Richard again. "A forensic knot specialist? There is such a thing?"

"Sure," I said. "Someone with specialised knowledge of ligatures and knots."

Nathan this time. "He should be able to tell if the knot was self-tied."

"And he may well be able to characterise the knot in such a way as to narrow down a suspect list," I added. "People usually tie knots based on their knowledge and skill. Nautical knots, for example."

Richard let out a long, low whistle. "Well, I'll be damned. You live and learn."

I said, "Hangings are nearly always suicidal; it's the third most common method. Homicidal hangings happen, but they're rare. But without specialist help, it's notoriously difficult to tell the difference."

Nathan said, "Anything you can tell us from the crime scene, Mikey?"

"I'll take a look around first," I said. "Get a feel for the place." I nodded towards a spot outside the window where a white Seat Tarraco was parked. "Is that Ferguson's car across the road?"

Richard confirmed it was. I nodded an acknowledgement and left him with Nathan while I took a look around.

Both the front and rear doors had keys in the locks and bolts on the inside. Ferguson was obviously safety conscious. Hardly surprising in a neighbourhood like this.

I stepped out of the rear door. It led on to an alley running the length of the terrace with access at both ends. A uniformed officer stood guard by the door. I nodded a greeting.

Back inside, I scanned the room. A thin stained carpet of indeterminate colour covered the floor, and ill-matched threadbare curtains framed the two small windows. A single lightbulb dangled from the ceiling on its cord. The room had clearly not been cleaned for some time, and the musty stale smell I'd noticed on my previous visit still permeated the air. Cobwebs hung in corners and where cluttered surfaces were exposed, layers of dust added to the general air of neglect.

The remains of a curry in a tinfoil tray, last night's dinner no doubt - at least, I'd hoped it was last night's - lay discarded on a table by the far wall. A small object by its side caught my attention. A gold locket on a chain. I leaned over it to take a closer look. Engraved on it were the initials WB.

I called over to Nathan and Richard. "You'll want to see this."

A moment later, we were all peering down at it.

Nathan said, "Willow Brookes."

"So that's what happened to it," said Richard.

To the two crime scene investigators patiently standing by, Nathan said, "I'll let you guys get on with your work. We'll bag this up later."

The photographer and scribbler took up their positions again, camera and sketchbook at the ready, as Nathan, Richard and I stepped outside. The air smelled cleaner out here.

Richard said, "At least, we now know he's definitely connected to Willow's murder."

"Strange that the locket was left in the open," I said, "as if we were meant to find it."

"If he did hang himself," said Richard, "could he not have left it there as an admission of guilt?"

"It's a possibility," I said, "but I think you were right to start with. It's a setup."

"What makes you think that?" Nathan asked.

"When I was here the other day," I said, "Ferguson was taking a day off work. He hadn't even bothered to dress. Yet, here he is, dressed and ready for work. Why would he do that if he's about to kill himself?"

"Wouldn't he want to smarten himself up?" said Richard. "Make himself presentable on his last day?"

"Did you take a good look around in there?" I said. "You really think he's the type who cares how he looks? He's in a line of work where appearances matter. But I doubt he'd bother to make the effort otherwise."

"Anything else?" said Nathan.

"Two things," I said. "First off, Ferguson's car is parked out front. So he's likely to leave the apartment that way. And yet, the front door was locked from the inside, and the back door was unlocked. That doesn't make sense. Unless he opened the back door to let someone in. I can't think of another logical reason."

Nathan raised a hand to shield his eyes and scanned the area facing the apartment. A chain-link fence ran alongside the pavement on the other side of the road, and beyond it were several industrial buildings.

"There's more chance of being captured on CCTV at this side of the building," he said. "So it would make sense for someone to use the back door if they wanted to avoid being caught on camera." He turned back to me. "And the other thing?"

"He hanged himself in full view of an open window. Death by hanging is quick. Minutes at the most. But why risk being seen before the job's done? Why not close the curtains?"

"You have an answer to that?" said Nathan.

"I think we were meant to find him as quickly as possible. To stop us looking any further."

"That was never going to happen," said Nathan. "But at least this opens up more lines of enquiry." To Richard, he said, "I want everyone known to Ferguson questioned. I want you to check his calls, his movements over the past few days, and anyone he's made contact with."

"And the sooner we have that knotwork checked, the better," I said. "If this is a setup, and I'm sure it is, it means someone thinks we're getting too close."

CHAPTER THIRTY

Following through from a long backswing, Karen released the ball in a fluid forward motion and watched it speed along the lane and take down all ten pins in a well-earned productive clatter.

"Got it in one," I said. "Another strike. You're on form today."

"It's all in the wrist action," she said.

We were enjoying an early morning game down at the local bowling alley. After the discovery of Ferguson's body two days earlier, both our men were working longer shifts, leaving us to rely on each other for company. Karen was taking some downtime before the holiday season started in earnest the following week, and I was in dire need of some relief from the pressures brought on by recent events.

At this time of day, and out of season, the place was rarely busy and only four of the twelve lanes were in use. But the animated chatter from around us, the distant clank of the pin-setting machines, the crash of wood on wood, and blaring music from the loudspeakers filled the air.

From nearby, another resounding crash of skittles was followed by a cheer.

"I thought about asking Owen to join us," I said, "but I'm not sure it's appropriate in the circumstances."

Karen said, "I suspect fun and games are the last things on his mind."

"I don't like to think of him sitting alone in his room and brooding."

"Nothing to stop you dropping round. He could use the company."

We were nearing the end of our game, and the electronic scoreboard above our lane told me I was seriously behind. I said, "Seems everyone is having a good day but me." I picked up my ball from the return and held it up in readiness for play.

"I'll call in on Owen later. But I needed to catch up with you first. We've not had much chance since you got back."

I took a long, low swing and sent the ball on its way. It made it almost to the end of the lane before veering to the left and taking down the seven pin.

"He's been asking questions," said Karen.

"What sort of questions?"

"Like why you lived a double life for so many years."

And what did you tell him?" I waited for the return to deliver my ball.

"Not a lot. It's something for you to discuss. I told him you'd had some issues."

I laughed. "Issues? Yes, I suppose being raised by a bigot could be called an issue." I took my ball from the lineup and moved back into place for a second throw.

"Like I said, it's something for you to discuss with him."

"I guess he needs to sort out his own problems first." I raised the ball, ready to step up to the mark.

Karen said, "You and Nathan need to sort out yours too."

Something about the pointed way she fired off the comment made me pause. I fixed her with a cool stare and said, "Are you having a dig?"

"You'd better believe it," she said.

Earlier, after meeting up in the coffee bar section, I had confessed the reason for my recent argument with Nathan. And now she was giving me a hard time about it.

"I told you how it went down," I said. "It was just bad timing and Nathan was in a sensitive mood."

"You have a habit of jumping into things feet first. It wouldn't be the first time."

I narrowed my eyes and said, "That's the exact same phrase Nathan used. Have you been talking to him?"

"Of course I have. I talk to him all the time."

"What's he been saying?"

"Are you going to play that ball or not?"

I rolled my eyes and turned my attention back to the game.

Moving up to the mark, I swung low, putting some spin on the ball as I let it go. It made the halfway mark before dropping into the gutter.

"Your mind's not on your game," said Karen.

"I wonder why." I folded my arms. "Okay, let's have it. What's he been saying?"

"He worries about you. He's always been the cautious type. You know that."

I stood away as she moved to the return to get her ball. She took her shot and got another strike.

"You really are on form," I said and took my ball from the return.

She moved away as I took up my stance. I stepped up to the line and released the ball. This time, I downed four skittles.

A moment later, the return deposited my ball in the lineup with a clunk. I picked it up, weighed it in my hand as I moved up to the mark, and swung it down the lane. This time, it took down the rest of the pins with a satisfying clatter.

"That's better," said Karen.

"Nathan's not said anything else, has he?" I stepped aside again, and she took up her position ready for another shot.

"Like what?" She took up her ball and steadied it in her hand before releasing it. Seven pins down.

While she waited for the return, I said, "He's not regretting us getting back together, is he?"

She paused in the act of reaching for her ball and glared at me. "What kind of question is that?"

"One I need an answer to."

She shook her head and sighed as she made her play with the second ball. Another satisfying clatter as she took down two more pins, ending the match way in the lead.

"Good game," I said.

"Never mind the game. What's all this nonsense? You and Nathan are getting on okay, aren't you?"

"We were until this case blew up. And now the local press are snooping around and raking over my past again."

Karen dropped into one of the nearby metal chairs and unlaced her bowling shoes. "You weathered the storm last time. You can do it again."

I sat in the chair next to her and removed my shoes. "It's not just about me, is it? I worry about Nathan too. Why should he take the flack for my past misdeeds?"

"And does he?" She took off her shoes, grabbed our jackets from over the back of her chair and stood up.

I rose, took my jacket from her, and we padded towards the desk. "It won't be long before the press are dishing the dirt. And our relationship makes him a target."

At the desk, we handed in the bowling shoes in exchange for our own. The young male attendant stopped chewing gum long enough to ask if we wanted a copy of our scores. I declined.

We seated ourselves at a nearby table, and as Karen pulled on her shoes, she said, "There's not much you can do to change the past. But you must know Nathan will always be there to support you."

I laced up my trainers and stood again to put on my jacket. "I wonder sometimes if he ever fully forgave me for the mess I made of everything. Just when it all seems settled, the past keeps coming back to haunt me. It can't be easy on him."

Karen rose to her feet and said, "Do you remember when we were in our teens? How close the three of us were?"

"Of course I do. We did everything together." I picked up her jacket and helped her on with it.

"I remember the way he looked at you sometimes," she said. "You'd be standing with a group of friends, holding court, laughing and joking, the centre of attention. And I'd see the way he looked at you. I knew then what that look meant, and I know what it still means now. I promise you, there's nothing to worry about."

We strolled together towards the coffee bar.

I said, "I was such an idiot to throw all that away. I'd think back to those days sometimes and wonder what he was doing, if he'd found someone else and settled down."

Karen ordered coffees, and we took seats at the counter while we drank them.

"Nathan had his moments," said Karen. "But nothing serious. He always shied away before it got too heavy."

"Something else I have to be grateful for."

"You have a lot to be grateful for. So don't go screwing it up. Be thankful you found each other again."

She was right, of course. As usual. But shaking off the past wasn't always easy. Especially at a time like this, when events conspired to reopen old wounds. Guilt had a way of taking hold of you, feeding into your insecurities, a constant reminder of the hurt you caused and the continuing need to make amends. I wasn't sure I would ever be able to let that go.

CHAPTER THIRTY-ONE

Nathan's call came through early.

The following morning, he'd left for work soon after breakfast, leaving me to settle down to some serious research for my next radio series on the forensic analysis of some true-life murder investigations. My main problem was in deciding which cases to choose from a depressingly large number of options.

I'd barely sat at my desk and opened my laptop when the phone rang. The preliminary findings on Ralph Ferguson's death had come through, and Nathan was calling a meeting to discuss a possible fresh lead. I was being summoned.

By the time I reached the station car park, Richard was drawing into one of the bays at the front of the building. I sounded my horn to attract his attention as I pulled in beside him and parked the Elan. He waited for me to lock up and we crossed over to the main entrance together.

"So what's this new lead?" I asked.

"Search me. I thought you might know."

"I tried to worm it out of the Chief on the phone, but he wasn't playing ball."

"Guess we'll find out soon enough."

Andrew Lynch and Sharon Worth were already waiting in Nathan's office when we arrived. We pulled up a couple of chairs and joined them, facing Nathan across his desk. He had the case file open in front of him.

"So what do we have, Chief?" said Richard as he settled himself in place.

"I went through the medic's preliminary report earlier," said Nathan. "It makes for interesting reading." He flipped through the report until he found what he was looking for. "The bruising around Ferguson's neck is V-shaped rather than straight-line bruising. So we know he died as a result of the hanging rather than by ligature strangulation."

Lynch interrupted. "So are we saying it was suicide after all?"

"We're saying it's difficult to tell from the hanging alone," said Nathan. "It's not unusual for a victim to be strangled first and then hanged to make it look like suicide. But we know from the bruising that's not what happened here."

"What about the wrist binding?" asked Richard.

"The knotwork doesn't tell us anything decisive," said Nathan. "It's a simple overhand knot that could have been tied by either the victim or someone else."

Richard persisted. "Mikey's observations about the crime scene suggest someone else was there. Wouldn't that be enough to make this a murder investigation?"

Nathan tapped the file. "We have more than that. Other bruising on the body is compatible with some rough handling at the very least. It looks as though the victim put up a struggle and suffered some injuries as a result."

I said, "If we are looking at murder here, I presume the locket was planted at the scene to suggest Ferguson left it in plain sight as a sort of confession, an indication he was Willow's killer." As an afterthought, I added, "Has Owen identified it, by the way?"

"The photo was missing," said Nathan, "but he was able to identify it from the style and the initials."

Sharon chimed in at this point. "He was more upset about losing the photo than anything else," she said. "It was a picture of him and his son, Simon. And he doesn't have a copy."

Richard said, "Whoever took the locket must have intended to sell it. It was the only thing on her of any value."

I asked Sharon how Owen was coping. "Are we keeping him up to date on developments?" I asked.

"Can't really name names at the moment, but he knows we're following up new leads."

I nodded. "I'll call round and see him later. Make sure he's okay."

Nathan rapped his knuckles on the desk to regain our attention. "If we could move on."

Lynch spoke up. "You said something about a possible lead, Chief?"

"I was coming to that," said Nathan. "We recovered Ferguson's mobile from the crime scene. One of the last texts on it was to Bryan Yates." He flipped to the next page of his file and read from it. "We need to talk. It's urgent." He looked up again. "That was three days ago."

I interjected. "Three days ago? That was the day I went to see him. What time did he send it?"

"That morning," said Nathan. "Just after eight."

"It must have been about the time I left," I said.

"And that's the point," said Nathan. "The timing suggests your visit prompted Ferguson's text. Which means Yates is mixed up in this too."

It was gratifying to know my suspicions about Yates had been vindicated.

Richard said, "It was a bit risky going round there on your own, Mikey. You should have made sure you had backup."

I exchanged a quick, guarded look with Nathan. "We've already had that conversation," I said.

"So are we pulling Yates in again?" said Lynch.

"We have enough for a warrant to search his farm," said Nathan. "If we get an application in straight away, we should be able to get over there this afternoon." To Richard, he said, "I'm going to need a team over there. Can you get onto that?"

The rest of the meeting was taken up by Nathan allocating duties between Richard and Andrew; applying for a warrant, coordinating a search team, bringing in Yates for further questioning.

I waited until all the arrangements were in place, the meeting was brought to a close, and the rest of the participants dispersed.

Once we were alone, Nathan slumped forward in his chair, hands clasped on the desk before him, his eyes dull. With a weak smile, he said, "Looks like we're in for a busy time." It sounded like an apology.

I reached across the desk and took his hands in mine. "It's only to be expected. I know that."

"I was hoping we could get away for a few days before the season started in earnest. We could both use a break right now."

I squeezed his hands. "I'm just sorry I add to your burdens."

"What?" He pulled his hands away and leaned back in his chair, his face creased in a frown. "What's that supposed to mean?"

"I know I can be reckless at times. And thoughtless. What was it you said? Jumping in feet first. Even Richard picked up on it earlier."

He leaned forward again, a wry smile on his face, and slow-punched my shoulder. "I worry about you, okay?"

"You shouldn't have to. You're under enough pressure without me adding to it. And the crap they've been printing in the local press doesn't help."

"There's not much we can do about that. We have to grit our teeth and get on with it."

"I thought we were getting past all that."

"We are. You're the one who won't let it go."

"It must worry you when it gets personal. I wonder sometimes if you wished you'd settled for someone who's less of a screw-up."

"Hey, enough of that." He stood up, leaned over the desk, took my head between his hand, and planted a kiss on my forehead. "Tell you what..." He settled back down in his chair. "...to hell with work. I'll knock off early tonight and grab some pizzas on the way home, okay? We could both use some downtime."

"You're bringing Yates in this afternoon, aren't you? Don't you want me at the interview?"

"You wanted to check in on Owen. So why don't you drop by the Fairview on your way home and you can go through Yates's recording later."

"Sounds like a plan." I rose from my chair. "We may as well make the most of it while we can."

As I was rising to leave, he reached over and took hold of my arm. "We could make even more of it and have an early night." He grinned up at me.

"My day just gets better," I said. "Don't you dare be late."

I said my goodbyes, left Nathan to wade through his mounting paperwork and headed off to the Fairview feeling less stressed.

Nathan was right. We needed some time to relax. I had a feeling the investigation was about to get a lot more heated and there would be little chance to take a break in the days ahead.

CHAPTER THIRTY-TWO

I arrived at the Fairview to find Owen on his knees, paintbrush in hand, a can of white emulsion by his side, touching up the front panel of the reception desk.

The smell of paint hung in the air.

"She soon had you on your knees," I said. "Why am I not surprised?"

He grinned up at me and struggled to his feet. "I can't sit in my room all day moping. Karen thought this would be good therapy, give me something to take my mind off things."

"Did she indeed? And where is our amateur therapist?"

"She had some shopping to do down at the market."

"Good. I was looking for a chance to talk with you. Alone."

Owen narrowed his eyes. "Sounds serious."

"Karen said you'd been asking questions."

His face flushed. "Sorry if I overstepped the mark. None of my business, really."

"It is your business. We were supposed to be friends. And I deceived you."

"Who am I to talk?"

"You were just hiding some inconvenient truths. I was living a total lie. Big difference."

Owen held up his hands, still clutching the paintbrush in one of them. "Let me go clean up and then we can talk."

"I'll be out on the terrace."

As Owen made his way to the cloakroom, I moved in the other direction and out through the sliding glass doors onto the terrace. At the far side, I leaned against the wooden balustrade, arms folded across the top. Beyond the concrete sea defences on the other side of the Esplanade, the ocean was calm. The Esplanade itself was deserted but, soon, the holiday season would start in earnest. The town would come to life, thronged with city dwellers enjoying the simple carefree pleasures of sun and sand and sea, oblivious to the drama unfolding around them.

Behind me, the deck's creaking wooden boards signalled Owen's return, and he joined me at the balustrade.

I leaned over the rail and pointed to my right, to where the coast curved away towards the sea, marking the spot where Tinkers Wood began. "You see that church tower over there behind the trees," I said, "I lived in its shadow for most of my early life. Did you know my father was the local priest?"

"That much I did know," said Owen, "but you never spoke about him."

"With good reason. My father was old school. All fire and brimstone."

"The hell and damnation type?"

I snorted. "Sure was. So you can imagine how it went down when he found out I was in a gay relationship."

"I think I'm beginning to see."

"Which is more than he did. As far as he was concerned, I was one step away from the fires of hell."

Owen nodded his understanding. "So you tried to conform."

"And ran away. Worst thing I ever did. I hurt a lot of people along the way. Including the one I left behind."

"I was surprised to learn it was the local Police Chief," he said. "But I'm glad to hear it's working out for you both."

"I've spent the last year trying to make amends. I guess I still have a way to go."

"It's easy for people like me. We grow up accepting the world as it is. Never question it. Just accept its values and the social norms that go along with them. But for you, it must have been hard. You had to find a place for yourself in a world that doesn't readily accept you for who you are."

I laughed. "Some of us take longer than others, but I got there in the end."

"And I didn't help any, did I?" He placed a hand on my shoulder and squeezed. "I wish I'd known what you were going through."

"But you didn't know." I turned around, my back to the tower, and leaned against the balustrade. "And, in the circumstances, your reaction was understandable."

"When it hit the media, all that... you know... it was a shock. It was as if I'd never really known you. And after that, we lost touch."

"I couldn't face anyone. Not then. But what happened - when I was outed like that - it was a wake-up call. I couldn't hide anymore. I could finally be myself. So maybe it wasn't such a bad thing after all."

"I had no right to confront you the way I did. It was shameful. I should have tried to understand."

Before I could allay his unwarranted concerns, the terrace door opened and Karen stepped out, followed by Laurel.

"We'll talk some more later," I said. "But, for now, know I'm here for you."

As she crossed towards us, Karen said, "Look who I bumped into on the way over."

After acknowledging me with a brief nod, Laurel turned to Owen with a look of apprehension. They faced each other without speaking, as if each was unsure how to address the other.

Laurel was the first to break the silence. "I wanted to see you, Owen, to tell you how sorry I was."

Owen found his voice. "It can't have been easy for you, coming here."

She took a step towards him. "None of what happened was ever your fault. Or mine. And I'm sorry it had to end like this."

They exchanged weak smiles, and whatever tension there had been between them seemed to melt away. Laurel opened her arms, and Owen stepped into her embrace, and they hugged.

As they parted, smiling more openly now, Karen said, "Let's go into my private quarters. We can talk there."

Laurel linked her arm through Owen's as we went inside. "How is Simon taking it?" she asked.

"He doesn't know yet," said Owen. "I keep in touch though. He's staying with his grandparents and seems contented enough for the moment."

"If it's all right with you," said Laurel, "I'd like to be there when you tell him. I'd like to give my support."

Owen squeezed her hand. "I'd appreciate that very much. You always were his favourite aunt."

Once in Karen's living room, we seated ourselves, Owen and Laurel sharing the couch and Karen and I taking the two armchairs.

"I wish this damn case was over," I said, "so we can all get on with our lives."

"Not sure if there's a connection," said Karen, "but I heard in the market that the police were all over Yates's farm this morning."

I snorted. "What is it with this town? The smallest event spreads like wildfire in minutes."

"Hardly small," said Karen. "Did you know about it?"

Now on my guard, I said, "I knew they were going to question him, yes."

Karen leaned towards me, eyes shining. "So there's a connection to the murder investigation then?"

"You know I can't discuss it," I said.

Satisfied, she leaned back in her chair. "So there is a connection. Interesting."

"Who is this Yates?" asked Owen.

Laurel was the first to respond. "He's local. Lived here all his life. He was always around on the fringes of the group we went around with all those years back."

"So Willow knew him?" said Owen. "He was a friend?"

"She knew him," said Laurel, "but I'd hardly call him a friend. He was one of those awkward types everyone made fun of. A hanger-on."

"Didn't he once fancy his chances with Willow?" said Karen.

"I remember him once making a pass," said Laurel. "She was outraged. Told him she was out of his league." She pulled a wry face. "I felt sorry for the guy." She turned towards Owen with a startled cry, her eyes wide. "Oh my God, Owen. I hope you don't mind us talking about Willow like this?"

"Not a bit," he replied. "It's comforting to hear your shared memories. I'd like to know how this guy is involved now though."

It was time to put any speculation to rest. I butted in. "It's best not to jump to conclusions. His farm is the nearest place to the crime scene. It's inevitable they'd need to question him more than anyone else."

My explanation seemed to satisfy them, and we drifted on to other topics of conversation.

Karen made a jug of coffee and, over our drinks, we chatted about other times. A group of old friends catching up on the past. And for a brief spell, we forgot about the horrors that had brought us all together and just enjoyed each other's company.

Eventually, I took my leave of them, pleading the need to buckle down to some work before Nathan came home.

As I bade my farewells and headed for the door, I felt lighter, as if some burden had been lifted from me.

It had been a day for coming together, putting old hurts to rest, and making amends.

CHAPTER THIRTY-THREE

I had just finished another chapter of my book and was humming along to White Stripes on Radio 1 when Nathan arrived home. I closed my laptop as he closed the door behind him.

"Perfect timing," I said.

He didn't get a chance to reply. Rocky was on him in a flash, a bounding blur of fur.

"Here, take these." He stumbled, almost dropping the two pizza cartons he was carrying, but managed to thrust them in my direction while trying to fend off Rocky.

I grabbed them, took them into the kitchen, and dropped them on the worktop while I fetched a couple of cans of beer from the fridge. Behind me, a few sharp commands brought Rocky under control and, a moment later, Nathan followed me through to the kitchen with Rocky following meekly behind.

"Is that how you keep your men in line?" I said.

"No, just you and Rocky."

I handed him a beer and pulled a face.

He took the beer and one of the pizzas, headed back to the living room and put them on the coffee table while he took off his jacket. He threw the jacket over the back of the couch, settled in place, grabbed his carton, and opened it. "I'm starving," he said.

"You're always starving." I followed him into the living room, dropped down beside him, and put my beer on the coffee table next to his.

Rocky followed us and curled up in his basket at the other side of the table.

The evening paper was sticking out of Nathan's jacket pocket. I reached over and pulled it free. "What fascinating stories have our boys of the fourth estate conjured up for us tonight?" I said.

Before I could open the paper, he snatched it from me and dropped it onto the floor at his side of the couch. "Later," he said.

He picked up a slice of pizza and was about to eat it when I put a restraining hand on his arm. "That was just a bit too hasty for my liking. What are you hiding?"

"What?" He stared at me, wide-eyed, eyebrows raised.

"Don't come the innocent. I know you too well. What's in the paper?" I held out a hand.

He opened his mouth to speak, thought better of it, and grimaced. Muttering under his breath, he leaned over the arm of the couch and retrieved the paper from the floor. As he handed it to me, he said, "It's just the usual speculative nonsense. It's obviously a slow news week. Don't take any notice of it."

I took the paper from him and unfolded it. The headline read 'Police Cover-Up?'. I screwed up my eyes and groaned. "Do I even need to read it to know what crap they've printed?"

Nathan held out a hand. "No, you don't. So you may as well give it back."

I turned away, holding the paper out of his reach. "I'm going to read it, anyway." I scanned the print under the headline, found the key point, and read it out. "Media Presenter Michael MacGregor, in a sexual relationship with the local Police Chief Nathan Quarryman, had assault charges against him suddenly dropped following the death of the complainant." I threw the paper across the room. "Why do we even bother to buy that scummy rag?"

"Because we rely on the press to disseminate information on behalf of the police. We need to keep them onside. So chill out."

"It's you I'm worried about. It makes you out to be a bent cop. And how dare they belittle our relationship like that. I shouldn't think your bosses would be too pleased either."

"I've already spoken to my Super."

I groaned. "What did he say?"

He pointed to my carton. "Eat your pizza. It's getting cold."

"Well?" I grabbed a slice of pizza, ripped a chunk off with my teeth, and chewed it vigorously.

"Mikey, It's well known we're in a committed long-term relationship. I've never made a secret of it. And my Super knows that. As for the rest of it, you think the police never had to deal with this sort of speculative nonsense before? It goes with the job. I'm just surprised they've held off this long." He bit into a slice of pizza and chomped on it.

"You'd think there was enough genuine news around to keep them occupied without them inventing it."

Nathan reached for his can of beer, took a long swig, and said, "Well, perhaps we'll have something for them soon enough."

I froze, pizza slice halfway to my mouth. "There are developments?" I slapped my forehead with my free hand. "Of course. Yates's farm. In the heat of the moment, I'd forgotten all about it. You found something?"

He finished chewing and said, "Nothing at the farm yet. But we're still searching. Forensics are over there."

"A confession?"

Nathan snorted. "No such luck. But we found something on his mobile." He took another bite of his pizza, keeping me in suspense, and then, "The morning Andrew Lynch dropped Willow off at the garage, she called Yates."

I stiffened. "That's odd. You'd think he'd be the last person she'd call."

He knitted his brows. "Why?"

"I'll tell you in a moment. I want to hear what he had to say about it." I reached for my beer and drank several mouthfuls.

"She called him to ask if they could get together. Seems they were romantically involved back in the day and she wanted to meet up for old times sake."

I spluttered halfway through taking a mouthful of beer. "No way. It doesn't make sense." I put the can back on the table and wiped a hand across my mouth. "He has to be lying."

"You can check the tapes tomorrow and judge for yourself."

"And did they meet up?"

"He says not. She asked if they could meet that morning at the old Coastguard Station at the end of the Esplanade."

"Why there?"

"It's a well-known local landmark, and it's off the beaten track. It was closed down last year and, since then, that end of the Esplanade hasn't seen much activity, so it makes an ideal meeting point for a clandestine meeting."

"And an ideal place for a murder."

I chewed on another slice of pizza while I thought this over. "I remember the conversation I had with the guy at the garage. Carl somebody." I snapped my fingers. "Carl Tanner. He told me Willow had turned left on the Esplanade. So that would have taken her in the direction of the Coastguard Station."

"We know Yates didn't meet her, anyway. The timing is all wrong. Willow's call came through just after Lynch dropped her off. So presumably she made it after she rounded the corner onto the Esplanade. But it was only a few minutes later Yates called the station about his possible break-in and Lynch went straight over there."

"And yet she was still heading in that direction?"

"He says she was insistent and rang off before he could object."

I snorted. "That sounds like Willow. She never was one to take 'no' for an answer. But I don't buy it. The whole romance thing is so unlikely."

"You seem sure of that."

"I am." I told him about my earlier conversations at the Fairview, the gossip about Yates's possible involvement in the investigation and how it lead to talk about Willow's rejection of Yates's advances.

"We need to check out the coastguard station, anyway. I've arranged for Forensics to go over there tomorrow once they've finished at Yates's farm. If Willow did go there, it could have been where she met her untimely end. In the meantime, Richard is arranging for the area to be cordoned off and patrolled until Forensics can get in there."

I closed the lid on my half-eaten pizza and rose to my feet. Rocky perked up, head raised and ears up, a hopeful gleam in his eyes, but settled down again when I carried the carton through to the kitchen. "I'll finish this later," I said.

Nathan followed behind me and dumped his empty carton into the recycling bin. "I suppose they could have gotten together later that morning," he said. "Yates obviously fancied his chances."

"No way," I said. "By all accounts, Willow had no time for him. And let's face it, you only have to look at the two of them to know how unlikely it is."

I made my way back to the couch, picked up my can of beer and dropped into place. "Willow went for the upmarket type. Yates is a bit too rough and ready for her tastes, I would have thought."

"Sometimes opposites attract." He came back into the room and joined me on the couch. "Look at you and me."

"You and me?" That came out of nowhere.

"We have very different personalities. You show your emotions much more readily. I tend to keep mine under wraps. Most of the time, anyway." He reached for his beer. "Unless you really piss me off," he said with a smile.

I squeezed his thigh and grinned back at him. "If that's your subtle way of telling me I go over the top at times, I'm not going to deny it." I took a swig of beer. "But as for Willow and Yates, I don't buy it. It's not just about personalities. They're different in every possible way."

"Seems to me, the biggest problem is trying to establish Willow's past relationships and then looking for more recent connections. But they were all so long ago. And that makes it more difficult to search them out." He leaned forward and rolled his beer can between his hands as he thought this through. "We need to dig deeper." He gulped down the rest of his beer and put the empty can on the table.

With my own beer finished too, I picked up his empty can, took both cans through to the kitchen, and dropped them into the recycling bin.

I called back to him. "Has Amelia Cole been interviewed yet?"

As I walked back into the living room, he said, "We're still working our way through the guest list."

"I'd like to have another shot at her," I said and regained my seat. "I think she still has a lot to tell us. We should make her more of a priority."

Nathan agreed. "Why don't you pay her a visit again, keep it informal for the moment? If you don't make any headway and still have some concerns, we can bring her in for questioning later."

"I was going to suggest that myself."

"Only this time, you don't go alone. I'll arrange for one of the local uniforms to go with you."

His tone didn't invite argument. Not that I was about to start one. "Sounds good to me."

"And in the meantime, we'll keep pushing Yates. But that can all wait. Enough about work." He rose to his feet. "Time to chill. I'll put on some music."

Before he could move, I grabbed him by the wrist. "Not so fast, fella." I pulled myself to my feet as he turned to face me and pressed up against him, my other hand on his chest. "I seem to remember something about an early night."

A lopsided grin spread across his face and he slipped an arm around my waist and pulled me closer. "Well, if it's some action you're looking for..."

I leaned into his embrace and pressed my lips to his neck. "Listen," I whispered, "You may well keep your emotions under wraps. But you know what they say; actions speak louder than words." I licked his ear. "And when it comes to action, you got 'em all beat."

He was right, of course; we were very different. He was the stable, sensible one, the one who kept his feet firmly fixed on the ground, the one who thought things through before acting. I was the opposite; impulsive and thoughtless, ready to act without proper consideration. Hardly surprising he acted up sometimes.

Even after all these months together, I occasionally wondered what he saw in me that made our relationship worth the long haul.

I leaned back, stared into those molten green eyes, and ran a hand down the strong square-jawed face, returning his grin.

Maybe it was time I learned to count my blessings.

CHAPTER THIRTY-FOUR

I replayed the recording. And replayed it again. And again.

Nathan stuck his head around the door, interrupting me as I replayed the same snippet for the fourth time.

"How's it going?"

It was the morning of the following day and I was in Nathan's office at the local station, seated at the front of his desk, rerunning the recording of Yates's interview from the day before.

"Can't make up my mind," I said.

He closed the door behind him, crossed the room, seated himself in the chair at my side, and peered at the screen on the desk. "What's the problem?"

I tapped the screen. "This is towards the end of the interview where Richard tells Yates we know about Willow's call and asks for an explanation."

"Yates answers readily enough. He seems sure of himself."

"And that's why I have a problem with it. The rest of the interview is the usual bluster and evasion we saw in his previous interview. But he seems on firmer ground here. None of that uncertainty."

Nathan rose from his chair, rounded the desk and sank into his chair on the other side of it. "Doesn't that suggest he was telling the truth?"

"I'm not so sure."

"Why not?"

"Disfluencies."

"That sounds like psychospeak. Not a language I'm too familiar with. You'd best explain."

I turned away from the monitor and leaned back in my chair. "A significant number of the words we use in conversation are random, meaningless interjections, verbal tics. You must have come across people who constantly use terms such as 'like' or 'you know' in their regular speech?"

"Sure. We all do it to some extent."

"We call those sorts of interjections disfluencies. They also include other sounds such as sighs or grunts. Even the number and placing of pauses in our speech. They're part of our regular speech, and each of us has our own distinctive pattern."

"As does Yates."

"For the most part, yes. And after sitting in on his previous interview and listening to this one, I've familiarised myself with his particular speech patterns. But the moment he starts to explain that telephone call, it changes. It's more confident with fewer interruptions. It seemed rehearsed. As if he was expecting the question and had a ready answer prepared. As if he'd been prompted." I leaned over, switched off the monitor, and fell back in my chair. Running through the recording again would be a waste of time. "I just don't know."

Nathan swivelled his chair back and forth a few times, a faraway look in his eyes, as if he were thinking through what I'd just told him. "The one thing we are sure of," he said, "is that Willow called him. And she was seen heading towards the Coastguard Centre."

"I've had some thoughts about that too," I said.

Nathan stopped swivelling and leaned forward, hands clasped before him on the desk. "Go on," he said.

"Just after Willow called Yates, he contacted the station to report a possible disturbance at the farm. I'm wondering if the two calls were connected?"

"I wondered about that myself. Too much of a coincidence. But I'll be damned if I can figure out what the connection could be."

"Let's presume there's a cause-and-effect relationship and think about how it could fit in with what we already know." I rose from my chair, crossed over to the window, and stared out into the car park, running over recent events in my mind. I turned and sat on the sill and leaned back against the window. "We found nothing at Yates's farm, no signs of disturbance. Right? And perhaps that's the point."

He nodded and said, "Go on. Let's hear it."

"We know that Sgt Lynch dropped Willow off near the Esplanade, that she then called Yates as she made her way in the direction of the old Coastguard Centre, and later that morning was murdered."

"Straightforward enough so far."

I continued. "We're presuming, for the sake of argument, that Yates was a party to the murder. Now suppose that, during that call, he learned Lynch was on patrol in that area and that's where he'd dropped Willow."

Nathan saw where I was going with this and took up the thread. "You're suggesting it was a distraction," he said. "There was no incident at Yates's farm. He put in the call to draw Lynch away from the Esplanade to make sure his patrol didn't take him past the spot where Willow was about to meet her end."

"Of course, Yates couldn't be directly responsible for her murder," I said. "But we don't know who else was involved. Apart from Ferguson. Have you checked Yates's other calls? And how about Ferguson? Do we know what his movements were?"

"The only other call Yates had that day was to an out-of-town animal feed supplier. And Ferguson's movements are accounted for. He was in a meeting at work." He reached over to the phone and, a moment later, he was asking for Lynch to be sent to his office.

As he put down the receiver, he said, "At least we have another line of enquiry we can follow up."

Some minutes later, we were joined by Lynch. Nathan offered him a chair facing his desk, and I went over to join him and settled into the other chair while Nathan brought the Sarge up to speed on our discussion.

Lynch wasn't wholly convinced by my supposition. "I'm not sure Yates would have the wit to be so devious," he said.

"Maybe not," said Nathan, "but we need to follow it up, anyway."

"So where do we go from here, Chief?" Lynch asked.

"We need to get back out on the streets," said Nathan. "I'll draft in more uniforms from HQ and make sure we have plenty of cover in the area where Willow was last seen. But this time, we're asking for details of anyone seen in the area, not just Willow."

Lynch said, "We still have details on file from the last sweep."

"We'll carry out new interviews anyway," said Nathan. "We may pick up more leads. Just make sure we cross-reference them with what we already have."

"And how about the old Coastguard Station?" said Lynch. "Anything on that yet?"

"Forensics should get over there this afternoon. Until they do, Richard has one of his officers posted over there to keep the place secure."

Lynch glanced at his watch. "I'm out on patrol shortly. I'll put it on my route. I'll take a quick look around. Make sure everything is okay and the place is still secure."

"We'll leave it there then," said Nathan. He rose to indicate the meeting was over. "Keep me informed of any progress."

Lynch assured his Chief he'd get things moving and hurried away. As he left the room, he almost collided with Sharon Worth as they passed each other in the doorway.

"Sorry to butt in, Chief," she said. "You wanted to see me?"

Nathan invited her in and asked for details of her schedule.

"I have my daily meet with Owen Brookes later this afternoon, not that there's much to tell him," she said, "but I'm on general duties till then."

"In that case, I have a task for you." He outlined our earlier discussion about my visiting Amelia Cole and asked her to accompany me. "Leave the talking to Mikey this time," he said. "We're trying to keep it informal, but I'd like a police presence there, anyway. Just for backup."

I wasn't sure what sort of backup he thought I needed, but Sharon readily agreed to his instructions, anyway.

"And who knows," he said, "if all goes well, you may have something to tell Owen after all."

CHAPTER THIRTY-FIVE

I was without my car that morning; we'd driven to the station in Nathan's Astra. As Amelia Cole's shop was on the way to the Fairview - more or less - Sharon agreed to drive us there and then head over to the Fairview from the shop, leaving me to walk the short distance home.

My mobile rang as we pulled out of the station car park. I dug it out of the pocket of my jeans and checked the screen. "I'd best take this. It might be important," I said. "It's Laurel Ford."

As it happened, it was a social call, an invitation to meet up at her place the following day. Owen had already accepted an invitation, and she thought it might do him good to enjoy our shared company. I accepted readily enough, and we agreed a time.

I finished the call and, as I slipped the mobile back into my pocket, Sharon said, "Owen and Laurel seem to be getting close."

It was difficult to tell from her tone if she was making an informative comment or having a disapproving dig.

"I'm just glad he has someone else around to offer him support," I said.

"At least it takes some of the pressure off me," she said. "Given the lack of progress so far, it makes my role difficult. Being kept in limbo like this is getting the poor man down."

"It's not having a positive effect on any of us," I said. "I'm hoping I might get some useful information from Amelia Cole to help move the investigation on."

We arrived at Salem Row, and Sharon turned the corner onto the Esplanade. She pulled over to the kerb on the far side of the road and I glanced over to the shop as I reached for the door handle. "That's odd," I said. "The place is in darkness."

Amelia Cole's Newsagent and Confectioner's, dark and silent, settled back into the gloom of a dull overcast day. It stood in sharp contrast to the illuminated shops on either side of it, all of them spilling light onto the pavement from brightly lit windows.

"Strange," said Sharon. "I've never known her close during the day."

I climbed out of the patrol car and headed across the road. Fortunately, the light rain that had fallen for most of the morning had stopped, but there was a chill wind, and I turned up my jacket collar as I hurried on my way.

At the front of the shop, I cupped my hands around my eyes, pressed them up against the window, and peered into the dim interior.

No sign of life.

Several bundles of twine-bound newspapers bearing delivery labels were stacked in the recessed doorway, suggesting the shop had been left unattended, suddenly and unexpectedly. The 'closed' sign hung against the inside of the glass door.

Sharon came up from behind me and said, "Amelia lives above the shop but it's in darkness up there too."

I stood back to get a better look. The blinds were drawn in the upper windows.

"There's an alley here leading to the back of the shop," said Sharon, and moved towards it.

I followed her through the narrow space between the shop and its neighbour into a shared courtyard at the rear of the buildings. The only light back there was from the window of the premises next door. The blinds on the upper rear windows were also drawn.

"She seems to have left in a hurry," said Sharon.

My thoughts exactly. "Maybe one of the neighbours might know where she is."

As if by magic, the rear door of the shop with the lighted window opened and a heavy-set, denim-clad, bespectacled man stepped out. "I saw your car out front," he said. "Anything I can do to help." As if by way of explanation, he added, "I own the hardware store next door."

We learned his name was Donald Perry and that he and Amelia were friends as well as neighbours. We also learned that he was concerned about her welfare. "She seems to have left abruptly," he said. "And it's not like her to keep me in the dark about her plans."

"Did you see her leave?" I asked.

He confirmed that he hasn't. "But I was worried when she didn't open the shop, It's so out of character." He swallowed hard, ran a hand through his thinning hair and said, "I went round there to make sure she wasn't injured or incapacitated. We have keys to each other's premises, see. Just in case."

"And nothing out of the ordinary?" said Sharon.

"Everything as it should be." He peered at me over the top of his specs and said. "It is Mr MacGregor, isn't it? Michael MacGregor? I've seen you on TV. She said you came to see her the other day."

"Did she say why?" I asked.

"Something about this murder, she said. It was a friend of hers. The police have been round all the shops asking questions."

"And did she discuss it with you?" I'd half-hoped she'd confided in him, told him things she'd been reluctant to tell me.

No such luck.

He shook his head and said, "She's been acting kind of strange lately though. And now this sudden absence. I just hope she's okay."

Sharon interjected. "What was so strange about her behaviour?"

Donald Perry shuffled uneasily and swept a hand through his hair again. "It might sound over the top," he said, "but if I had to describe how she's been acting, I'd say she was paranoid." He looked at each of us in turn, as if waiting for a reaction. In the absence of a response, he continued. "She asked me if I'd seen any strangers hanging around the shop. Or if I'd seen any unfamiliar cars parked nearby."

"And had you?" Sharon asked.

He shook his head. "If there were any suspicious characters hanging around, I didn't see them."

I said, "Did she give you any reason for her... er... her concerns?"

Another negative response. "She just asked me to keep my eyes peeled."

Sharon reached into her breast pocket, took out a card, and handed it to him. "This is the number of the local station," she said. "If you hear from her or you think of anything that may interest us, give us a call."

He glanced at the card, nodded, and shoved it into his trouser pocket.

Sharon and I said our farewells and took our leave, making our way back along the alleyway to the front of the building.

"I hope she's not landed herself in any trouble," said Sharon.

I pounded a fist into the palm of my other hand. "I knew something wasn't right when I first spoke with her," I said. "I should have insisted we follow up on my concerns earlier. We may well have lost our chance now. I just hope she's safe."

"I'll put in a report when I get back to the station," said Sharon. "We can, at least, make some enquiries." She glanced at her watch. "And in the meantime, I'd best get over to the Fairview. Owen will be wondering where I've got to." She added, "Are you sure I can't drop you off somewhere first?"

I declined the offer. "I'm heading back along the High Street. Tell Owen I'll call round for him tomorrow."

We parted company. She crossed over to her car, and I turned back and headed towards the High Street, silently fuming. I was still angry with myself for not following up on my interview with Amelia sooner.

On the way, Lynch hove into sight in his patrol car, driving in the direction of the old Coastguard Centre. I signalled a greeting as he passed by and then turned around and trudged after him. The Station was only a few minutes walk away and it wouldn't do any harm to look around the place before it was overrun by police and Forensics.

I'm not sure what I hoped to find there, but after such a disappointing day, I felt I should be doing something.

CHAPTER THIRTY-SIX

On the way over to the Coastguard Centre, I called Nathan to let him know about the situation with Amelia Cole. He shared my concerns about her disappearance and agreed to raise it as an issue at the next briefing.

Once he'd learned where I was heading, he told me the forensics team had finished their examination at Yates's farm and he had arranged to meet them at the Station. I ended the call after agreeing to wait for him there.

A patrol car was positioned on the Esplanade a short distance from the Coastguard Centre, securing entry to the final stretch of road. Behind it, blue and white duct tape cordoned off the area beyond.

I stopped to pass the time of day with the driver, Bob Carver, an officer I recognised from the local force. The local station had just radioed to let him know the Chief and forensics team were on their way.

Much to his relief.

"The tedium was starting to get to me. Apart from you and the Sarge, I've not seen a soul for hours," he said.

I laughed and said, "I think that's rather the point."

"Even so, it's always good to see a friendly face to lighten the burden," he said, and added, "The Sarge is still back there somewhere checking out the place."

"Which is why I'm here too," I said. "I'll go find him and compare notes." I signalled goodbye, sidestepped the duct tape, and went on my way.

The coastguard's compound stood back from the road at a point where the Esplanade came to an abrupt end by the sea wall.

Yet another victim of Government cutbacks, it had been closed a year earlier, and the main building, a white stucco-coated terrace of converted cottages, was now falling into disrepair, its doors and windows secured by steel shutters.

Tyre tracks set in the compacted wet sand that had blown over the sea wall led me around to the back of the building where Lynch had parked his car. He was peering through the grimy windows of a long, low brick-built shed on the other side of the open ground behind the two buildings. I called out a greeting as I crossed towards him.

He acknowledged me with a wave and, as I reached him, he said, "Not much to see here. The main building is secure. No way would anyone have gotten in there, at least not without leaving some obvious traces."

I nodded towards the shed. "Anything there?"

"It seems a more likely prospect," he said. "It's the original tool store and repair bay. The door has been forced but going by the degree of rusting and weathering, it looks to have been done some time ago. And the interior shows no signs of any recent activity. I doubt anyone's been here in a long time. I was hoping we might find something useful." He didn't sound too happy.

We agreed to leave any further investigation to Forensics. He'd already learned they were on their way and offered me a seat in his car pending their arrival.

As we crossed towards where he was parked, he brightened up somewhat and said, "How did you get on with Amelia Cole? Any luck?"

I quashed any hopes he'd had of a breakthrough there, telling him of Amelia's disappearance. "Looks like we've both had disappointing days," I said.

We didn't have long to wait for new arrivals. Nathan was first. He pulled in alongside Lynch's car and was closely followed by three men in an Audi, no doubt the forensics team.

With introductions over, Lynch led the forensics team away to show them around the compound.

Once we were alone, Nathan said, "Have you had a chance to look around?"

"Briefly. Before you arrived. But enough to know you're not likely to find anything."

He furrowed his brow. "Why so certain?"

I glanced over to where Lynch was in conversation with the forensics guys and, satisfied that Nathan's input wouldn't be needed for a while, took him by the arm and, leading him around to the road at the front of the compound, said, "I'll show you."

Pointing down the road to where the patrol car was positioned, I said, "You see where Bob Carver is parked? That's the only point of access to this compound. Right?"

He grunted his agreement.

"Now look along this stretch of road. See how the sand has built up against the sea wall? It's spread across the road and compacted over time. Probably because it's lain undisturbed for so long."

"Until now, that is," he said. "It's been churned up by our cars."

"Exactly. And yet when I first arrived, the only signs of disturbance were the tyre treads from Lynch's car. I was able to follow them along the road and around to the muddy ground at the back of the main building."

"I can see where you're going with this," said Nathan.

"It means no one has been in this area for some time," I concluded.

"But surely any signs of disturbance could have been blown away by now. You can see how exposed we are here. This area gets the worst of any bad weather. And besides, Willow was on foot. She would have walked down on the other side of the road, avoiding the sand. Same goes for anyone she may have met here."

"We've had several light showers over the past few days," I said. "Enough to solidify the wet sand against any possibility of being blown away. And it's fairly sheltered, anyway, up against the sea wall."

He grunted and kicked at the nearby sand. The wet mass swallowed the front of his boot but remained intact.

I continued, "And as for anyone on foot, sure, they could have passed this way without leaving any trace. But if Willow was killed here - and I presume that's what you're thinking - the only way anyone's going to get her away without being seen is by some sort of transport."

Nathan hunched his shoulders and stared out to sea. The sound of waves hitting the sea wall rose from the other side of it, and spray flew high into the air.

"I'm apt to agree with you," he said. "What I find odd though is that despite intensive enquiries, no one saw Willow either making her way here or going back."

"I have my own theory about that," I said. "Amelia Cole's shop is just around the corner from where Willow was last seen. I'm beginning to think that's where she went."

The furrowed brow again. "You seriously think Amelia Cole is involved in all this?"

"The more I think about it, the more convinced I am. Especially after what I learned about her recent behaviour."

"Her sudden disappearance doesn't help."

"Which just makes me even more sure she's involved."

He nodded. "We need to make some enquires in that direction. I'll get onto it."

A shout from the far side of the compound interrupted us. It was Lynch. He waved over to us. "You'll need to see this, Chief," he said.

As we hurried towards him, one of the forensics guys stepped out of the repair shed. He was bagging a piece of material into a plastic wallet with a latex-gloved hand.

"It's a woman's scarf," said Lynch. "And it's in good condition. Looks like it was dropped here recently."

"Where did you find it?" asked Nathan.

Forensics guy led the way into the shed. One of his colleagues was photographing the interior and the other taking notes.

"It was here," he said, and pointed to a rusted hose reel on the wall. "There's a tear in the fabric. It looks like it snagged on the spindle and was pulled off. I'll make sure it's fast-tracked for DNA."

"Let's have it checked by the victim's husband first," said Nathan. "He may recognise it."

"And look over here," said Lynch. He motioned towards a rotting wooden rack against the far wall. Several small rusting hand tools were displayed on its shelves. "Something like this could have been our murder weapon."

Nathan shot me a wry look. "Seems we could have been wrong after all," he said.

CHAPTER THIRTY-SEVEN

"Looks like we're getting somewhere at last," said Richard. "Now we just need Forensics to throw a few leads our way." He sounded buoyant. A bit too buoyant.

It was the day after the search at the Coastguard Compound, and Nathan had called in his team for a briefing. We were seated in a circle in one of the smaller meeting rooms, Nathan and I, Richard Lowe, Andrew Lynch, and Sharon Worth.

Once word about Willow's scarf had gotten around the station, it had caused a stir, an air of optimism, as if the investigation was finally on track, and movement towards a swift conclusion was just a matter of time.

It was difficult to understand the positive vibes encouraged by the find but, given the lack of progress so far, I guessed anything would seem like a major achievement.

I didn't share in the general enthusiasm. "We are sure it's Willow's scarf?" I said.

Sharon said, "Owen identified it this morning. It was a particular favourite of hers, so he was quite sure."

"And does Owen know the circumstances in which it was found?" I asked. "I'm meeting him later and I don't want to put my foot in it."

"Not the details," she said. "Just that it was near where she was last seen."

"And for the moment, we'll keep it under wraps until we know more from Forensics," said Nathan. "I've asked them to fast track their analysis, so we should have some results soon. In the meantime, we're proceeding on the assumption it was either worn by Willow or in her possession at the time of her murder."

"And are we also working on the assumption she was killed at the Coastguard Station?" said Lynch. "It seems the most likely possibility."

I butted in and voiced my doubts about the compound being the murder scene. I went through the concerns I'd raised with Nathan and said, "The ground conditions would have shown clear signs of vehicular activity. And it would have been impossible to remove Willow's body without transport and not be seen."

"Could she not have been moved by boat?" said Richard. He leaned toward me, eager for a positive response.

"No way," I said. "The Coastguard Compound is on an incline and there's a deep drop over the sea wall at that point. Which suggests that manoeuvring a body over into a boat would have left signs of disturbance in the build-up of compacted sand alongside the wall. There was none."

"It might be possible though," said Richard. His eyes pleaded for confirmation.

I squirmed in my chair. "Sorry, I know how much everyone would like to think we found the crime scene," I said, "and I hate to put a dampener on your expectations, but I don't think you should raise your hopes too high."

Nathan said, "Forensics are still over there. So we should know one way or the other soon enough."

"She was heading in that direction," said Lynch. "And the coastguard house is as far as she could go."

The only answer I had to that was a shrug. "I'm sure she didn't die there."

Lynch again. "So what about the scarf?"

"There's a pattern building here," I said. "First, the call from Yates's farm. Then the locket found at Ferguson's place. And now the scarf."

"Distractions," said Nathan and nodded.

Richard said, "You mean someone is playing us?"

"'Someone' being Bryan Yates," I said. "I'm fairly sure his original call to the station was meant to hinder any future investigation. So it follows he would play a part in any subsequent attempts to throw us off the scent."

Lynch slumped back in his chair and folded his arms. "If you knew him as well as I do, you'd know he doesn't have the wherewithal to be that devious."

I wasn't about to give ground. "I still think he's at the centre of this."

Nathan broke in. "Let's look at what we know for sure," he said. "Willow was last seen rounding the corner of the Esplanade in the direction of the Coastguard Station. We also know that, on the way, she called Yates. And it was the last anyone saw or heard from her."

"But we know Yates didn't meet her," Lynch added. "So someone must have got to her after she rounded the corner."

"She's not likely to have been attacked or abducted in broad daylight in a busy shopping area," said Richard. "So, she either met someone she knew and went with them willingly or she went into one of the shops."

"What about that friend of hers, Amelia Cole?" said Richard. "Her shop is just around the corner. Did we get around to interviewing her?"

"I was coming to that," said Nathan. He swallowed and pulled at his cuffs. "Unfortunately, Ms Cole seems to have disappeared."

One of the chairs squeaked, and someone shuffled their feet.

Richard said, "Disappeared?"

Lynch nodded. "Mikey told me about that. I take it she's not turned up yet?"

I took over the conversation and explained the circumstances of my visit the previous day. "She seems to have left unexpectedly and in a hurry."

"Obviously, we'll need to find her," said Nathan. "Enquires about and interviews with any known family and friends."

"I'll get onto it," said Richard.

Sharon said, "You think this has something to do with our investigation?"

"I'm not sure," said Nathan. "But we need to talk to her, anyway." To Lynch, he said, "Where are we with our more recent sweep of the area? Any new sightings? Any reports of suspicious behaviour?"

"Nothing new," said Lynch. "We're no further on than we were before."

Turning next to Richard, Nathan said, "What about Owen Brookes's assault? Where are we on that?"

Richard grimaced. "Sorry, Chief. We're still looking out for similar incidents. But, so far, we've drawn a blank."

"We are sure Owen Brookes is in the clear?" said Lynch.

Nathan confirmed he was. "His alibi stands. We have a witness statement and local CCTV confirming his whereabouts."

"I think we need to put more pressure on Yates," I said.

"We're already onto it," said Richard. "We're following up on his recent activity and re-interviewing his wife and anyone he's likely to have had contact with."

With nothing else to discuss, Nathan drew the meeting to a close.

As the others left the room, I reminded Nathan I was meeting up with Owen and driving over to see Laurel. "It might help him take his mind off all this," I said.

Nathan suggested it would help me unwind too, and we parted company after agreeing to catch up later at home.

Owen was waiting for me on the terrace at the Fairview. I was a few minutes late and, as he climbed into the passenger seat, I apologised. "We were having a briefing over at the station," I explained.

"Anything new?" he asked as he fastened his seatbelt.

I let out an exasperated sigh as I slipped into gear and pulled away from the kerb. "I wish I could tell you we were making some progress," I said, "but we're not much further forward than we were."

"The more I think about it, the more I'm coming round to the conclusion it was a random attack after all," he said. "I can't understand why someone she hasn't seen for years would want to kill her. It makes no sense."

As I turned onto the road to Colton Drey, I cast him a quick sideways glance. "How much has your Liaison Officer told you?" I was reluctant to point the finger at possible suspects until we could be more certain.

"She told me about the guy at the wedding party. The one they found hanged. The one who had Willow's locket. But I still don't understand how he was involved."

During the rest of the journey, I filled him in on as much of the investigation as I could without giving too many details away. But by the time we arrived at Laurel's kennels, he was as confused as ever. "Why don't we forget about the investigation for the time being and make the most of our visit."

Laurel came out of the house to greet us as we drove into the yard. There was no welcoming smile and, as we climbed out of the Elan, I noticed how edgy she was, clasping and unclasping her hands, unable to stand still, jittery. And when she spoke, her tone was curt.

"Let's go inside," she said. "It's cold out here."

For someone who had suggested a social get together, she didn't seem well disposed to being sociable.

"Everything okay?" I said.

"Of course." Short and sharp.

She glanced around in a manner I would describe as furtive, eyes darting everywhere, before leading the way to the house.

Something wasn't right here.

Once inside, she led us across the hall and paused with her hand on the handle of the door into the living room.

She swallowed hard, betraying her nervousness, and said, "There's someone I want you to meet."

She pushed open the door and moved aside to let us in. As we stepped over the threshold, a figure rose from an armchair by the fireside and turned towards us, her face creased and worn.

It was Amelia Cole.

CHAPTER THIRTY-EIGHT

Keeping my eyes on Amelia, I said, "I presume this is more than just a social occasion, Laurel?"

"I'm sorry for the subterfuge," she said. "But it was necessary."

Owen's gaze settled on each of us in turn. Frown lines creased his brow.

"Let me introduce you," I said to him. "This is Amelia, Willow's childhood friend."

"Pleasure to meet you," he said, not very convincingly.

An embarrassed silence was interrupted by the sound of distant barking from the direction of the kennels.

Amelia said, "I was sorry to hear about Willow's... about what happened to Willow."

Owen nodded but said nothing.

Somewhere outside, several more dogs joined in the barking.

"Why don't we all sit," said Laurel, "and we can tell you what this is about."

"That would be a start," I said.

I sank into the battered old fireside armchair I had used on my previous visit. Owen seated himself in its companion on the other side of the hearth, and Willow and Laurel shared the couch between us, facing the hearth.

Laurel turned to Amelia and held out a hand. "Let me have the letter," she said.

Amelia rummaged in the canvas bag held in her lap, produced a folded envelope and gave it to Laurel. She, in turn, reached over to where I was sitting and handed it to me.

I unfolded the envelope and drew out a typewritten sheet of paper. It read, *If you know what's good for you, you'll keep your mouth shut. It would be a shame if your shop burned down. Especially if you were in it at the time.*

I breathed in and exhaled slowly. "Short and to the point," I muttered.

Owen leaned forward. "What is it?"

"Just the usual run-of-the-mill threatening letter," I said. "You don't need to read it." To Amelia, I said, "Why didn't you take this straight to the police?"

"I was frightened. If someone is watching me, they'd know if I called the police," she said. "Laurel is the only person I felt I could trust, so I asked if I could stay here for a while. I feel safer here."

"This meeting was my idea," said Laurel. "We're all old friends, so getting together like this is less likely to raise any suspicions. The last thing we need is the police swarming all over the place. That might put Amelia in even more danger."

"I'll take this with me," I said, holding up the letter. "I'll make sure it gets into the right hands." I put it back in its envelope, refolded it, and slipped it into my jacket pocket.

Amelia tightened her grip on the canvas bag in her lap. When she spoke her voice trembled. "I never wanted to get involved in any of this."

No longer the self-confident woman I had met two weeks earlier, she seemed shrunken, vulnerable.

Laurel squeezed her shoulder. "Sorry, pet, but you're involved whether or not you like it."

"I don't understand what's happening here," said Owen. "Is this something to do with Willow's murder?"

"It has to be," said Amelia. "Willow and I were best friends for a long time. We did everything together."

"But why you?" I asked. "Willow had other friends."

Amelia's hand went to her throat, and she toyed with the silver chain around her neck, twisting it back and forth between her fingers. She stiffened, clasped her hands in her lap, and sat upright, her face set firm, as if she had come to a decision. "Because Willow and I shared a secret," she said.

"Just tell them what you told me," said Laurel.

Amelia nodded. "Back in our teens, Willow and I were no different from any other girl our age. If there was a party going, we'd be up for it. If not, we'd be down the pub with the rest of our crowd, hanging out and having a good time. And at the weekends we'd be out clubbing, dancing and drinking till the early hours." Once again, her hand flew to the chain at her throat and she clutched it tight. "We liked to enjoy ourselves."

Her eyes dimmed as she was transported to the past, reliving those earlier times. "One night, we went to the Vortex Nightclub in Charwell. It was Saturday night, club night. All the local crowd were there. It was just a typical weekend rave-up."

"It was a popular club back then," interrupted Laurel. "We all went there."

Amelia continued, "Willow and I travelled over by bus and usually caught the late-night service back. But not that night." She squirmed in her seat and a slow flush crept across her cheeks. "I met someone and went back to his place." Her hands fell into her lap, and she looked down. "I left Willow to make the journey home alone." She looked up and stared straight at me, her face twisted in pain. "I would never have left her if I'd known."

"What happened?" I said.

"She had to cross some waste ground on her way back to the bus station. It was dark. They must have followed her. She didn't stand a chance." Her eyes welled up with tears and she screwed them shut.

I interrupted her, keeping my voice low and calm. "You're telling us she was raped?"

Amelia nodded rapidly, her eyes still tightly shut. "Three or four of them."

Owen sank back in his chair. "Dear God."

I said, "Did she know who they were?"

"No. They made sure of that. They pulled her coat over her head while two of them held her down. She heard their voices, but she didn't recognise them."

"Did the police have any leads?" I said.

"She didn't report it."

Owen groaned, his eyes closed, face drained of blood. "I can't believe I'm hearing this," he said. "I had no idea."

"She didn't want anyone to know," said Amelia. "She was embarrassed and ashamed. I tried to get her to go to the police, but she wouldn't."

"Ashamed?" said Owen. "Of what? What did she have to be ashamed of?"

"They called her names," said Amelia. "Slag. Whore. Told her she was a cheap drunk. Said she'd been asking for it."

"Sexual assault is dehumanising," I said. "There's a lot of shame attached to it. And that shame can lead to self-blame. We live in a culture that all too often blames the victim. Hardly surprising so few women report rape."

"I blamed myself too," said Amelia. "If I hadn't left her to go home alone, it would never have happened. After that, it was never the same between us. I tried to be there for her but, in the end, we drifted apart."

"It would explain the suicide attempt too," said Laurel. "And it can't have been long after that she moved to London with our parents. I wonder if that's why. I wonder if they knew about it."

"That's the last thing she wanted," said Amelia. "She made me swear never to tell. They were already at her all the time about her so-called wayward behaviour. She knew they'd blame her. They weren't the most supportive of parents." She blushed and cast a glance Laurel's way. "No offence intended."

"None taken," said Laurel. "Our parents would have been much more concerned about their public standing than Willow's welfare. They probably moved away to save face after Willow's suicide attempt. Hardly surprising we both cut them out of our lives."

Owen pushed himself up from his chair and moved over to the window. He stood with his back to us and stared out into the fading light without speaking.

It was impossible to imagine how gruelling this must be for him. Bad enough he should lose his wife to such a harrowing death, and now he had to endure hearing of all the horrors that had preceded it.

I rose from my seat, crossed over to him, and placed a hand on his shoulder. He stiffened momentarily and then relaxed again, half-turning to face me with a weak acknowledging smile.

"I'm sorry you had to go through this," I said.

"If it helps get to the truth," he said, "then so be it." He turned to face the rest of the company and said, "But why now? Why, after all this time? I don't see the connection."

"There has to be one," I said. "Why else would someone threaten Amelia? It was something only she knew about. There has to be a connection."

"Something you said earlier," said Laurel. "Something about Willow not recognising her rapists' voices. Maybe she did. Maybe she finally heard a voice she recognised."

"After all this time?" said Owen.

I said, "Some things you never forget."

"Maybe someone at the wedding reception?" said Laurel.

I made my way back to my chair and seated myself. "Ralph Ferguson was at the reception," I said. "And he was definitely involved."

Owen followed me back across the room and sank into his own chair. "What about this Yates guy?" he said. "You think he could have been one of her rapists?"

"It wouldn't surprise me," said Amelia. "He fancied his chances with her and she rejected him. It might well have been payback."

"We've not made much headway in that direction so far," I said. "But at least we have more to go on now. It's worth taking another shot at him."

"Does that mean I'll be involved?" asked Amelia. She twisted her hands together in her lap.

"The police will probably want a statement from you," I said. "But there's no reason anyone else should know."

"And you know you can stay here as long as you need to," said Laurel. "You should be safe enough here."

"The police should be able to do something about that too," I said. "I'll ask if they can arrange for surveillance."

"The dogs will let us know soon enough if anyone comes sneaking around here," said Laurel. "And not all of them take too kindly to strangers."

"No harm in being doubly sure," I said. "And in the meantime, I'll take all of this back to the Chief and we can then plan the way forward."

I wasn't sure where we were going with this, where this new information might lead. But after hearing what Amelia had to tell us, of one thing I was certain, Ferguson and Yates weren't the only ones involved. Someone else out there had been a party to Willow's rape, and, just like Ferguson and Yates, that somebody had every reason to silence her.

CHAPTER THIRTY-NINE

I pushed the empty cereal bowl to one side, reached across the breakfast table, and helped myself to a slice of toast from the toast rack. "I thought we could get away for a while when this whole sorry mess is over. Somewhere hot with plenty of sun and surf. Maybe Malta. I've always fancied Malta."

"Hmm." On the other side of the table, Nathan sat with both hands wrapped around his coffee mug. He stared with unseeing eyes at a distant spot somewhere over my left shoulder. His face was impassive.

"Well, what do you think?"

"Hmm." His focus didn't change.

Over on the sideboard, the radio burbled the local news. I tipped my head towards it and said, "They're reporting sightings of Martians landing in Hounslow."

"What?" He came to with a start.

"Oh, good. You are finally listening to me then? I've been chatting to myself for the last twenty minutes."

"Sorry, I was miles away."

"And I was just wishing we were." I reached for the butter dish. "You were in one of your fugue states. So what's on your mind?" I buttered my toast and bit into it.

"I was thinking over your chat with Amelia Cole."

Once we'd left Laurel's place the previous day, I'd dropped Owen off at the Fairview and made my way back to the station to see Nathan and to report on our meeting with Laurel and Amelia. It had obviously given him a lot to think about and, after sleeping on it overnight, it was still on his mind.

"Trouble is," he said, "Willow was secretive about so many things. Even her husband knew next to nothing about her past. It makes you wonder how many other secrets she kept."

"It's the only one we've unearthed so far that gives us a motive for murder. If Willow recognised one of her rapists, he'd want to silence her."

A scratching at the back door signalled Rocky's readiness to come in from his morning scramble around the garden.

Nathan pushed away from the table, rose from his chair, and crossed through to the sitting room. As he made his way over to the door, he called back, "And it's why he'd want to silence Amelia too." He opened the door and stood aside as Rocky bounded past him and headed for the kitchen where he knew his bowl of biscuits would be waiting.

Nathan followed him back and, as he reseated himself, said, "He didn't do himself any favours sending that note. It drew attention to something that may otherwise have stayed hidden in the past. It shows he's running scared." He reclaimed his mug of coffee and rocked back in his chair. "One thing puzzles me. How could he have known Amelia knew about the rape?"

I swallowed my last piece of toast, and said, "He didn't. The way the note is worded tells us that. 'If you think you know something...'." I reached for the coffee pot and refilled my mug. "Willow kept her ordeal a secret. She didn't even tell her parents. So you have to ask yourself why, of all people, would she tell Amelia?"

"They were close back then. Best friends. They did everything together. Everyone knew that."

With appetite sated, Rocky licked his chops and settled himself under the table, spreading himself across our feet.

"Everyone who knew her," I said. "And that's the point. Whoever our mystery man is, even if he wasn't sure, he knew them well enough to know that Willow would almost certainly have confided in Amelia." I picked up my coffee mug, blew on its contents to cool it, and sipped from it.

Nathan said, "That could help us narrow down the search for

suspects. It has to be someone who was part of that group, one of the guys they regularly socialised with." He glanced at his watch. "Time I was on my way." He pushed his chair back from the table, extricating his feet from beneath Rocky, and earning himself a rolling grumble in response.

He gathered up the empty bowls and his coffee mug from the table and, as he carried them over to the sink, I said, "Pity we don't have any more tangible suspects."

Nathan said, "We already have Yates in the frame. And after hearing what Laurel had to say, I'm convinced he's at the centre of this. And armed with this new information, we can bring more pressure to bear. See if he finally cracks." He rinsed the dirty crockery under the tap and dropped them in the bowl.

"Good luck with that," I said.

He turned to face me, brow wrinkled. "You don't sound so sure."

"Yates isn't one of the sharpest knives in the drawer."

He leaned back against the sink and crossed his arms. "I'm not sure I see the relevance."

"Anyone with half a brain would go one of two ways. Either fabricate some alternative reality in an attempt to extricate themselves from a difficult situation. Or realise the game's up and try to minimise the effects of any potential consequences. Either way, it would give us something to work with. Something to grasp hold of and use against them."

"And Yates?"

"Lying well needs a modicum of intelligence. And Yates is a bit deficient in that department. He's the sort to batten down, play stubborn, and just deny everything with no attempt to explain or elucidate. Pretty much like his last interview."

"So you're saying we'd be wasting our time?" He glanced down at his watch again, headed into the living area, and grabbed his jacket from its hook on the back of the door.

I turned in my chair to follow his progress. "And getting nothing in return to work with, yes. And we have nothing to tie him directly to Willow's murder, which just makes our task even harder."

As he slipped into his jacket, Nathan said, "From what Amelia told you, it seems like we're looking at a number of rapists. If Yates is one of them, he could well be covering for others we don't know about."

I left my chair and followed Nathan into the living area. "One of whom is probably our killer," I said. "And I'm presuming Ferguson was one of their number."

Nathan buttoned his jacket and said, "Doesn't explain his murder though."

"Maybe he got cold feet. Maybe he was about to blow the whistle."

"Maybe. Unfortunately, we're not able to question him now, are we?" The criticism in his tone wasn't lost on me.

Before I could respond, Rocky appeared from under the table, stretched and yawned, crossed over to the door, and looked up at Nathan in anticipation of his morning run on the beach.

Nathan reached down and ruffled the fur between Rocky's ears. "Sorry, boy. Mikey's on dog duty today." He grasped the doorknob, ready to leave, and said, "We're going to have to bring in Yates, anyway. He's our only lead." He opened the door.

I said, "Can I make a suggestion?"

"Make it quick or I'll be late."

"Instead of bringing him in and treating him as a potential suspect, let's go visit him at home where he'll feel on safer ground. He's already told us he had a relationship with Willow - though I'm sure that's a lie - so we can interview him on the pretence of asking for information about her past."

Nathan pulled a face, seemingly unconvinced, and so I hurried to explain. "If we don't treat him as a suspect, he won't be on the defensive. Which means he'll be easier to manipulate. And we can use his claim of a relationship with Willow against him. Ask for details of the places they met and who they socialised with. It could help to trip him up. He'll be off guard and more likely to slip up, and with the right questioning, we may learn more."

Still clutching the doorknob, Nathan thought over my words for a moment and then nodded. "Okay, it's worth a try I guess."

"So you're okay with me going out there to question him?"

He let go of the doorknob and raised a warning finger in my direction. "I'm not letting you go on your own."

I held up my hands in mock surrender, palms facing out to him. "I didn't suppose you would. Lesson learned, okay?"

"Lynch is on patrol today. I'll get him to drive you over there."

"Make it this afternoon when Yates' wife is back from the market stall. It will be interesting to see how Yates reacts when she's around."

"Come over to the station after lunch," he said as he opened the door. "I'll get it set up."

Reaching down, I took hold of Rocky's collar to stop him following Nathan out of the door and said my goodbyes as Nathan headed out to the car.

I took down Rocky's lead from its hook on the back of the door as I closed it and said, "Let's go for that walk, boy. I need to think through how best to play this."

CHAPTER FORTY

By the time I reached the station that afternoon, Nathan was briefing Lynch on the proposed visit to Yates's farm. Which probably explained Lynch's tetchy response to my greeting when I met up with them both in Nathan's office. He was not happy. He was standing over Nathan's desk when I arrived, complaining about wasted manpower. In Lynch's book, focusing attention on Yates was a distraction, a false trail leading us away from the investigation proper.

But Nathan was having none of it.

I stayed out of the argument; I'd heard it all before and knew Nathan was unlikely to give ground. Plus, I was eager for them to get it over with so I could raise some concerns of my own.

Whilst out exercising Rocky that morning, I'd reflected on the events of the past few days, trying to make connections amongst disparate events. And out of that mix, something gelled, a pattern, a series of coincidences. Something I needed to discuss with Nathan.

But perhaps now wasn't the time. He was clearly not too happy about having his instructions questioned by Lynch, and the frown lines on his face were deepening by the second.

Nathan dismissed Lynch's argument as groundless and sent us on our way. As we were about to leave, I turned back to Nathan and said, "Are we any further forward on Owen's mugging?"

He looked up from the files scattered across his desk, exasperation written on his face. "Not that I know of. Why?"

I hesitated and said, "Something I'd like to discuss with you, but it can wait. I'll check back with you later."

Lynch and I left the station and on the way to the vehicle compound, I said, "I see the Chief's not in the best of moods."

"He's not the only one," Lynch said. "So what's your take on all this? You seriously think Yates is involved?"

The querulous tone told me he'd already formed his own answer to that question.

"There are too many pointers in that direction for him not to be," I said. "The phone call from Willow, the incident report to the station - which I still think was a diversionary tactic, the text from Ferguson. He has to be involved. And that crap about being in a relationship with Willow. What a total crock."

Lynch pulled his keys from his pocket as we crossed the compound to his patrol car. "It wouldn't surprise me," he said. "Willow did put it about a bit. And she wasn't exactly discriminating. I feel sorry for her husband. It can't be easy for him hearing about his wife's sordid past."

I shot him a dark look across the top of the car before opening the door and sliding into the passenger seat.

As he climbed in the other side, I said, "And you never played the field in your early years?"

He switched on the ignition and said, "Sure, but you expect that of a guy. Not a woman."

There were times I despaired of men like Lynch. But now wasn't the time for a face-off. I gritted my teeth and snapped on my seatbelt.

"I just feel sorry for the guy is all," he continued. "He's not had the best of times in our town, has he? First the mugging. And then a murder charge dropped on him. Makes you wonder why he stays around." The automatic gates opened, and he drove out onto the slip road behind the station. "You told the Chief you wanted to discuss the mugging. Sorry to disappoint you, but there's nothing new there. It's not a priority at the moment."

Glad of a change of subject, I said, "I wasn't looking for a progress report. I'm more concerned with what was taken."

"It was just the usual stuff. Wallet. Mobile." He pulled round onto the main road and turned the car in the direction of the clifftop. "It's not as if he lost much. He said himself it was loose change, a bit of credit and some photos."

"It was the loss of the photos that interested me."

"What?"

"Something Willow's sister said yesterday. It got me thinking." My mind was elsewhere now, making connections. "You never found Willow's mobile, did you?"

"We searched every inch of the beach. And, no, we never found it."

"And the photo was missing from Willow's locket."

"Where are you going with this?" Lynch sounded exasperated. "Are you suggesting there's some connection?" He slipped down into second gear as we took the steep incline onto the clifftop road.

I said, "Willow's sister suggested Willow may have overheard one of her rapists and recognised his voice. But suppose it wasn't his voice but his face."

"My understanding is she never saw any of them."

We reached our destination, and Lynch drove into the car park. It was empty. He pulled over to one side, parked up, and switched off the ignition.

"I was talking with the Chief earlier about David Masters, Willow's previous partner," I said. "He's not someone she ever talked about. Not even to her husband. Not even after all this time."

"It can't have been easy for her."

"Maybe. But it puzzled me. At first, I thought perhaps she'd been driving the car. That she had been responsible for his death. She wasn't the best of drivers. She could be reckless. And I thought perhaps her death had been a revenge killing."

Lynch drummed his fingers on the steering wheel. "It's a possibility, I guess. But we've not been able to trace the guy. He's fallen off the face of the earth."

"Exactly. And the more I think about it, the more I think there's another reason Willow was reluctant to talk about him. Maybe he never existed in the first place. Maybe he was a fiction she invented to hide the truth."

Lynch stared at me long and hard, his brow creased in a frown. "Sorry, I don't understand."

"It's all in the timing," I said. "Check the dates. Willow is raped and nine months later has a child."

Lynch shook his head slowly, keeping his gaze fixed firmly on my face. Seems he was having a hard time accepting my theory.

I tried to press my case. "Her closest friend was the only one she confided in. She chose to keep the rape a secret. So, if I'm right, she would need to create a fiction to explain the pregnancy."

Lynch still didn't seem convinced.

"It's not like she'd want anyone, including her son, to know he was the product of a rape," I said. "It would make sense to invent an alternative history."

"Even if it was true," he said, "how does it impact on our investigation?"

"Because Willow may have seen enough of a resemblance to her son to identify the rapist."

"Seems a bit far-fetched to me." He unfastened his seatbelt and opened the door.

I put a hand on his arm to stay him. "It's not uncommon for children to share the physical characteristics of a parent. Sometimes the resemblance is uncanny."

"Is that you wanted to discuss with the Chief?" he asked.

"Yes," I said. "But in the meantime..." I dug into my pocket and pulled out my mobile. "I know it's a long shot but there's only one way to find out for sure. I need some pics."

"You're not calling Brookes?" His voice rose a notch. "You can't dump a half-formed theory like that on him. Have you any idea the distress it could cause?"

"I've no intention of giving him the real reason," I said. "Karen and I broached the idea of a book of remembrance with him recently. There are still people around from the old days who remember Willow and may want to contribute. So it wouldn't seem out of place to include some recent photos of Willow and her family."

I brought up Owen's number on the screen and called him.

Lynch closed his door and waited for my call to go through. It went to voice-mail.

I left a message asking Owen for some photos and explaining why I wanted them, finished the call and rang off. "Looks like we'll have to wait to see if I'm right or not," I said.

"What were you hoping for?" asked Lynch. "A spitting image of Yates?" The touch of sarcasm in his tone wasn't lost on me.

"It would give us something to work on and sure would make our interview easier."

"We'll have to make do with what we have." He opened the door again and climbed out of the car.

I climbed out of the other side and followed him across the car park towards the farm path.

Lynch raised a hand to shield his eyes from the glare of a sinking sun that hung low over the horizon and squinted over to where a distant figure was bent over, hoe in hand, raking the earth at his feet.

"Looks like Yates is at work in the field," said Lynch. "You stay here. and I'll go get him."

"I'll head over to the house and see if I can get anything out of the wife."

"She's away," he said. "The car's not in the yard."

"Pity," I said. "I was hoping to get a different take on the alleged break-in. See if she backed him up."

He responded with a disapproving grunt.

Getting him to accept my view on the incident report was a no-go. Never going to happen. "I'll take another look around the outbuildings," I said. "See if there's anything we missed."

He raised a hand in acknowledgement as he took the path that led down the side of the farm and to the open ground beyond.

I watched after him for a few moments as he made his way to the distant figure and then headed towards the main house, passed through the gate, crossed the farmyard, and knocked at the door. There was just an outside chance that Yates's wife was at home after all.

There was no response. Not that I'd really expected one. I peered through a side window to make sure no one was inside and then made a tour of the outbuildings. Not that I expected to find anything there either. It was a way of passing the time until Lynch returned with Yates.

Once I'd checked out the interior of the last building. I crossed to the far side of the yard from where I could see across the tract of land beyond the farmyard. Lynch and Yates were heading my way, Yates trailing Lynch by a short distance.

I moved back towards the house, taking shelter from the stiff breeze blowing from across the cliff top, and waited for their return.

My mobile buzzed.

It was a message from Owen attaching some family shots his parents had recently sent to him.

I flipped through them; holiday snaps, family photos, some of Willow alone, some with Simon.

My heart sank.

Simon bore not the slightest resemblance to Yates. The dark saturnine looks and angular face were in sharp contrast to Yates's long face, pale complexion and light wispy hair. So much for my grand theory.

Half-heartedly, I flipped through the rest of them.

And stopped at a full-on portrait of Simon.

My breath caught in my throat, and my hand tightened on my mobile.

It was a face I half-recognised. One I'd seen before.

Recently.

I searched my mind, trying to remember where I'd seen that face.

And then I had it.

I stared down at the image. And in my mind's eye, the face of Willow's young son, open and smiling and full of innocence, morphed into something else.

Something I was in no doubt about.

Staring back at me was the face of a killer.

CHAPTER FORTY-ONE

Yates was trailing Lynch by a few feet and carrying a heavily laden sack. He scowled at me over Lynch's shoulder as they approached. Clearly, not happy at the prospect of yet another interrogation.

Luckily for him, he was off the hook for now. Everything had changed. We had a more urgent concern to deal with.

Before I could let him know I was postponing the interview, he made his excuses and trudged past us, dragging his sack behind him. "I'll go put these carrots in the shed and be right back."

Seeing an opportunity to speak to Lynch without being overheard, I waited until he was out of earshot on the other side of the yard and said, "We need to get back to the station. Yates's interview will have to wait for now."

"What's the problem?"

"This." I held up my mobile, displaying the image for him to see.

He stared at it, blank-faced, and without comment.

"Well?" I said, inviting a response. "You have to admit I'm right now. You recognise him?" I'd expected a more enthusiastic response.

"Yes, I recognise him." His voice was flat, emotionless. "Carl Tanner. I've known him for years."

"She must have seen him at the Fairview after the wedding. Remember? He dropped your car keys off at reception. One of the guests was helping Willow to a chair nearby."

Lynch nodded, stony-faced.

"She looked shaken, and we all presumed she was feeling the effects of the booze. But it must have been him. Seeing him." I glanced down at the image again. "The likeness is remarkable. It would have been such a shock, coming face to face with the man who had blighted her life for all these years."

I turned off the mobile and slipped it back into my pocket. "You'd think it would have encouraged her to go to the police finally. It would have been the obvious..." I stopped, cutting myself short as the words dried in my throat.

And I froze, silenced by the sudden rush of thoughts that surfaced into awareness and coalesced into a sudden shocking realisation.

Moments of clarity sometimes seem to come unbidden, appearing of their own volition out of nowhere. A sort of sixth sense or intuition. But, of course, they don't. They're the result of the mind's constant quest to make sense of the world, forming patterns out of seeming randomness. And sometimes, all it needs to make sense of it is that final piece of information falling into place as seemingly unrelated events finally come together into a perfect whole.

And once I knew the moment Willow first saw her killer, the man who had raped her, everything else flowed from it.

I looked up and stared into Lynch's face, and in his cold, hard gaze, I saw the truth of it. An icy shiver ran down my spine. "But of course she did go to the police, didn't she? The very next morning. She saw you."

He didn't speak. Just that cold unblinking stare, and a slight, almost imperceptible nod in silent acknowledgement of what he read in my face; that I finally understood.

Time slowed, and we stood in silence, eyes locked.

"Her complaint wasn't about me, was it?" I said. "It was about Tanner."

A slow shake of the head, and he said, "You were too fucking stupid to let it go, weren't you?" There was a contemptuous curl to his lips, and the narrowed eyes were full of scornful pity. "Anyone else would have been happy to walk away from an assault charge. But not you. You had to make a big deal of it."

This was not the man I had come to know over the past weeks. The jovial banter and infectious grin had gone, replaced by something cold and dark.

"You were one of them, weren't you? One of the gang that raped her?" It was more a statement than a question. I already knew the answer. I just needed to hear him say it.

A sharp metallic click from behind me.

I whirled around.

Yates stood a few feet away, facing me down the barrel of a shotgun. He levelled it at my chest.

"You too," I said.

To Lynch, Yates said, "I called Carl. He's on his way."

I half-turned and took a step back, keeping them both in my line of sight.

"And Ferguson?" I said. "Another one of your happy band? What happened? Did he get cold feet? Threaten to drop you in it?"

"Something else we have to thank you for," said Lynch. "But it's payback time. You really should have kept out of it."

"You're making a big mistake," I said.

All too aware of the precarious position I was in, I scanned my surroundings, hoping against hope there was some means of escape, some nearby cover.

Nothing.

We were in the middle of the yard with the nearest exit point some distance away between two of the outbuildings. Even if I could have made it that far, there would be too much open ground to cover before I could reach the relative safety of the trees on the other side of the clearing.

"You're the one who made the mistake," said Lynch. He nodded to Yates. "Get him into the barn."

Yates took a step back and waved the barrel of the gun in the direction of the outbuildings. "Move it." His voice trembled. He didn't seem at ease with his new role as enforcer.

I held out a hand towards him, imploring. "You don't have to do this."

He took another step back and shot Lynch an anxious look.

Lynch was more assertive. "Get moving," he barked.

My mind went into overdrive, racing through my options. Although Yates had the shotgun, Lynch was the one in charge here, the driving force. Yates was less certain, unsure of himself. I needed to work on him, play on his uncertainties. I was fighting for my life here.

"Listen to me. Bryan. I know you had nothing to do with Willow's death. You weren't even there. But this is different. If anything happens to me, you'll be part of it. Is that really what you want?" To Lynch, I said, "It was Tanner's garage, wasn't it? That's where you killed her? You drove her to her death. Literally."

Yates ran his tongue over dry lips and shot Lynch another anxious glance.

Lynch moved to his side and, keeping his eyes firmly fixed on me, took hold of the barrel of the shotgun. "Let me have the gun," he said.

Muscles tensed, I readied myself for action.

Relinquishing control of the shotgun, Yates stepped away as Lynch took the weapon from him.

I sprang forward.

Too late.

Lynch swung the gun around, finger on trigger, and slammed the barrel into my chest.

I winced and fell back, hand pressed against my chest.

Face flushed with anger. Lynch barred his teeth, and for one sickening moment, I thought he was about to shoot. I took another pace back and raised my hands in surrender.

"That was fucking dumb." He spat the words at me.

"You can hardly blame me for trying." My limbs were turning to jelly, but I fought to stay in control.

Through clenched teeth, Lynch said, "Now move it." He nodded towards the barn on the other side of the yard.

Hands still raised, I crossed the yard towards the open door of the dilapidated wooden structure and stepped into the dim interior. It smelled of dung and wet straw.

My stomach churned, and the acid taste of bile filled my mouth. I turned to face Lynch. Yates stood behind him. shifting uneasily from foot to foot.

"Now what?" I said. "If you think you can shoot me and get away with it, you're mad."

He ignored the comment and waved the gun towards one of the wooden supports holding up the raised hayloft above. "Over there," he said. "On the floor."

"Get some rope," he said to Yates.

Yates dithered as if unsure what to do, and, finally, said, "I'll get some from the store next door," He disappeared into the yard, leaving me to face Lynch.

I did as I was ordered, crossed over to the support and sat on the floor at its base with my back to it.

"So whose idea was it to kill her?" I asked. "Yours? Or was it Tanner?"

"What does it matter?" he said. "We were all in this together. And we weren't about to let some two-bit slapper ruin our lives."

"Your lives were ruined the night you raped her."

"Raped? This is Willow we're talking about, remember? Good-time easy-lay Willow. Girls like her don't get raped. They get used."

I flinched.

"She was out for a good time," he said. "Like the rest of us. She knew the score."

"Is that why you had to hold her down?"

"Don't try to make this sound like she was some innocent victim. She'd been around the block a few times. She knew what she was in for."

"You make me puke. Is that how you justify what you did? Blame the victim?" I spat on the floor in front of me. Maybe it wasn't the best of times to aggravate him, but sometimes it's impossible to hold back.

He raised his voice. "It was over fifteen years ago. We've all moved on, made honest decent lives for ourselves. You think any of us wanted to throw all that away for the sake of some ancient misdemeanour."

"Misdemeanour?" I couldn't keep the incredulity out of my voice.

Before he could respond, Yates reappeared carrying some short lengths of rope.

"Tie him up," said Lynch.

Still looking unsure of himself, Yates moved into position behind me and dropped to a crouch. He grabbed my hands, crossed them at the wrists behind the wooden support, and bound them with the rope.

I winced as the rough hemp dug into my flesh. "Easy," I said. "I'd like to keep my hands intact."

"That's the least of your worries," said Lynch.

"Before I could respond, we were interrupted by the sound of an approaching vehicle.

"That'll be Carl," said Lynch. "I'll go get him." As he hurried out of the door, he called back to Yates. "Get his phone. We don't want those photos falling into the wrong hands."

Yates patted down my pockets until he found what he was looking for, dipped into my jacket pocket, and pulled out my mobile. He was sweating and his hands trembled as he slipped it into his own pocket.

I tried to make eye contact as he stood up and backed away, but he avoided my gaze, glancing towards the door or staring at the floor, rocking imperceptibly.

This was a man ill at ease, someone caught up in a situation he was clearly not comfortable with. And now I had him on his own, away from Lynch's influence, I needed to work on him fast before Lynch returned, try to persuade him of the consequences of his actions before he got in too deep, before there was no way back.

This was my last chance.

CHAPTER FORTY-TWO

Yates hovered by the half-open barn door, shoulders hunched, shuffling, staring down at his feet.

The sound of muffled voices drifted in from outside. I needed to work fast before Lynch returned with Tanner.

"It's not too late, Bryan," I said.

He turned away, refusing to face me, and peered out through the doorway into the yard beyond, as though eager to be outside, out of my sight. Seems he couldn't even bear to look at me.

"You know what's going to happen here, don't you?"

He raised a hand and rubbed the back of his neck but said nothing.

"You know what they're going to do, Bryan."

A sharp intake of breath and he let out a strangled sob.

"Is that why you can't face me?"

He whirled towards me, his features twisted in anguish. "Shut up. For fuck's sake, shut up." He clenched his fists.

"Listen to me." I leaned towards him, straining against the pull of the rope that bound me to the wooden support. "This is the only chance you'll get. If you end this now, turn the others in, the courts will show some leniency. They'll go easy on the rape charge."

"I didn't rape her. It was nothing to do with me. I didn't even want to be there."

I raised my voice. "Then why the hell are you doing this? They're going to kill me, Bryan. You know that, don't you? And this time, you'll be a part of it. Conspiracy to murder. Is that what you want? Can you live with that?"

He didn't get a chance to reply.

The door swung open and Tanner stepped into the barn with Lynch following close behind him.

Tanner was wearing his overalls, and there was grease on his face and hands. Yates must have pulled him from a job, and he didn't look too happy at having been interrupted.

The scowl changed to a smirk as he sauntered towards me, arrogant and self-possessed.

"So, the famous Michael MacGregor finally meets his match." He crouched down in front of me, his face inches from mine, and sneered. "You're about to become one of those unsolved murders you're so fond of spouting about." He laughed and rose to his feet, glancing back at the others, seeking to share with them what passed as a joke in his twisted mind.

"Unsolved?" I said. "You reckon? One thing I've learned is that arrogant scum like you always get caught in the end."

The grin faded to a look of contempt. "Gobby fucker, aren't you?" he said. "I'm not sure you're in a position to get too clever with me right now."

"Is there going to be a better time?"

"Not for you, there ain't. Time's up, fucker."

Tanner's attitude was in sharp contrast to those of his co-conspirators. Lynch had been aggressive, but grim, cheerless and defensive. Yates was a scared emotional mess.

Tanner was different.

I stared up into the hard square face, looking for the signs I would surely find there; the cold unblinking gaze, dead eyes devoid of emotion, the sneering grin that betrayed the callous indifference to the fate he had in store for me.

The face of a psychopath.

Appealing to the troubled conscience of someone like Yates, someone deeply conflicted and struggling to come to terms with the morality of his actions, might have worked. I might have persuaded Yates to change his mind. But not so with Tanner. This was a man devoid of conscience. My only option now was to work on the others through him.

I said, "Not forgetting, of course, you have a couple of fall guys ready to take the rap if anything goes wrong. Like you tried to do with Ferguson."

The grin faded. "Ferguson was about to rat on us thanks to you."

"Bryan would be your best bet," I continued. "He's already under suspicion. And he's conveniently placed right next to the clifftop. It would be easy to shift the blame onto him."

"Shut the fuck up." Over his shoulder, he said, "Don't listen to him, Bryan. He's trying to wind you up."

Yates didn't look too convinced. He wiped his hand across a sweating brow and stared at the back of Tanner's head wide-eyed, his mouth hanging loose.

Lynch squeezed Yates's shoulder with a reassuring hand. "Ignore him. He's playing games with us." To Tanner, he said, "How are we going to do this?"

Tanner spat on the ground at my feet before turning away. He nodded to Lynch and Yates as he walked towards them and said, "You two need to get your stories straight. We don't want you tripping over yourselves later."

Yates and Lynch exchanged puzzled glances. Yates shrugged. "Like what?" he said.

"Think about it," said Tanner. He jabbed a thumb behind him in my direction. "This interfering git was here to question you, wasn't he? You need to cobble something together. Who said what to who. Get on the same page."

"And him?" said Lynch, nodding towards me.

"You should drive back to the station," said Tanner, "and tell them you finished the interview. Boyo here wanted to take another look around the clifftop. Wanted to check out the drop where the bitch went over. Unfortunately, in his eagerness to show what a clever twat he is at reading crime scenes, he got too close to the edge and fell over."

He turned to face me again. "And so Elders Edge's finest lose one of their best in a tragic accident."

A grin spread across his face. "But not to worry. I'm sure they'll give you a good send-off. Big showy funeral. Lots of blah about how you died in the line of duty." The grin widened. "You'll be a hero."

I snorted. "You're getting stale. You think you'll get away with that tired old ploy a second time. Didn't work too well the first time around, did it?"

"Well you know what they say," he replied, "practice makes perfect."

He turned away, addressing the others. To Lynch, he said, "You scout around, make sure the coast is clear. Me and Bryan will deal with Boyo." He glanced at his watch. "How long have you been here?"

"Not sure," said Lynch. "Maybe half an hour. Forty minutes."

"We'll give it a while longer," said Tanner. "Make it look like the interview took some time." He dipped into his overall pocket and pulled out a pack of cigarettes. "It'll give me time for a fag break before we dump this jerk."

He turned away, laughing, and made his way out to the yard, lighting a cigarette on the way and followed by the other two.

I was fast running out of time.

The wall to my right was only a few feet away. Hanging on it, dangling from a hook on a loop of string, tantalisingly close, was a scythe.

I shuffled around, stretched myself to the limit, and tried to reach it with my foot, hoping to dislodge it. No such luck. I was shy of it by a couple of feet.

A scan of my surroundings showed no other tools within easy reach.

I was getting desperate.

The smell of damp, rotting wood suggested an alternative means of escape. The barn was old, badly maintained and in poor condition. If the support was rotten, maybe I could pull it loose. I grasped it with my hands and tugged hard. It didn't shift. The outside walls may be rotten, but the internal structures seemed to be constructed of sturdier stuff.

The support had sharp edges, and I tried to use one of them to cut through the rope. But it was too tough.

I was running out of options.

Without warning, the barn door opened, and I stiffened, ready to face the inevitable.

It was Yates. Over his shoulder, he shouted, "I forgot to get his mobile."

He was alone.

And in a hurry.

He seized the scythe from its hook as he raced towards me, reached down, and sawed through the rope that bound me, freeing me from the support.

A moment later he was digging into his pocket and pulled out my mobile. He threw it at me and, in a low strained voice, said, "Get in the loft now."

I grabbed my phone and ran across the barn.

As I climbed the ladder, Yates pushed open the window on the back wall and then hurried towards the door.

As I moved out of sight towards the back of the loft, I heard him shout across the yard. "He's gone. He's heading into the trees across the clearing."

From the safety of my hiding place, all I could hear from that moment on was a cacophony of sounds; shouted recriminations, howls of rage, Tanner's voice rising above the others, hollering and screaming abuse.

"Get after him," Tanner yelled. "If he gets down to the beach, we're done for."

I strained to follow the sound of their running as they headed through the narrow passage to the rear of the yard and across the clearing towards the trees.

The sounds slowly died away, fading into the distance.

I held my mobile steady with a shaking hand and tapped out the number of the station.

CHAPTER FORTY-THREE

"Are you sure you're up to this?"

Nathan leaned across his desk to where I was seated on the other side and took my hands in his. Worry lines creased his face.

I nodded and squeezed his hands. "I'd rather be here right now. I need to get this over with."

"You're sure they didn't hurt you?" His voice trembled.

"I'm just shaken, is all. But I'll be okay."

The past couple of hours had passed in a blur, and I was only just getting my head together. Those last fifteen minutes in Yates's hayloft had been an eternity, minutes seeming to stretch into hours as I lay trembling in the dark, holding my breath and praying I wouldn't be discovered before the police arrived. Only when the distant sound of sirens grew to an ear-splitting wail as patrol cars raced into the yard outside did I finally break down and weep.

I tried a wan smile. "I guess I must have looked a bit of mess when you found me."

Nathan had been the first to burst through the barn doors, closely followed by Richard Lowe. After climbing down from the loft, I had turned towards him, my face crumpled, hair full of straw, and, a moment later, I was in his arms, holding him tight, never so pleased to see him.

He returned the smile. "I've seen better sights," he said. "You don't smell so great either." His expression became serious again. "We'll get away somewhere when this is over. You're going to need a break. We both are. Maybe that trip to Malta you talked about."

"You do listen to me then?"

The smile returned. "Only when you have something sensible to say."

My mobile was on his desk. I'd left it there after showing him the photograph of Willow's son. He glanced down at it and said, "You could swear that pic was an old snap of Tanner. The likeness is remarkable. Willow must have made the connection the moment she saw him."

"Which, presumably, is why they went to such lengths to get rid of any photographic evidence. I'm guessing that's why Owen was mugged."

"Just one of many leads we need to follow up."

"Has Yates said anything yet?"

"Not yet. Richard's setting up an interview. He'll call me when he's ready."

"And the other two? Any sign of them?"

"No, but they won't get far. I have a team out scouring the woods and we have the beach covered in case they try to go down there. At least Yates had the sense to give himself up."

His eyes dulled and he stared out, unseeing, at a spot over my shoulder. "I still can't believe..." He paused. "I can't believe that one of our own..." His voice trailed off.

He looked down at his desk briefly and then looked up again. The worry lines were back. "You were supposed to be safe in his company."

"No one could have known."

Before he could respond, the insistent ring of the desk phone interrupted us. It was Richard. He was ready to start the interview.

The video link to the interview room had been set up in Richard's office. We made our way over there and by the time we had settled down in front of the monitor, the interrogation had already begun. Yates faced Richard across the desk, shoulders hunched, rocking back and forth in his chair as Richard talked him through the preliminaries and read him his rights.

A recording device sat on the side of the desk, its power-on light glowing red. By its side stood a water carafe and two glass beakers.

Richard poured himself some water and sipped it. "You sure you don't want a solicitor?" he asked.

Yates shuffled in his chair. "What's the point? I got nothing to hide anymore."

Richard reminded him that he could ask to have a solicitor appointed at any time and, after glancing down at the open file in front of him, said, "Okay, let's go back a couple of weeks to…" he ran a finger down the top sheet of the file. "…to the eighth of April. If it helps jog your memory, it was the day you reported a break-in at the farm."

Yates swallowed hard. "I remember."

Richard leaned back in his chair. "It was also the day Willow Brookes was last seen alive. And it seems you were the last person she spoke to."

"That never happened. I didn't even know she was back in town."

Richard furrowed his brow and tapped the file. "We have it on record that she called you that morning. A call you later confirmed."

A pause. Yates tugged at his shirt cuff. "It was Andrew Lynch. He used her mobile so the call couldn't be traced back to him."

Again, Richard checked his file. "So your claim that Willow Brookes asked to meet at the old coastguard house was false?"

"Andrew asked me to say that. And he planted her scarf later to make it look as if she'd gone there. He said it would throw the investigation off the scent."

"So what was the purpose of the call?"

Yates's agitation increased. "Could I have some water, please?"

Richard filled the other beaker and pushed it across the desk. With a shaking hand, Yates picked it up, gulped down its contents in one go and put it back on the desk.

He drew in a deep breath and said, "Andrew asked me to call the station and report a break-in. Said he was on patrol and needed a reason to drive up to the cliff top. Said he needed to cover himself in case anyone saw the car up there."

Leaning forward, Richard clasped his hands together on the desk and said, "That must have seemed an odd request. Surely it must have raised some concerns? Did you not think to question him?"

"Of course I did." Yates ran the back of a hand across his mouth. "He said there wasn't time to explain. It was important I helped him out, and he'd fill me in on the details later." He squirmed and his voice rose several degrees. "But I swear I had no idea what they were up to. Not then. I swear it."

"And what were they up to?"

Yates tugged at his cuff again. "Andrew told me to stay out of the way. I didn't even know Carl was with him. It was only later when… you know… when they found Willow's body. I put two and two together."

"And what did it add up to?"

"Andrew told me later." Yates was becoming more and more agitated. Beads of sweat broke out on his forehead. "She'd found out it was Carl what raped her and had gone to see him to report it. Andrew called Carl and then drove her down there. Told her he wanted her to take a closer look at Carl, just to make sure."

He pulled a crumpled tissue from his pocket and dabbed at his forehead as he spoke. "Carl was ready for her. Andrew drove her into the garage and Carl felled her with a wrench. Killed her straight off. Then they took the body up to the cliff top in the boot of Andrew's car." His voice rose again. pleading. "I swear I didn't know anything about it. I swear."

"Then why didn't you come to us once you did find out?"

"He said it was too late. That we were in it together. He told me and Ralph that if it came out about the rape, we'd all go down for it. He got Ralph to make up the story about Willow saying MacGregor had assaulted her. Said it would shift attention off us and explain Willow's visit to the police station."

"Ralph Ferguson was mixed up in this too?"

"There were four of us left the nightclub together that night. Me, Carl, Andrew and Ralph."

"Let's move onto that then shall we." Richard flipped through his file and opened it at another page.

We were interrupted by a sharp rap at the door of Richard's office. So involved had I been with the drama unfolding on the monitor screen, I had lost all sense of place and now came to with a start.

A uniformed constable stuck his head around the door. "A moment of your time, Sir," he said.

Nathan squeezed my shoulder as he left his seat and followed the constable out into the corridor, closing the door behind him.

I turned my concentration back to the screen.

Yates was still protesting his innocence, claiming he hadn't taken an active role in Willow's rape. "The four of us was on our way home and she was ahead of us, crossing the waste ground behind the shops off the main road. Carl got up behind her and had her on the ground and her jacket over her head before she knew what was happening. It's not like it was planned. Once Carl had her on the ground, the others joined in. Held her down and raped her in turn. It just happened. They were all drunk."

"It just happened." Richard fixed Yates with a cold, hard stare as he repeated the phrase, his voice edged with distaste. He continued, "So if this assault just happened and you didn't participate, why just stand by and let it happen and not report it to the police at the time?"

Yates flushed and looked down at the desk. "I was too scared. Carl said I'd get blamed, anyway. We all would. I just wanted to forget about the whole thing."

"Well, that didn't go too well for you, did it?"

The door opened behind me and Nathan came back into the room. "How's it going?"

"I think I've seen all I want to see," I said.

Nathan dropped into his chair and turned down the sound on the monitor. "You'll be pleased to know we caught up with Tanner and Lynch," he said. "Tanner is on his way to the station as we speak."

"And Lynch?"

"Lynch is on his way to the morgue."

CHAPTER FORTY-FOUR

It wasn't one of the liveliest get-togethers I'd ever taken part in. But then farewells in such circumstances are hardly joyful occasions.

Karen and I were having a last drink with Owen on the terrace of the Fairview before he left for London and home.

The weather was improving. It was a mild spring afternoon with clear blue skies and a warm breeze that told of the coming summer.

We were seated around a patio table by the steps leading down to the Esplanade, Karen and I sharing a bottle of white wine, Owen drinking orange cordial, as we waited for Owen's taxi. He had his bags packed and ready and standing by his chair.

As Karen topped up our glasses, Owen thanked us for looking after him during his stay.

I said, "I only wish the circumstances had been better."

"You've both made my time here more bearable," he said. "I'll always be grateful to you for that."

"And we'll always be here for you, Owen," Karen responded. She squeezed his arm as if to emphasise the point.

"I have to come back for the trial anyway," Owen said, "but for the moment, I need to be with my family. This will hit Simon hard. I'm going to have to tell him the man who killed his mother is his biological father." He finished his drink and pushed the empty glass away from him across the table.

"You're his father," Karen said. "You always have been."

She picked up the carafe of cordial to replenish Owen's glass, but he waved it away. He said, "Simon will need me more than ever right now."

I was struck by how steadfast had been Owen's attachment to his son through all of this. Despite the circumstances of Simon's birth, circumstances that had cost Willow her life, Owen's devotion had never wavered. The relationship of a lesser man could have been torn asunder by a revelation such as this.

"Simon couldn't want for a better father," I said.

Karen said, "I don't suppose there's any way to keep this from him?"

"His grandparents are trying to restrict his access to the media," said Owen. "But he's going to find out, eventually. It's best if he hears it from me."

"At least you'll finally get some justice," said Karen.

I said, "Tanner is still asserting his innocence, but forensic evidence is stacking up against him. We have blood splatter at the garage that tested positive as Willow's. Same in the boot of Lynch's patrol car. All of which ties in with Yates's testimony."

"Is he being charged with Ralph Ferguson's murder?" Karen asked.

"The investigation is still ongoing," I said. "But it's not looking good for Tanner. And Lynch's suicide just helps reaffirm everything Yates told us. Otherwise, why take his own life?"

"It was definitely suicide?" Karen asked.

"No question," I said. "Several of the search team witnessed it. They had him backed up against the cliff edge and were closing in. He turned away and stepped over the edge before they could reach him."

"A final act of cowardice," said Owen.

"When I think back," I said, "there were several times when he tried to steer the investigation off course."

"Didn't that make you suspicious?" said Owen.

"No reason why it should," I said. "And he seemed such an okay guy. I'm just glad Yates finally found the guts to come clean, or Lynch might have got away with it."

"What will happen to Yates?" said Owen.

"He'll still have to face some charges," I said, "but I suspect they'll go easy on him. He saved my life after all."

Karen shuddered. "It doesn't bear thinking about."

"I'm trying my best not to," I said.

"It must have been a terrifying experience," said Owen.

It wasn't an episode I cared to dwell on. Fortunately, before I could respond, we were interrupted by the arrival of Owen's taxi, saving me from having to dredge up memories of an experience I preferred to forget.

Owen grabbed his bags as we said our goodbyes, and Karen reminded him she would keep a room ready for his return. We left our seats as Owen descended the steps to the Esplanade and waved him off from the front of the terrace.

As the taxi headed away in the direction of the railway station, Karen said, "After all the poor man has put up with over the years, you'd think it couldn't get any worse. And now he has this to live with too."

We made our way back to the table and Karen replenished our glasses as we seated ourselves. "At least you're in the clear," she said. "All that nonsense about assaulting Willow can be put to rest. No one who knows you believed it, anyway."

As I picked up my glass, I said, "It didn't stop the media dredging up my past again, did it? Will I ever be allowed to forget?" I took a swig of my wine.

"Nothing you can do to change the past. You have to learn to live with it."

"It's not me I worry about. Nathan has to cope with the fallout too. Just when our relationship is back on track, the past comes back to haunt us. I still wonder sometimes if he regrets our getting together. It can't be easy for him."

"Not that tired old refrain again?"

"It matters."

"Only to you." She pushed her glass of wine to one side and leaned towards me, arms folded on the table. "Listen, Mikey. The only one who has issues over your past mistakes is you. You need to get over yourself. Nathan forgave you a long time ago."

"I hope so."

"And right now, he needs your support. Both our men are going to be busy for a while yet with this case. The last thing Nathan needs is you putting pressure on your relationship."

"Okay. I hear you." I glanced at my watch. "And busy or not, he'd better not be late. He promised to pick me up on the way home."

Even as I spoke, Nathan's Astra drew up and parked on the far side of the Esplanade. "Talk of the devil," I said, "and he appears."

Nathan climbed out of his car and waved up at us, a big grin on his face. He was carrying a brightly coloured folder.

"He's looking very pleased with himself," I said. "I wonder what he's up to."

He bounded up the steps towards us, leaned over the table, planted a kiss on Karen's cheek, and dropped into the chair next to me, still grinning.

"Okay, let's have it," I said. "Something's got your mojo working."

Without a word, he handed the folder to me. I opened it and took out its contents; a couple of airline tickets and a brochure for a hotel in Malta.

Something melted inside me. I reached out and stroked his cheek with the back of my hand. "See, this why I love you," I said. "Just when I need it, you know exactly how to cheer me up."

"It's not until the end of next month," he said, "but it will give us something to look forward to."

Later, after taking our leave of Karen, and driving home, my thoughts drifted back to our conversation, to Karen's comment about not being able to change the past. Obvious of course. We can't change the past. But the past has no real power. It cannot hurt us unless we let it. All we can do is change how we see it, find new ways to remember it and learn from it.

I kept thinking back too to Owen's troubled relationship with Willow. Easy now to see how the traumatic events of her early life had damaged her and her relationship with Owen. But despite her rash behaviour, her constant mood swings, her reckless affair with her sister's husband, he forgave her all of it. Every time.

And yet, for too many years, she had wrongly blamed herself for all that had befallen her and failed to find a way to forgive herself.

But forgiveness is a two-way street. Being forgiven isn't enough. We have to learn how to accept forgiveness and learn to forgive ourselves too. A lesson I should have learned long ago.

As we walked the short distance from the car to the front of

Woodside Cottage, Nathan hummed a tune, some jaunty ditty that matched his mood. I watched him as we made our way along the garden path, taking pleasure in his sunny smile.

How could I have ever doubted him?

He caught my look and furrowed his brow. "What?"

"Nothing."

Narrowing his eyes, he said, "Why are looking at me like that?"

"I like looking at you. You're nice to look at."

"Oh, yes?" Grinning broadly, he slipped an arm around my waist and, pulling me close, leaned in towards me, his breath warm against my ear, and said, "Does that mean my luck's in for later?"

Returning his grin, I said, "Your luck's always been in."

We were still laughing as we made it through the door.

* * *
IF YOU ENJOYED THIS BOOK

I'm already working on the next title in this series. If you enjoyed this book, you may wish to add your name to my mailing list to receive notification of publication.

Please see details on my Website GrantAtherton.co.uk

And I'd love it if you could post a review about the book on Amazon or another website. Getting reviews would give me a lot of pleasure and I look forward to reading what you think. Perhaps you could mention which parts you liked best.

I look forward to hearing from you.

Grant Atherton

Printed in Great Britain
by Amazon